How had she [...]
bed with her [...]

Dawn felt mortified. Yesterday she'd married Quentin Bayliss. She'd gone to bed with Quentin, explored Quentin's body and nearly made love to him.

But now sexy Ross Duke was in her bed. He was watching her carefully as if she were a strange, potentially dangerous species of animal. This had to be a nightmare—a reasonable enough explanation considering all the champagne and rich food at her wedding reception. Or was Dawn going insane? Maybe she'd sleepwalked....

And yet the fact remained: If Ross was in her bed, then her husband had vanished.

Dawn's heart suddenly pounded against her ribs, and she stared at Ross. "What are you doing in my bed?" she demanded in a lethal tone. "And what have you done with my husband?"

Dear Reader,

Imagine you've traveled far away, to a place of heady danger and luxurious romance nestled high in the Colorado Rocky Mountains. The bellhop has left your bags and you're about to unpack. You've finally reached the exciting Elk River Resort, the setting for Sheryl Lynn's first book in her new duet, HONEYMOON HIDEAWAY, brought to you this month and next.

Sheryl Lynn lives in a pine forest atop a hill in Colorado. When not writing, she amuses herself by embarrassing her two teenagers, walking her dogs in a nearby park and feeding peanuts to the dozens of Steller's jays, scrub jays, blue jays and squirrels who live in her backyard. Her best ideas come from the newspapers, although she admits that a lot of what she reads is way too weird for fiction!

Harlequin Intrigue invites you to escape with Sheryl Lynn to the HONEYMOON HIDEAWAY! Next month don't miss *The Case of the Bad Luck Fiancé!*

Regards,

Debra Matteucci
Senior Editor & Editorial Coordinator
Harlequin Books
300 East 42nd Street
New York, New York 10017

The Case of the Vanished Groom
Sheryl Lynn

Harlequin Books

TORONTO • NEW YORK • LONDON
AMSTERDAM • PARIS • SYDNEY • HAMBURG
STOCKHOLM • ATHENS • TOKYO • MILAN
MADRID • WARSAW • BUDAPEST • AUCKLAND

For the gang, Tom and Tristan and Abby

ISBN 0-373-22424-9

THE CASE OF THE VANISHED GROOM

Copyright © 1997 by Jaye W. Manus

Printed in U.S.A.

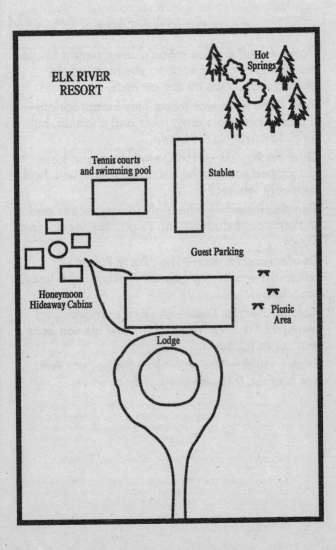

ELK RIVER RESORT

Hot Springs

Tennis courts
and swimming pool

Stables

Guest Parking

Honeymoon
Hideaway Cabins

Picnic
Area

Lodge

CAST OF CHARACTERS

Dawn Lovell-Bayliss—She'd been taught to use her head, not her heart, so she married the perfect man. Was he *too* perfect?

Ross Duke—He was thoroughly inappropriate—a black sheep, playboy, joker and charmer, but he'd do anything for Dawn.

Quentin Bayliss—Had Dawn's husband been kidnapped, or was he a smooth talker who had suddenly left her?

Connie Haxman—The high-society mover and shaker would do anything to protect her darling Dawn.

Desdemona Hunter—The "Party Patter" columnist was always on the lookout for a juicy scandal.

Colonel Horace Duke—A stern patriarch and owner of Elk River resort, he knew his son Ross was up to no good.

Janine Duke—She won't let anyone, not even her brother, threaten the family business.

Chapter One

Brad picked up Galena's purse. He was dying for a smoke, but his fiancée was such a puritan she'd faint if he lit up in her presence, or even if she smelled it on him. If he recalled correctly, Galena smoked like a chimney.

"Hey!" Galena shouted, grabbing her purse out of his hands.

But not before Brad saw the unmistakable gleam of a firearm. He jumped and drew up his hands to protect his chest. He stared wide-eyed at her. "Is that a gun? Are you nuts?"

She pulled a blue steel .32 automatic from her purse. She glared steadily at him. "I must be, for trusting you."

He flopped onto a cheap chair, hating this sleazy motel room, and hating Galena. But if she got a whiff that he had a penny of his own, she'd go straight to Dawn and ruin everything. He watched her pace like a tigress, caressing the gun barrel as if it were a pet.

"I'm pretty good with this thing. I've changed a lot in five years, Brad—"

"Quentin," he corrected. "My name is Quentin Bayliss. I told you, the Witness Protection Program insists that I stay in character all the time."

She stopped in the middle of the room and hung her head. Her shoulders shook. It took him a few seconds to realize she was laughing. He softened his tone. "I know what I did was wrong, baby. I wouldn't have done it if I had a choice, but those mobsters were out to kill me. I loved you more than I've ever loved anybody, or ever will. I still love you. If I could turn back the clock, I would."

Her head snapped up. "Liar!"

"I don't blame you for not believing me. If you'd run out on me, I'd have been—"

"Run out on you? You ruined me, Brad! I lost the gallery, I lost my house. I lost everything because of you." She extended her right hand, and sighted down the barrel of the pistol, aiming it straight at his head. "Five years, *baby.* Five long years and the only thing I've done is hunt for you. If you don't give me back my money, I will kill you."

He huffed a heavy sigh. When he'd married her, she'd been a flaky artist, an appealing eccentric who always wore black and drank only Dom Perignon. Now she was just plain flaky, and obsessed—and dangerous. The only way to shake her off his tail would be to give up Dawn and her millions, but that he refused to do. "Look, Dawn promised to give me the money."

"Sure."

"She thinks it's a business debt, and she's agreed to pay. A hundred and fifty grand, a cashier's check. She promised to give it to me as soon as we're married, but she won't give it to me until we're legal. Ten days, baby. Just hang on until the wedding. Then we'll be square."

"You better not be lying. Because you can't hide from me anymore. No matter where you go, no matter what lies you tell, I will find you." She lowered the pistol.

"And if I have to find you again, you won't have time to open your big mouth. I'll put a couple of holes in your head and then we'll really be square."

"You won't need money if you're in prison," he grumbled.

"I won't care, as long as you're dead."

WONDERING IF she made the biggest mistake of her life, Dawn Lovell entered the lobby.

From the outside, the main lodge of Elk River resort looked rustic. Constructed of logs and stone, the lodge seemed to sprout from the rocky forest along with the towering pine trees.

Inside, Dawn gazed in wonder at the exposed beams high above the lobby and the posts sporting antlers and Old West memorabilia. As a native of Colorado, Dawn knew about Southwestern style. Only in theory, though, or from what she'd seen in magazines. Mother had not approved of "rustic charm."

With guilty pleasure, Dawn approved heartily of the decor. She liked the brightly colored rugs on the pine floor and the squat furniture covered in geometric-patterned upholstery. Knotty-pine wall paneling had aged to a golden patina. Western art depicting cowboys, Native Americans, North American wildlife and sweeping landscapes enchanted her with earthy colors and lively subjects.

She twisted her engagement ring around her finger and wished Quentin had agreed to join her for this prewedding vacation.

A young woman behind the reception desk smiled curiously at Dawn. Another young woman carried a tray of drinks across the lobby to a man and woman seated before a window. A catch gripped Dawn's throat as she stared at the pair. She hoped once she and Quentin were married, he'd settle down enough so they'd make a happy-looking couple. As much as she loved him, his hyperactivity distressed her.

"Dawn Lovell?"

The warm masculine voice startled Dawn. She caught her pocketbook in both hands. Turning her head slowly she stared into a pair of bright gray eyes.

Beautiful eyes sparkling to match a sunny smile. Dawn forgot her nervousness about being in a strange place. Forgot her loneliness. Forgot the curious looks of the girl behind the reception desk and the happy couple enjoying the panoramic view of the Rocky Mountains.

Deep in the secret place where she allowed her spirit freedom, she heard the crystalline whispering of bells.

The man lifted one thick eyebrow and his smile softened, turning crooked. "Are you Dawn Lovell?" he asked, but hesitantly, his voice lower.

Snapping back to herself, she lowered her gaze. She noted the man's light gray trousers were of expensive fabric and cut, breaking perfectly over his shiny black loafers. "Uh, yes." She cleared her throat. "I'm Miss Lovell."

"Ross Duke." He thrust out a hand.

Ross Duke, Quentin's best friend since high school and the owner of this mountain resort. Quentin had assured her Ross would see to her every comfort this week, but he hadn't told her his friend was so attractive. Or how the sunshine filtering through the windows appeared to dance against his chestnut hair.

Keeping his hand out, Ross said, "Quent didn't describe you very well."

She clutched her pocketbook more tightly. With eyes blinded by love, Quentin had most likely described her as an angel gracing the earth. Now Ross saw firsthand she was nothing special at all. By sheer force of will, she made her fingers release her pocketbook, leaving it to hang by the shoulder strap. She surreptitiously swiped her palm against her skirt before extending her hand for a proper handshake.

Ross touched her fingertips. Electric chills tickled her skin. He slid his hand across her palm and folded his fingers over the side of her thumb. While she puzzled over his unusual hold, he bent at the waist, lifted her hand to his mouth, and kissed the back of her hand.

The chills raced up her arm all the way to her shoulder. Gooseflesh rose on her arms. Her face warmed. She opened her mouth to protest, but a sigh emerged.

"Quent never said you were so pretty."

Drowning in the smooth river of his voice, she stared helplessly at his handsome face.

"I'm pleased to meet you, Dawn. Where's your luggage?"

Pretty? This man with movie-star good looks called her *pretty?*

He glanced at the wide doors where a young man wearing a white Western-style shirt and black trousers pushed a cart into the lobby. The sight of her dark brown luggage brought Dawn back to her earth.

Of course Ross Duke was charming. He had a resort to run and his job required flattering the guests. "There's my luggage," she said. "I'm about to check in. It's— it's—it's kind of you to greet me." Suddenly feeling conspicuous and out of place, she looked about. "This is the first time I've ever taken a vacation without my parents. Mother was very good at arranging the details."

Ross cocked his head and gave her a curious look.

She mentally replayed her words. What a silly thing to

say. At thirty years old, she was capable of arranging her own vacation plans.

"I prefer big pictures to details myself." Ross grasped her elbow. "Here's the desk." He guided her across the lobby and presented her to the clerk. "Miss Dawn Lovell, sweetheart. She goes first-class all the way."

The young woman, whose name tag read Kara, rolled her eyes and gave Ross a tense, admonishing smile. The rude expression vanished before she turned her attention on Dawn. Dawn noticed, however, and it made her uneasy. In her book, the boss shouldn't call employees "sweetheart" and hired help shouldn't make disrespectful faces at the boss.

After accepting Dawn's credit card, Kara typed deftly into a computer. "Welcome to Elk River, Miss Lovell. All of us are looking forward to your wedding." She placed the credit card, a room key, brochure packet and a maroon folder on the counter, then tapped the folder with a fingernail. "Mom made the arrangements for you. It's all in here. I'm sure she'll want to speak to you as soon as you're settled."

"Mom?" Dawn questioned.

Grinning insolently at Kara, Ross leaned against the counter. "Tsk, tsk, sweetheart, have to remember your professionalism." He added in aside to Dawn, "She's a trainee."

"I mean Elise." Kara's cheeks turned pink. "Ross, dear, get lost. Don't pay any attention to him, Miss Lovell. My brother thinks he's a comedian."

Ever since Quentin had insisted they hold the wedding and spend their honeymoon at Elk River Resort, Dawn had spoken many times to Elise Duke—Ross's wife, she'd assumed. Now she realized she had misinterpreted the relationships. Ross and Kara were siblings and Elise was their mother. She felt a prickle of annoyance. As talkative as Quentin was, he could be terribly vague at times.

Quashing her irritation, she picked up a pen to sign the computerized slip Kara placed on the counter. Seeing clearly in her mind's eye her father's disapproval, she hesitated. "Conspicuous consumption is a certain sign of poor breeding," he'd often told her.

What could be more conspicuous than to spend an idle week at a luxurious mountain resort? Quentin had been perfectly reasonable in his arguments. "You deserve it, darling. I'll be busy the entire week and I can't bear to think about you rattling around in that big lonely house, getting on your own nerves. Do it for me. Have fun. Walk in the woods. Play some tennis. Soak in the hot springs. I want you relaxed, suntanned and happy for our honeymoon."

"Is there something wrong?" Kara asked. "Is your name spelled correctly?"

Dawn swallowed hard and signed the registration card.

Ross picked up the room key and nodded as he read the number. "The view will make you think you've died and gone to heaven, Dawn. Come on, I'll show you where it is."

Kara's eyes narrowed. "Stefan will show her to her room. Don't you have something to do, Ross?"

He gave the question a moment's thought before widening his eyes and shaking his head. "Nope. Only thing on my agenda this week is showing Dawn a good time." He tossed the key and caught it in a graceful downward swipe.

"You better watch out for the Colonel." Kara slammed a drawer under the counter.

"I'm shaking in my boots, sweetheart." Ross swept Dawn toward a staircase.

Bemused by the interchange, Dawn waited until they reached the second floor before asking Ross about the Colonel.

"You'll meet him. He's my dad."

"You call him the Colonel?"

"Everybody calls him the Colonel." He gave her a conspiratorial grin. "He even calls himself the Colonel. I bet every morning when he goes in to shave, he salutes himself in the mirror."

She supposed every family had its eccentrics. Except hers, of course; her parents had been the epitome of social grace and exemplary decorum. Eccentricity had never been tolerated in her home.

He stopped before Room 208 and dropped his hold on her arm. His release relieved her. His warm hand had been too possessive for comfort. When he turned his back to her, she rubbed her inner elbow briskly.

"It's most generous of you to have your family living and working at your resort." She admired the carpet; its Southwestern design made the windowless hallway cheerful.

Ross pushed open the door. "My resort?" He laughed. "Elk River is the Colonel's baby, not mine. I only visit when I get nostalgic for some abuse from Mom and the girls. Do you have sisters?"

Now thoroughly confused, she shook her head. She'd completely misunderstood Ross's connection to the resort.

"You've already met the baby, Kara. She's still in college, so she only works here in the summertime. You'll meet the other two soon enough. Janine's the oldest. She runs the joint. Don't let her cutie-pie looks fool you. She has the soul of a riverboat gambler holding four aces. Megan is in the middle. Don't let her sucker you into a tennis match. She'll take your head off.'' He swept an arm in a wide, graceful gesture. "Ta-da! The Jesse James suite. Welcome.''

She crept inside. Her breath caught at the sight of so much sunshine drenched loveliness, and yes, rustic charm. The outer wall consisted of a massive bank of windows—Ross had not exaggerated about the view. Mountain peaks rose, baldly majestic, in the background. Despite its being June, snow was frozen in rivulets on the highest peaks, glittering like liquid pearls. Over the dark pine forest, checkered with bright patches of aspen trees, a hawk soared weightlessly.

''The Jesse James suite?''

''Do you know how the outlaw died?''

The vulgarities of history—especially concerning the notorious—had never been considered a fitting interest for a Lovell. She shook her head.

''Shot eight times and left for dead. Somehow, he managed to climb onto his horse and make it here. This used to be a brothel. The highest-class cathouse in the Rocky Mountains. Cattle barons traveled for days to sample the fancy women Madame Belle imported from Europe. Jesse and Belle were longtime friends, so she hid him from the posse in this very room and did her best to keep him alive.'' Ross turned a mournful gaze upon the bed. It had a wrought-iron headboard crafted into a trellis of climbing roses and singing birds. ''He died right there.''

Dawn took a few steps closer to the bed. Tingles of pleasurable fear squeezed her diaphragm. ''He died *here?*''

''It's not the same mattress. Some folks have seen

Jesse riding a black horse down the hallway. His ghost always disappears into this room.''

''A ghost?'' She turned to him with wide eyes. ''This room is haunted?''

Ross made a strangled noise, then burst into laughter.

She looked between him and the bed, his laughter distracting her from coherent thought. The only thing she could focus on was the rich warmth of the sound and his handsome face creased in good humor.

Then she got it. ''Mr. Duke, you made it all up.''

He shook a finger at her. ''One of these days I'll get that story out without cracking up. Definitely need to work on my delivery. And call me Ross.''

''Honestly! You shouldn't tell tales about ghosts.''

''People *like* ghosts.''

He had a point. Until Ross began laughing, she'd been enjoying the idea of a sharing a room with a ghostly outlaw. She chuckled, and covered her mouth with a hand. Imagining her credulous face as she drank in Ross's tale turned the chuckle into a laugh. She distracted herself by examining the beautifully crafted bed.

''The resort has history, but not of the shoot-'em-up, wild-west variety. The original lodge was built in the 1920s for a hunting club. They sold it to some back-east investors just in time for the Great Depression. The place was deserted until the fifties when Jute Hallstone bought it.''

''The cowboy actor?''

His smile dazzled her. ''You're a B-grade western fan?''

She blushed. Few people knew about her affinity for great old, bad movies.

''Jute turned it into a dude ranch. When he died, his kids didn't want it, so they sold it to Ralph Beerson. He upgraded it into a resort and added the wings. The Colonel bought it from him.'' He waved a hand in dismissal. "I'll be glad to tell you about it later.''

He moved across the room. Trying to keep at bay the schoolgirlish urge to stare openmouthed at his every move, she watched him. Tall and lean, he moved with an athlete's smooth grace. His casual knit shirt fit snugly over his broad shoulders, but draped elegantly on his torso. He looked much younger than Quentin's forty-two years. She liked the way his hair curled in back, barely brushing his shirt collar.

She caught herself twisting her engagement ring and made herself quit.

He opened a cabinet, revealing a television set and stereo. "In case you get bored. But I don't intend to let you be bored for a minute.'' In a slightly mocking manner, as if imitating a bellhop, he showed her the wet bar and the well-stocked cabinet of drinks and snacks. After a demonstration of the light switches, the bedside clock radio and the television/stereo remote control, he informed her the housekeeper's name was Nancy.

His good humor put her at ease. In the spirit of the game, she tested the faucets in the bathroom and caressed the soft towels. She declared everything perfectly acceptable.

"Good.'' His gray eyes gazed intently into hers; she wanted to sigh. "Stefan will be here in a minute with your luggage. Put on your play clothes, then join me in the lobby. We'll have lunch before I take you on the grand tour.''

She supposed her linen suit wasn't proper resort wear. "All right.''

His smile faded, and his expression turned thoughtful.

His suntan gave his complexion a golden cast, contrasting with his pale eyes.

The bells pealed inside her soul.

Ross gave a start and turned away. "I'll meet you downstairs, Dawn. We're going to have a blast this week."

She nodded slowly and pressed a hand between her breasts. Her heart raced as he closed the door behind him.

A shaft of sunlight flashed against the large diamond in her engagement ring. Guilt filled her throat and she swallowed hard. Ross Duke had definitely been flirting.

As she was certain she'd flirted in response.

And her wedding was less than a week away!

She hurried to the telephone. She must tell Quentin the resort vacation was a mistake. If he felt strongly about not holding the wedding at a church in Colorado Springs, then they could go downtown to the justice of the peace.

As she lifted the phone, she realized how silly she would sound. Surely Ross wouldn't betray his best friend by flirting with his fiancée.

Quentin had been her godsend, rescuing her from the lonely grief of losing both her parents within the space of a year. He loved her. He worshipped her. He wanted the very best for her.

She hung up the telephone. Her gaze traveled the room and settled on the breathtaking view out the window. She loved the mountains. Her most pleasurable indulgence was the sound of her boots on rocks and the crisp taste of mountain air in her lungs. This vacation was Quentin's way of indulging her—his gift. She could not toss a gift of love back in his face.

She smiled at her own foolishness. All her life she'd been warned about men like Ross Duke. Too handsome, too glib, too charming, and far too interested in her money. "Use your head, never your heart," her father had told her time after time. "Emotion causes nothing but trouble. Logic and reason are the criteria for a successful life."

Quentin Bayliss was the logical choice for her husband: a successful businessman whom she suspected was even wealthier than she. He had good manners, impeccable breeding and courage. Father and Mother would have approved. Logic also told her Ross had a vested interest in her satisfaction with Elk River Lodge. Even if he didn't own the resort, his family did, and all resort owners needed happy guests.

She fingered her engagement ring, watching sunlight create rainbows around the diamond.

Hearing bells was foolishness, illogical, ridiculous. Ross Duke meant nothing to her and he never would.

"I THINK I'M GOING to be sick to my stomach," Dawn said. She gazed haplessly at Connie. Her friend knelt, scrubbing at a tiny spot marring the scalloped hem of Dawn's wedding dress.

Connie Haxman lifted her eyes. "Don't you dare."

"I shouldn't be getting married. It's a mistake." She stared at the clock radio next to the bed. In one hour she and Quentin would exchange their vows in the Sweet Pines Chapel. "Quentin doesn't know me well enough. What do I have to offer? I don't even know any jokes!"

Connie rose to her feet and tugged at her pale fawn jacket. "You're the nicest girl I know." She grinned saucily. "Kind of neurotic, but perfectly nice."

Feelings ruffled, Dawn sniffed. "I am not neurotic."

Connie glanced at the small tape recorder lying on the bed. "You're the only person in the entire world who actually uses one of those things to make memos. And don't forget, I've seen your Daytimer. You could single-handedly organize an entire country.''

Dawn peered with worry at the tape recorder. Making verbal notes to oneself made perfect sense. She could reuse the cassette tapes countless times, helping the environment by cutting down on the use of paper. ''That makes me neurotic?''

''In a nice way.'' Connie laughed. ''Chin up, my darling, you're a gorgeous bride. This is nothing but jitters. Even I feel the jitters when I get married, and I've had plenty of experience.''

Dawn managed a small smile, but debated how much to tell Connie. They'd been friends since the day Dawn began volunteering for the Children's Betterment Society, which Connie had founded. Mother had always dismissed the socialite by saying, ''One can drape a hound in jewels and even take it to the ball, but it remains a hound.''

Despite Mother's opinion, Dawn loved Connie. She laughed too loud, drank too much and wore vulgar clothing, but she had tremendous energy and a generous heart.

Dawn twisted her engagement ring. ''I'm not—I mean—I don't know…I'm not sure if I love him.''

Connie folded her arms, pressing her impressive bosom higher. ''This *is* moving kind of fast. You met him at the Valentine's Day ball, so that makes it what, four months?''

''It's not that fast,'' Dawn said hesitantly. Quentin swore love at first sight and had proposed three weeks after they met. ''I am thirty, and I want children. I don't have time to waste on a long engagement.''

''Are you asking my advice, opinion, what?''

Knowing only that she didn't know what she wanted, Dawn considered. ''Assurance?''

"All right. Quentin is good-looking and obscenely wealthy. He can charm the socks off a brass statue. He's funny, bright, and I think your father would have approved."

"Really?"

Connie chuckled. "One shark always approves of another."

Not understanding the joke, Dawn peered closely at Connie's face.

"Oh, please, my darling. Your father was a Great White. He didn't get where he did by being sweet." She held up a hand, displaying an impressive number of diamond, sapphire and emerald rings. "Do not get me started on your parents. We'll both be sorry. We're discussing Quentin."

Dawn hung her head. Connie had disliked the Lovells as much they had disliked her. Occasionally she indulged in tirades, calling Edward Lovell a bully with ice in his blood and a stock-market ticker for a brain. Worse, she called Deborah Lovell a stuck-up, snobbish, bluenosed twit without an ounce of compassion. Worst of all, Dawn sometimes secretly agreed.

"Quentin has a lot of energy. He'll force you to come out of your shell." She held her hands wide in a gesture of welcome. "Maybe he'll succeed where I've failed and draw you out into the open where you belong. You'll make beautiful children, to whom I give permission in advance to call me Auntie."

"Oh, Connie..."

"Oh, my darling, forget these silly jitters." She sniffed and lifted her chin. "Unless you'd care to postpone this ridiculous wedding in the sticks and let me throw a proper bash for you? I still can't believe you're not inviting anybody. Not even one reporter!"

Dawn sheepishly shrugged. "I have too invited people. Important people." Her short guest roster included those people who had been especially close to her parents. She and Quentin had argued about including any guests at all, and about having a reception. He claimed anything other than a small, private ceremony would turn into a media circus. She argued that her parents' friends would be irreparably offended if she failed to hold some kind of celebration. They'd compromised by holding the wedding out of town and keeping the guest list under thirty. "Quentin doesn't like publicity. I don't care much for it myself. Besides, considering my age, a huge wedding seems rather—"

"Watch it. I'm a year or two past thirty myself."

Dawn hid a smile by lowering her face. "The wedding itself doesn't bother me at all. I find it all very romantic." Screwing up her courage, she admitted, "It's another man."

Connie gasped. When Dawn looked up, she realized it was a delighted gasp.

"I don't mean it *that* way! You see, Quentin's best friend has been my companion this week. He's been…wonderful."

Connie tapped her lower lip with a talonlike fingernail.

"We've gone hiking and horseback riding. I don't know how many games of tennis we've played. We've gone swimming and had picnics. We've watched movies. I was reluctant to take this vacation, but now I'm glad I did. I've never had so much fun in my life."

"You haven't…you know?"

"Oh, no! Nothing like that. He's been a proper gentleman. He's Quentin's best friend, after all. I don't know why he wasn't at dinner last night, but you'll meet him at the wedding and I'm sure you'll agree, he's very nice."

"You're attracted to him."

She nodded miserably. "I shouldn't be. He hasn't a serious thought in his head. Even his own family apologizes for his behavior. We haven't talked about anything personal, but I gather he doesn't hold an honest job. I think he's a professional gambler. He's rude to his own father. He teases his mother and sisters unmercifully. He has no ambition. He tells outrageous lies, then laughs when he's caught in them. Altogether an inappropriate man."

"But you fell in love with him anyway."

"No!" Dawn closed her eyes. "It's just that...around Ross I feel, I feel—"

"Pretty? Special?"

"Yes," Dawn whispered in a sigh. "I feel so guilty and disloyal. What am I to do? I can't marry Quentin under false pretenses."

Connie laughed. She grasped Dawn by the shoulders and made her turn around to face a mirror. "Late-breaking news bulletin, my darling, you are both pretty and special."

Dawn stared wide-eyed at the vision in the mirror. Appliqués of white roses and twining leaves overlaid the sleeveless, fitted bodice. Matching appliqués covered the tea-length, scalloped hem, and a pair of embroidered roses fastened the narrow sash. Her hair was upswept into a French twist held by combs festooned with tiny rosebuds; a single strand of pearls encircled her neck. Cosmetics expertly applied by Connie made her eyes large and luminous.

"I think you're beautiful," Connie said softly. Her eyes glistened with tears. "My little mouse has blos-

somed. I wish you were my own daughter." She snatched
a tissue from a box and dabbed at her eyes.

Dawn wondered if Ross saw her this way when he
stared so intently at her. She prayed Quentin saw her this
way, too.

"Don't worry about being attracted to another man.
Despite your mother's best efforts, you're a perfectly normal young woman. It's only natural to get the hots over
a hunky man."

Dawn frowned at Connie's reflection in the mirror.

A soft knock on the door caused both women to turn.
Dawn steadied herself with a deep breath. "The car must
be here. I'm ready."

Moving toward the door, Connie asked, "Are you
sure? There's still time to back out."

Dawn clasped her trembling hands over her fluttering
stomach. "Marrying Quentin is the right thing."

"Good." She opened the door.

Hands in his pockets, his tuxedo jacket hanging open,
Ross Duke stood in the doorway. "Hi." He extended a
hand. "You must be Mrs. Haxman."

Connie exchanged a glance with Dawn. Then she
straightened her shoulders to better show off her bosom,
cocked a hip, and laid her hand against Ross's. "And
you must be Ross."

He kissed the back of her hand. Connie giggled like a
girl.

"I'm sorry I couldn't make the rehearsal dinner last
night. We could have gotten properly acquainted."

"You can't possibly be sorrier than I am." Connie
dreamily rubbed the back of her hand.

"What are you doing here, Ross?" Dawn asked.
"Shouldn't you be with Quentin at the chapel?"

"May I speak to you for a moment?"

He looked serious, even solemn, without a trace of his usual teasing sunniness. She just knew he'd come to tell her Quentin wanted to call off the wedding.

Connie looked between them. "I'll go check on the car."

Before Dawn could protest, Connie was gone. Ross glanced at the hallway behind him before slipping into the room and softly closing the door.

"You shouldn't be here." Her heart shouldn't be pounding and she shouldn't be thinking how devastatingly gorgeous he looked in a tuxedo, either. The summer-weight fabric draped gracefully over his broad shoulders and the stark white shirt set off his tan to perfection.

"Are you sure about all this?"

She focused on her restless feet, willing them to stay still. She didn't dare look at Ross. The bells she longed to hear belonged to Quentin, not to this rascally playboy. "Sure about what?"

He lifted his shoulders in a quick shrug, then shifted his weight from foot to foot and smoothed a hand across the side of his head. He stared at the floor. "Marriage." The word emerged in a rush, as if it pained him to speak. "It's a major commitment."

"I know about commitments," she said coldly. "Is something wrong with Quentin?"

He looked up sharply. "You can do better than Quent."

Dawn gasped.

Ross's eyes widened and he clamped his hands on his hips. The action pushed back his jacket, revealing a cummerbund snug about his narrow waist. "That didn't come out right."

"I should say not." The fear of Quentin deserting her faded away as she realized she'd heard about this kind of thing before. Ross must be one of those determined bachelors who considered marriage something akin to a prison sentence. Ross hated the idea of his friend falling into such a miserable fate.

"You're not at all what Quent led me to believe. Maybe he isn't the right guy for you."

Emotion swelled in her throat and burned her eyes. She suddenly hated Ross for daring to speak what she felt. She especially hated him for being so attractive, for making her feel attractive, and for making her uncertain about the man she loved.

"Leave, please."

"This is the rest of your life, Dawn." He held out a hand and his fingertips twitched, beckoning. "You're special. You deserve the best."

What he possibly hoped to gain from this confrontation was beyond her comprehension. "I love Quentin, and he loves me. If you'd listen to your mother instead of fooling around all the time, you might understand what that means. Now, leave."

His thick eyebrows lowered and his eyes narrowed. A dark flush rose on his cheeks. He turned for the door. "Guess I stepped out of line."

She gazed upon his broad shoulders and lowered head, and suffered a pain so deep it threatened to double her over. She pressed an arm to her aching stomach. "Let's not argue. Please. You've been very kind to me this week and I appreciate it more than you can know. I'd like us to be friends."

He turned his head enough to see her over his shoulder. "Kind? You're either stupid or completely clueless." Shaking his head, he left the room.

He called her stupid? What did she expect from the likes of him? He'd spent the entire week undermining her confidence in Quentin. An experienced, worldly man such as he must have recognized her lack of experience with men. He was one of those predators she'd always been warned about, amusing himself at her expense—at Quentin's expense.

She grabbed a tissue from the box and carefully dabbed at her burning eyes. She didn't cry; she never cried. She certainly wasn't going to start because of a man like Ross Duke.

Chapter Two

"Surprise!" Connie Haxman hooted a laugh as she tugged the arm of a tiny woman.

Seated at the head table in the reception hall, Dawn tensed. She stared at the newcomer's emerald-green satin suit and the marabou-festooned hat perched at an angle on her carroty hair. Desdemona Hunter, society reporter and author of the biweekly "Party Patter" column, was one of Connie's dearest friends. Desdemona—called Dizzy by her friends—graced every guest list that mattered in southern Colorado. None of Connie's countless charity balls, dinners or holiday celebrations could proceed without Desdemona's reporting.

Next to Dawn, Quentin choked on the champagne he was in the midst of swallowing. Desdemona's photographer snapped pictures. The popping flash blinded Dawn, and red spots danced in the air before her eyes. Quentin coughed into a napkin.

Dawn thrust a hand toward the photographer. "Please! No more photographs. Please."

"It's my gift to you, my darling. The wedding of Dawn Lovell-Bayliss is front-page news." Connie looped an arm around Desdemona's shoulders. "Don't you agree, Dizzy?"

"Or at least, worthy of an entire column. My, my, my, just look at all these lovely people! Is that Judge Gideon? It *is* him! Ooh, and Elizabeth Masterson. Whatever is your connection to her?" Desdemona nodded vigorously, making her marabou feathers jiggle and bob. "Your dress is exquisite, Dawn. Is that a Karan, dear?"

"Uh, no, it's an Angelo. It's not an original, though, I didn't have time to order a custom—"

Quentin pressed his mouth against Dawn's ear. "Get rid of that idiot right now!"

Dawn recoiled from Quentin's red face and glittering eyes. As she stared in horror at the purple splotches spreading across his cheeks and the vein pulsing in his forehead, she realized she had much to learn about her new husband.

The wedding ceremony in Sweet Pines Chapel had been accomplished without a hitch. Two dozen of Dawn's friends had come from Colorado Springs, and the small gathering had nearly filled the tiny chapel. The only low spot had been Ross Duke. He'd performed his best-man duties exactly as he was supposed to, but he'd been grim-faced throughout the ceremony. Now everyone gathered at the Elk River lodge where Elise Duke and her daughters had arranged a sit-down reception dinner worthy of royalty. Everyone except Ross; he'd disappeared.

Despite Ross's peculiarities, the evening reception had unfolded with the watercolored loveliness of a sweet dream. The tables were laid with snowy cloths and silver service, and draped with garlands of silk roses. Dawn had giggled throughout toasts to the happy couple. She and Quentin had fed each other wedding cake. They'd danced. They'd eaten a dinner of venison medallions and chanterelles prepared by a master chef. They drank champagne and gazed into each other's eyes.

Now Connie had turned the dream into a nightmare by bringing in a reporter. To make matters worse, Dizzy Hunter and her photographer acted like a magnet, drawing the wedding guests near. They were the cream of Colorado Springs society: judges, high-powered attorneys, doctors and CEOs. Dainty purses unsnapped as women checked their lipstick and hair; men straightened ties and smoothed jackets. Dawn feared the quiet, dignified celebration she'd promised Quentin was about to turn into the media circus he had feared.

Dawn did not understand Quentin's aversion to media attention, but she did realize he was serious about it. She stood abruptly, waving both hands at Connie and Desdemona.

"Stop taking photographs right now!"

Glaring suspiciously at Dawn, Desdemona made a curt hand signal. The photographer lowered his camera. People hushed, watching Dawn. Some appeared offended by her outburst, but most looked surprised.

"Excuse me." Quentin leapt off his chair. Holding the napkin close to his face, he hurried toward the men's room. With his hunched shoulders, shuffling walk and the napkin pressed to his face, he gave the impression of a man about to be sick.

Desdemona clamped her fists on her hips. "Well!"

"Oh, my darling, I'm so sorry." Connie hurried to Dawn's side. "I didn't mean to make him angry. What did I do?"

"I—I'm not sure. Oh, Ms. Hunter, I'm so embarrassed. I had no idea Quentin would…" Dawn stared helplessly in the direction her husband had gone. She hadn't the faintest idea how to apologize for what had happened, or even if an apology were required. "I believe my husband has a phobia."

"This is my fault, Dizzy," Connie said. "Dawn told me not to invite reporters."

"A phobia about reporters." Desdemona's face was skewed by a skeptical grimace. "Oh, right."

The photographer turned his camera over in his hands. "Maybe it's the flash, Dizzy. He could be a war vet or something. You know, having flashbacks about mortar rounds."

The Colonel appeared. Wearing a somber black tuxedo, with his silver hair cropped short and his back as erect as if he wore a brace, he cut an imposing figure. He glared down his nose at the photographer. The young man quailed under the Colonel's fearsome gaze.

"Is there a problem, Mrs. Bayliss?"

It took a few seconds for Dawn to realize the Colonel was addressing her. She glanced at her guests. She sensed pity mixed with censure, for Quentin Bayliss was not one of them and his actions now highlighted his not belonging in their society. She imagined the gossip that would soon be rippling along golf courses and through country clubs, and deeply regretted not following Quentin's advice in forgoing a reception. She forced a smile to assure her guests all was well. "Uh, no, sir, Colonel, sir. No problem."

Desdemona pressed forward. "Colonel Horace Duke! Sir, it is a pleasure to finally meet you." She grabbed his right hand in both of hers and pumped it. "Desdemona Hunter. Surely you follow my column. I adore what you've done with the lodge. Ralphie Beerson let it go to pot, and it was a crying shame. I'd love to see this place make a comeback as *the* place to party."

Connie drew Dawn away from the table. "I'm so

sorry, my darling. I only meant to give a gift you could keep in your scrapbook. Can you ever forgive me?''

''There's nothing to forgive. I'm certain Quentin is finding the humor in this by now.'' She eyed the Colonel, whose crispness was fading fast under the onslaught of Desdemona's rapid-fire compliments. A smile appeared on his craggy face.

The smile reminded her of Ross, who, in height and build, resembled his father. Ross had disappeared from the reception soon after the toasts had ended and before the dancing began. He hadn't spoken a word to her since the confrontation in her room.

''Dawn?'' Connie's voice was low with concern.

She shook away thoughts of Ross. ''I don't think anybody approves of Quentin. Look at them whispering.''

''Don't be silly. Everyone thinks he's charming. They're concerned for you, that's all.''

Feeling pity for me, more likely, Dawn thought. She hated being the target of pity, and avoided the country-club-golfing circuit because she knew people pitied her. Mousy, awkward and unfashionable, she'd never lived up to her mother's beauty and flair, or her father's intelligence and ambition. Now they probably thought she had married beneath her. They did not understand Quentin loved her for herself. ''Do you think it's too early for Quentin and me to retire to our cabin?''

''That's a marvelous idea. I'll ask someone to go in after Quentin and make certain he's okay.'' She smiled broadly. ''I bet his nerves finally caught up to him. I have never in my life seen such a coolheaded groom. Ha! I knew it had to be an act.''

When Connie left her, Dawn looked around the hall for any sign of Ross. As people tried to catch her eye, she regretted even more deeply inviting them to her wedding. She'd done so out of obligation, because if her parents were alive they would have invited these people. Their jostling around Dizzy Hunter in the hope of a photo opportunity proved Dawn's wedding was merely another chance to be seen in the company of the right people. Unlike Ross, who had never seemed to care a whit about her breeding or who she knew or the size of her stock portfolio. She hated herself for wanting one last glimpse of him, for wanting to hear his rich, good-humored voice one more time. She especially hated how much his coldness hurt her feelings.

She lowered her gaze to her wedding ring, a simple gold band nestled against the gaudy engagement diamond. She was Mrs. Quentin Bayliss until death do them part. From this day forward only her husband deserved her love, attention or concern.

Ross Duke was nothing but a memory.

"MRS. BAYLISS," Quentin said. He held Dawn's hand and squeezed her fingers. He gestured at the front door of the Honeymoon Hideaway cabin.

"Mr. Bayliss," she replied. Enchanted, excited and a little bit afraid, she squeezed his hand in return. "It's so pretty."

"I knew you'd like it. Those sensible clothes of yours hide a romantic streak as deep as the Grand Canyon."

Discomfited he'd noticed and pleased he had, she giggled. "I can't imagine anything more romantic than this."

Tiny white lights draped in the bushes and trees lighted the gravel path leading from the lodge to the cabins. The four Honeymoon Hideaway cabins were angled and landscaped so each had a private entryway. Spotlights illuminated a central pond where triple fountains gleamed like quicksilver.

He unlocked the door, then bowed to her. "Might I have the honor of carrying my lovely bride over the threshold?"

Her knees wobbled, and her heart pounded so hard that she felt positive it might beat its way free of her body. "Please."

He pushed open the door, then scooped Dawn into his arms. She wrapped her arms around his neck. Laughing, he carried her into the cabin, and set her carefully on her feet. For a moment she thought he was going to embrace and kiss her, but he turned toward the bar where champagne was chilling in a silver bucket.

Disappointment filled her. Quentin was always a perfect gentleman and never pressed her sexually. She considered his restraint one of his best qualities. Predators wanted either sex or money from a woman, and Quentin was no predator. Still, she'd hoped marriage would make him more affectionate.

She wandered slowly, fearing to blink lest this beautiful room disappear. Her shoes sank luxuriously into the velvety carpet. She eyed a low table with a pickled finish that gave the wood a rosy glow. The entire room seemed to glow. She edged closer to the bed.

Bed seemed far too mundane a noun to describe the plush wonder of the king-size mattress covered with a confection of pink satin and ecru lace, piled high with pillows. It seemed to invite her to jump into its plumpness.

"Would you like me to start a fire, darling?" Quentin asked.

"It would be pretty, but much too warm. I think not."

She enjoyed his handsome smile. Despite a tendency

to fat, he presented a solid, masculine figure. She loved his thick, black hair and couldn't wait to run her fingers through it. He held out a flute of champagne and a silver tray piled high with chocolate truffles.

At his urging, she selected a truffle. "No more champagne, thank you. I've already imbibed enough."

His eyebrows raised and the corners of his mouth turned down. "A private toast."

"You're the true romantic, not me." She accepted the champagne. Behind her the bed seemed to whisper her name and she tingled with anticipation. "To what shall we drink?"

"To you. You've made me a very happy man today. You have given me riches beyond compare."

"I do love you," she whispered, gazing into his warm brown eyes. Desire tickled her deep inside. With it came guilt. Her one affair had happened a long time ago when she was in college, but the shame from then mingled with her recent infatuation with Ross Duke. A horrible urge filled her to confess everything.

"Dawn? What's the matter?"

She had to look away. She had never meant to deceive him, but now she was trapped in her lies. "There are things about me you don't know." She pressed the rim of the flute against her lower lip. The fuzzy sweet-sourness tickled her nose. "I should have told you before. I—I—I have done something I'm rather ashamed of."

"I know everything about you I need to know." He touched her chin with a fingertip and gently urged her to look at him. "Darling Dawn. You are precious to me. If what you mean to say is you have acted a bit indiscreetly in the past, rest assured it makes no difference to me. What matters is now."

She searched his eyes, fearing she'd find anger or insincerity or jealousy. She found warmth, compassion and shining love. The urge to confess withered.

He touched her champagne flute with his. Crystal against crystal rang like a bell. "A toast to the happiness you have given me by becoming my bride."

He drank deeply; she followed suit, draining her champagne. An aftertaste tightened her cheeks. The wine had soured, leaving an acrid taste in her mouth. She smiled quickly so as not to spoil the moment.

Seconds later her head began to spin and nausea roiled in her belly. She regretted every drop of champagne she'd swallowed this evening.

"Darling?"

Quentin's voice seemed to come from a hundred miles away. Rosy lights swirled and danced, offering no opportunity to focus on anything. She swayed and was vaguely aware of dropping the truffle. She knew she had dropped it, but could not make her hand grab for it. Before she realized it, she was sitting on the bed while Quentin loomed over her. Her vision doubled and his image swam before her eyes.

"Are you all right?" he asked, smiling as he held her shoulders.

"The champagne…" Her voice sounded froggy and slow. Her head felt as if it weighed a thousand pounds and it took every ounce of willpower she possessed to hold it upright.

"An excellent vintage, wouldn't you agree? Only the best for you, darling, only the very best…"

DAWN OPENED her eyes slowly, painfully. Gradually her vision adjusted enough to give her a shadowy view of curtained windows. As her head cleared, she remembered she was in the honeymoon cabin with her new husband.

Chilled, she rubbed her bare arms. Stiff fabric against her forearms roused her curiosity. She felt her bosom and belly, tracing the patterns of leaves and roses. She recognized her sash and the embroidered-rose fasteners.

She was still wearing her wedding dress!

She gingerly felt about her and figured out she lay atop the covers on the bed. Which meant the large shape under the covers next to her was Quentin.

She covered her eyes with both hands. Only she—clumsy, inept, ridiculous she—could get drunk on her wedding night and pass out on her groom. She swore she'd never drink another drop of champagne as long as she lived.

"Quentin?" she said softly. "Dear?" She sat up and looked over his body. The cold blue light of the clock showed it was not yet five in the morning.

She eased off the bed. With both hands outstretched, she groped her way to the bathroom. Only after she had shut the door did she turn on the light.

The light seemed as bright as a phosphorous flare, piercing her eyeballs with needles. Eyes squeezed shut, she sagged against the door and groaned. So this was what a hangover felt like. Lovely.

The pain faded quickly and by degrees she opened her eyes, testing her tolerance. Except for a mild throbbing in her sinuses she felt fine.

She glowered at her reflection. Her beautiful dress was rumpled and dingy-looking. Half her hair had come loose and now hung in scruffy hanks around her face. What remained of the twist had tangled into a lopsided knot. Mascara was smeared under her eyes and her face was blotchy. The string of pearls had left a red imprint along her neck, giving her the appearance of a strangulation victim.

Groaning, she turned away from the mirror, and faced another. The bathroom was lined with mirrors and inset lighting. The afteraffects of her overindulgence were thrown back at her in triplicate and quadruplicate.

Her gaze rested on the bathtub, an oval gold- and-pink-marble delight big enough for two. If she hadn't been such a lush, she and Quentin could have spent an hour or two frolicking in the tub. "But, no," she muttered. "You have to drink too much and spoil everything."

She stripped out of her clothing, praying a good dry cleaner could repair the damage she'd done to her dress. She stepped into the shower stall and turned on the water full force in hopes that the hot, pulsating spray would make the remainder of her headache vanish.

When she was done, she peeked out of the bathroom. The room had lightened enough for her to discern Quentin's bulk under the covers. Not enough, though, for her to figure out where the employees who'd transferred her belongings from the lodge to this cabin had put her negligée.

She mustered courage. They were married, which meant no secrets—or shyness—between them. She looked down at her nude body. A strict regimen of exercise and proper diet kept her trim, but her breasts were too small and her hips were angular.

For better or worse, she thought. Quentin knew he hadn't married a beauty queen. Giving herself no time for cowardice, she stepped out of the bathroom. She left the door ajar and followed the narrow strip of light to the bed.

Quentin lay on his side with his back to her. The morning was cool, but not cold, yet the covers were bundled to his ear. She eased pillows out of the way, and slid under the sheets.

The heat radiating off him took her aback. She laid a hand against his bare shoulder, finding him damp with sweat. She marveled he could bear the weight of the sheets, blanket and comforter. A smile tugged her lips. Perhaps he had overindulged in the champagne, too. Perhaps she wasn't the only one who had been in no shape last night to take advantage of the bridal bed.

Perhaps he might forgive her.

She folded back the covers, baring him to the waist. Between the pale glow of the clock, the silvering light of dawn seeping through the curtains and the light from the bathroom, she had a view of a shadow man. He smelled hot and distinctly masculine. She caressed his shoulder and was amazed by how hard his muscles felt in repose. She explored his ribs and waist, finding him lean and muscular without a trace of softness. For a man who showed not the slightest interest in exercise or sports, he was in surprisingly good shape.

Heat flooded her midsection, centering deep within her belly. She pushed the covers all the way off, kicking the comforter off the bed. Wide-eyed, she sat up and admired his long, sleek body, now outlined in gold and silver.

"Quentin?" She poked his shoulder with a finger. "Quentin, it's morning, dear. Time to wake up."

He remained exactly as he had been.

Irked by his lack of response, she considered her options. Leaving him alone seemed the most considerate thing to do. Unlike her, Quentin was not a morning person. She could order coffee and breakfast. Surely the smell of coffee would rouse him in a gentle, friendly manner. Or, she could take a morning jog through the forest and he'd be awake by the time she returned.

She poked him again. This time he grunted and shifted

his arm. "I love you, dear," she said. "I'm sorry I drank too much last night. I have no head for alcohol."

She ran her tongue over a hard ridge of muscle along his triceps. His skin had a faintly salty taste, with a woodsy undertone. He shifted again and pawed at his face. She kissed the side of his neck and his hair tickled her nose. He made a soft *mmm* sound, and she decided it meant approval.

Amused, but frustrated, she wondered if there were boundaries of taste in marital relations. This one-sided exploration was beginning to make her feel as if she were molesting him.

She grasped his shoulder with both hands and pulled him over onto his back. He lolled, his right hand flopping onto the mattress.

"Are you playing a joke on me?" She peered closely at his face, longing to see his features. "Wake up, dear."

She delicately touched the center of his chest, resting her fingertips over his heart. His chest rose and fell, and crisp hairs parted before her caress. His skin had cooled. She followed the cleft between his pectorals, up to the bony ridge of his clavicle, detoured in the intriguing musculature at the base of his throat and then to his chin. Beard stubble rasped her fingers. She found his lips supple and soft.

She pressed a kiss to his mouth.

She drew back a few inches. He smacked his lips.

"I knew you were awake," she whispered. She kissed him again, savoring the erotic sensitivity of her lips and the warmth of his.

He touched a hand to her shoulder. Triumphant, grown giddy with excitement, she pressed the kiss and he responded by parting his lips. She touched the tip of her tongue to his and fire burst within her, filling her with liquid heat. He clutched her shoulder, his fingers touchingly awkward, but very strong.

Unable to bear either the silence or darkness, she reached over his chest and groped for the nightstand. He slid his hand over her back and pressed her closer to him. His mouth turned hot against her neck, kissing her with wet lustiness. She shivered.

"Let me find the light, dear." Her body was twisted into an awkward position, so she struggled for balance. He resisted her efforts, holding her against him with one arm. Her breasts burned against his chest. She almost gave up on finding the lamp when his hold relaxed and she lunged over his body.

He mumbled unintelligibly and stroked his hand flat along her spine, ending up resting it boldly on her bare bottom. She gasped and found the lamp. She turned on the light.

Turning about, resting across his body, she smiled down at her groom.

She realized instantly the situation was not right, but it was *so* not right her brain locked up, unable to process what she saw. Instead of falling in heavy, jet-black, straight hanks, his hair was brown and soft with a curl. His face, instead of being rather full with heavy jowls, was lean and chiseled with high cheekbones and a squarish jaw. The eyes were all wrong, too. Instead of warm brown, they were bleary, bloodshot and pewter-gray.

He squinted as if the light pained him.

Dawn remembered a time she'd absentmindedly walked into a men's room instead of the ladies' room. It had taken several seconds for the sight of urinals and the absence of a vanity to sink in so she could realize her mistake. Once she had, she'd been horrified.

But not half as horrified as she was now.

Ross Duke grimaced. "Dawn? What are you doing in my room?"

Chapter Three

A reasonable explanation existed. One always did, even if it didn't appear exactly reasonable at first glance. Or so Dawn told herself as she stared at Ross's confused face.

But explanations, reasonable or otherwise, eluded her completely. Ending up naked in a bed with her husband's best man defied explanation. Scarcely daring to breathe, her heart drumming in her ears, she inched backward, cringing as her breasts collided with his chest. She groped blindly for a pillow, found something fluffy and snatched it to her bosom. Never taking her eyes off Ross's face, she crawled slowly, clumsily across the bed.

Ross watched her as if she were a strange, potentially dangerous species of animal.

The mattress seemed a hundred yards wide, but finally her feet found empty air and she slid onto the floor. Hunched over, holding the pillow over her breasts and belly, she backed toward the bathroom.

Ross suddenly dropped an arm over his eyes.

She scooted into the bathroom and slammed the door, fumbling with the lock until it turned. She looked wildly around the bathroom. Spying a pair of fluffy, terry-cloth robes hanging on the back of the door, she grabbed one, dropped the pillow and clothed herself.

Half-fearing Ross would come bursting through the door, she kept a fierce gaze on it as she sank onto the rim of the bathtub.

"A nightmare," she whispered. Her heart thudded, making her chest ache.

This had to be a nightmare—a reasonable enough explanation considering all the champagne and rich food she'd indulged in last night. If she went to the door and peeked out, the man on the bed would be Quentin. She'd married Quentin, she'd gone to bed with Quentin, she'd explored Quentin's body and nearly made love to him.

She was going insane.

Or perhaps... Her eyes widened, and her heart began hammering anew. She'd had a nightmare and sleep-walked, something she'd done often as a child. This wasn't the honeymoon cabin, it was Ross's room in the lodge. By now, Quentin must have realized she was missing and he'd never understand how she'd ended up in his best friend's bedroom.

Sharp raps on the door made her moan. She clutched her knees, certain she was going to be sick. *Please be Quentin,* she prayed, *let me wake up and discover the man banging on the door is Quentin.*

"Dawn? What's going on? Open the door."

Ross! Tears rose, but she choked them down, leaving her throat sore and her eyes burning. She rocked on the tub edge.

"I'm in trouble here," he called. "Please open the door."

He was in trouble? As far as he was concerned, this situation held the potential for a funny story to tell all his friends. She, on the other hand, had awakened from a somnambulist nightmare in another man's bed and hadn't the faintest idea how to explain her near-adultery to her husband!

"Dawn? Sweetheart, answer me. Are you all right? Dawn!"

The edge of fear in his voice reached her. She crept to the door. "Please go away," she called through the wood.

"I can't. Open the door."

Steeling her nerves, she unlocked the door and opened it about an inch. She peered out. To her relief Ross had wrapped a sheet around his waist.

He held up a hand, showing her his empty palm. "I swear to God, I don't know how I got in here. Where's Quent?"

She opened the door wide enough to take a good look at the room. She recognized the honeymoon cabin. So it *was* her bed, not Ross's. She opened the door all the way.

With one hand clutching the sheet, Ross held his head with his other hand and staggered toward the bed. He sat heavily, bent over so his face nearly touched his knees. "Where's Quent?"

Good question. She tiptoed out of the bathroom and turned on a nearby light. Ross winced away from the new source of illumination. He rubbed his eyes with the pads of his fingers. Glancing frequently at him to make certain he didn't try anything funny, she searched the room. No Quentin.

She did find her belongings. Her luggage was stacked neatly inside a closet and her garments had been draped on hangers or folded and placed in dresser drawers. But she didn't find anything belonging to her husband. Not a suitcase or a shirt or a hairbrush, nothing. Feeling a rise of panic, she dropped onto a chair and lowered her head between her knees. She breathed deeply until she could think again.

"Dawn?" His eyes were a little clearer. "Do you feel sick, too?"

"Where is my husband? What have you done with him?"

"I didn't do anything." He gave his head a shake, and winced. "Feels like two weeks' worth of bad booze."

"Get dressed and get out! If this is a joke, it isn't funny. So you—"

"Quit yelling at me." He pressed his hands to his ears. "I can't think."

Dawn jumped off the chair and rushed to the bed. She tore through the covers around the floor, looking for Ross's clothing. She didn't find so much as a sock. "I don't want you to think. I want you out of here. Where are your clothes?"

"I don't know." He held out a hand, but she skittered away, putting as much distance between them as possible without actually leaving the room. He groaned and dropped his hand. "Fine. I'll just march my naked butt across the grounds to the lodge. Everybody will get a big laugh out of that."

She gazed at the window. The sun was up. "You don't know where your clothes are? You don't know where my husband is?"

"No."

The mournful look he gave her went straight to her heart. Acknowledging his status as a victim did little to calm or assure her. She clutched her knees with shaking hands. "There is a perfectly reasonable explanation for this."

"Okay?" He eyed her expectantly. "What?"

"To start with, how did you get in here?"

He turned his attention to the door. Neither the chain nor the security catch were fastened. "I think I got conked on the head." He lifted a hand to his head and poked around the back of his skull. He winced. "I've got a bruise."

Warily, hoping he was telling a tall tale—the implications of his telling the truth were too horrible to contemplate—she moved to his side. He leaned forward and she examined the back of his head. She found a tender spot and a bump on his scalp.

"Do you think you have a concussion?"

"Maybe, I don't know. I saw a prowler sneaking around the honeymoon cabins. He must have hit me."

She sat on the edge of the bed, but away from him. Even touching his hair reminded her too vividly of how closely she'd come to unwitting adultery—how much she'd desired him. Even looking at him was dangerous.

"I was helping out Stefan last night. Playing valet and fetching cars for your guests—"

"You were working?"

"I made twenty-eight bucks in tips." A ghost of a smile appeared on his haggard face. "Anyway, your last guest left around midnight. I was about to turn in when Stefan said he saw someone carrying luggage to the parking lot."

"Why is that unusual?"

"It's unusual at midnight when there aren't any guests checking out. But when I reached the parking lot, I couldn't find anybody. It bugged me. Stefan is just a kid, but he doesn't make things up. He and I hung out in the parking lot for about an hour. I finally sent him to bed, but then I saw somebody on the walkway headed toward the Honeymoon Hideaway."

She made herself look closely at his face while he

spoke. The story had a fishy ring to it, beginning with him helping Stefan fetch cars for the guests. None of this led to an explanation as to where her husband had gone.

"The lights were on inside this cabin. I thought I saw somebody peeking in the window."

Dawn inhaled sharply. "A peeping Tom?"

"I don't know for certain," he added quickly. "The bushes and trees are thick. Shadows are funny. What I really had was a feeling."

"A feeling?"

"Call it a hunch." He averted his gaze. "I was worried about you. The Colonel doesn't have professional security people. He thinks he can handle any problems himself. So I snooped around." He touched the back of his head, his expression turned thoughtful. "Somebody hit me."

He looked much, much better than he had only a few minutes ago. His color was normal and his eyes had cleared. Dawn shook her head in denial. If he'd been struck hard enough to render him unconscious for hours, then he would have a severe concussion. Yet at the moment he didn't display a single symptom of a head injury.

He narrowed his eyes. "You don't believe me."

"My husband is missing. You're not. I'm sorry, Ross, but your story has a few holes in it."

"I'm telling the truth."

"Like the Jesse James suite was the truth? Or what about the white stallion your father caught trying to steal mares from the stable, which turned out to be a valuable circus horse kidnapped for ransom? I believed those tall tales, at first." She jumped to her feet and paced. The snakes in her belly writhed painfully. "If this is some kind of horrible joke you and Quentin have concocted, it isn't funny. It will never be funny."

"Dawn, look at me. Do you see me laughing? Do you see one teeny-tiny *ha ha* anywhere in this scenario? Yeah, I like a good joke, but I'm not cruel."

She paused in her pacing and stared miserably at the floor. "Then where is Quentin?"

"I don't know." He combed his fingers through his hair and frowned, his gaze distant. "Look around. See if he left a note. A message on the phone. Anything."

She had already looked, but did so again. Confirming that all of Quentin's luggage and other belongings were missing only heightened her fear. "Robbers," she said. "They stole all of Quentin's belongings and took him hostage. I must call the police."

"Robbers," he echoed, making no attempt to soften his skepticism. "I can think of a lot easier things to steal than your husband. Maybe it was Quentin who Stefan saw carrying luggage to the parking lot."

"Are you saying he deserted me?"

He lowered his face.

"He wouldn't do that. He loves me. We're newly-weds!" She rushed to the telephone. "I must call the police. Quentin could be hurt. Oh my God, he's been kidnapped—"

"Haven't you forgotten something?"

She pressed the handset to her breast. "What?"

"I'm in my birthday suit."

His meaning sank in. A naked man who was not her husband, but inside her honeymoon cabin, might distract investigators. Not to mention the embarrassing scandal it would cause when Ross's family and the resort employees found out. Her only consolation was that all her guests had returned to Colorado Springs. Deliberately scandalous acts were usually forgiven, but stupidity rarely was. Ending up with the wrong man in her bridal bed reeked of idiocy. She caught her lower lip in her teeth.

The more she considered it, the more Ross's words rang with truth. This situation was cruel. Not to mention the fact that her valuables weren't missing. If robbers had invaded the cabin, why wouldn't they have stolen her wallet and jewelry? She hung up the telephone. "Did you say something to Quentin?"

He drew his head warily aside. "Like what?"

Guilt tangled with her fear. Quentin could have intuited her doubts about the wisdom of their marriage, or worse, somehow sensed her attraction to Ross. Quentin could have punished her by arranging for Ross to end up in her bed.

"About us. Did you say something to make him jealous?"

Her question appeared to offend him. He rose from the bed and straightened the sheet about his waist.

"Answer me."

"You don't deserve an answer."

"You can't deny you tried to stop me from marrying him."

"Any aspirin around here?" He headed for the bathroom.

"Answer me!"

He turned her a black scowl. "Yeah, I didn't want you marrying him. He's a sleazebag and you're too good for him. But I didn't say a word about you to him. I'd never hurt you like that. Not in a million years."

"If you're trying to convince me of your nobility, it's not working. That's a mean, rotten thing to say about your best friend."

"Best friend?" He snorted. "I barely know the guy."

Before she could demand an explanation of what he meant, he entered the bathroom and closed the door.

ROSS EXCHANGED the bulky sheet for a bathrobe. As he tied the belt, he gazed at the Elk River logo embroidered on the robe. Harassing the colonel was a lot of fun, but this mix-up held the potential to give the old man a stroke. Not to mention the harm it might do to Dawn. What a mess.

He cursed himself for not listening to his gut instincts concerning Quentin Bayliss.

Steeling himself, grateful that the fuzziness in his head had abated, he opened the bathroom door.

Dawn was perched on the edge of a chair, her hands clenched in her lap and her feet pressed together on the floor. The Elk River robe swaddled her slim shoulders and the hem pooled around her feet, making her look smaller than she was. Her calm was an illusion. Her big, blue eyes spoke loudly of her pain and fear. For one of the few times in his life, words eluded him.

"I called Janine," she said.

His mouth fell open.

"I had to call someone."

He dropped onto a chair. "Why my sister?"

"You'd rather I'd called the Colonel? Janine is bringing clothing for you." Her chin quivered and her eyes glistened. "I didn't tell her anything. I didn't know what to tell her. Should I call the police? What shall I tell them?"

"I don't know." He closed his eyes, not looking forward to confronting Janine. She was almost as hard-headed as the Colonel.

"There must be a reasonable explanation."

Her quavering voice threatened to break his heart. He

didn't see anything reasonable about any of this. He fingered the half-dollar sized tender bump on the back of his head. He couldn't figure out how an injury so minor could have knocked him out. Or given him a headache that had temporarily felt like the world's worst hangover. Since he hadn't drunk a drop of alcohol last night, it made no sense whatsoever.

"Everything has a reasonable explanation," she said. "With a bit of thought and applied logic, an answer can be found for any mystery."

Her determined efforts to make sense out of senselessness made his heart ache. "Did you and Quent argue last night? Stefan told me there was some kind of disturbance at the reception."

She played with her wedding ring. "We didn't argue. He became a trifle upset when Connie brought Desdemona Hunter to the reception. Her photographer upset Quentin."

"Desdemona... The name is familiar."

"She writes the 'Party Patter' column in the newspaper. Society news. Quentin didn't want any reporters covering the wedding. But he wasn't angry with me. I know he wasn't. He was perfectly happy when we came to the cabin. He—he carried me over the threshold." She pressed a fist to her mouth. "I was...intoxicated. Everyone was making toasts. Quentin and I had champagne here, and it proved the final straw. I fell asleep." She looked away. "I passed out."

Ross frowned at a champagne bottle on a table. He'd seen the newlyweds leave the lodge last night. Dawn hadn't been acting as if she were drunk. He went to the table and picked up the champagne bottle. It was nearly full. He checked waste baskets. No other bottles. His nape prickled. "You left the lodge around ten."

"How do you know that?"

"I told you, I was out front helping Stefan with the parking. You didn't look drunk to me."

"I was." Hot color flushed her cheeks and she hunched over, hugging her elbows. "I must have been. The last thing I remember is drinking a glass of champagne. I slept in my wedding dress!"

Ross made an effort to ignore the implication that Dawn and Quent hadn't consummated their wedding vows. Knowing Quent hadn't made love to her pleased him too much. But seeing Dawn upset and near panic didn't please him in the least, so he lifted the champagne bottle to the light, searching for clues.

A knock on the door startled him. He nearly dropped the bottle. Dawn leapt to her feet, shifting her gaze wildly between him and the bed. He recalled vividly the sight of her small, perfect body hovering over him and the feel of her silky skin. Despite his grogginess, he'd been ready and willing to make love to her, and would have if she hadn't turned on the light.

"Be cool," he said.

She patted her head. Her hair was damp. "What am I going to say?"

The knocking turned insistent.

"It's Janine." He hoped. At the moment he wouldn't be surprised if Quent, playing a sick game of outraged husband, burst into the cabin.

Before he could suggest she get dressed, Dawn answered the door. Clutching an armload of clothing, his sister stood on the porch. Barely acknowledging Dawn, Janine swept inside and deposited the clothes on the bed. Ross recognized his jeans, a T-shirt and his tuxedo.

Janine turned on him. "What the heck are you pulling now, Ross? What are you doing here? Why was your tux in the bushes? You've pulled some bonehead stunts before, but this beats all. Do you have any idea what the Colonel is going to say? And what about Mom?"

Ross backed away from the finger Janine shook in his face. Even though she was two years younger than he, Janine had always acted older. Strong-willed, ambitious, and outspoken, she was their father's daughter. He wished they were twelve and ten years old again so he could sit on her and make her shut up.

"Pardon me, Janine," Dawn said. She stood rigidly, holding the neck closed on her robe. "Janine!"

His sister tossed her mane of thick brown hair and gave a start as if just now noticing Dawn.

"Quentin is missing. Ross and I are the victims of a crime."

"Crime? What kind of crime?"

Ross grabbed his clothing and made a hasty escape into the bathroom. While he dressed in the jeans and T-shirt, he frowned at his tuxedo. Pine straw and bits of bark clung to the black fabric. He frowned, too, at Dawn's rumpled wedding dress, which hung on a hook on the bathroom door. Someone knocking him out, stripping him naked, tossing his clothing into the bushes then putting him in bed with the bride was too twisted for one of Dawn's hoped-for reasonable explanations. An explanation existed, but he doubted if it would be reasonable or pleasant.

When he emerged from the bathroom Janine had calmed down considerably. She gave him a suspicious glance, but continued listening to Dawn explain what had happened.

Dawn passed a hand wearily over her eyes. "I want to deny it, but I can't. Quentin has been kidnapped."

Janine twisted a strand of hair around her fingers.

"You claim you saw a prowler, Ross. Why didn't you call the Colonel?"

Stung by her skepticism, he said, "I didn't have a phone."

"Don't be a smart aleck."

"I didn't have time to call in the SWAT team. It was after one o'clock in the morning when I saw someone headed for the Honeymoon Hideaway. I thought I saw him peeking in the windows. For all I knew it was a pervert checking out the newlyweds. Should I have left him there while I ran back to the lodge?"

Janine reversed the twisting of her hair. "Let me see your head. Dawn says you're injured."

He sat so she could examine the back of his skull. Her ministrations weren't nearly as gentle as Dawn's had been. "Ow! Watch it." He pushed her hand away.

"That's not much of a bump." Janine grasped his chin, forcing his face up. She peered critically into his eyes. "You look okay to me."

"Ever consider nursing, Ninny? You'd be a natural."

"Don't call me Ninny," she murmured absently, twisting her hair again.

"Ross was knocked unconscious. I can vouch for that much," Dawn said. "You haven't seen Quentin at the lodge?"

Dawn's hopeful note tugged at him. If Janine hadn't been here, he'd give in to his urge to offer Dawn a shoulder to cry on.

"I haven't seen him." Janine glanced at her wristwatch. "The dining room isn't open yet. He wasn't in the lobby drinking coffee, either. I just can't believe he's been kidnapped. Is there a ransom note?"

Dawn hung her head. Her shoulders hitched.

Ross stepped between them and gave his sister a pointed look. "Dawn, get dressed. We'll figure this out."

As if her joints were made of wood, Dawn gathered clothing from the closet and dresser drawers. When she entered the bathroom and closed the door, Ross turned on his sister.

"Ease up. Can't you see how upset she is?"

Her blue-gray eyes flashed. "I'm starting to catch on to why."

"What is that supposed to mean?"

"Don't play stupid." She poked the center of his chest with a rigid finger. "Everybody saw how lovey-dovey the pair of you were last week. Did Quentin catch you playing patty-cake with his blushing bride?"

"Keep your voice down."

She lowered her voice, but her temper seemed to increase. "Maybe it's a big joke to you hitting on every woman you meet, but she was engaged. Quentin found out you'd been having an affair with his fiancée, didn't he?"

Only Janine, who generally spoke first and did damage control later, would have had the guts to say that. But if she said it, then others would be thinking it. His pride was stung. Sister or not, she had no right to accuse him of acting like a creep. "You're lucky you're a girl. I'd deck you—"

"Go ahead!" She put up her fists.

Sisters! Not doubting for a moment she'd love a chance to pop him on the nose, Ross clamped his hands on his hips. "Dawn and I aren't having an affair."

"Then why did Quentin leave?"

He glanced at the bathroom door. Grasping Janine by the shoulder, he lowered his head until their faces were only inches apart. "Think what you want about me, but don't you dare say a single word about Dawn. I'm not taking that from you or anybody. Got it?''

"What am I supposed to think? I know what I—"

"Shut up and listen to me. Quent lied to me. He—"

"Lied about what?"

"About her. He told me their marriage was a business deal. Merging two households for tax purposes. A marriage-of-convenience kind of thing. He made her sound like a dried-up old lady, always keeping a sharp eye on the bottom line."

She began twisting her hair again. "Why would he say that? Every time I spoke to Dawn about the wedding arrangements I got the impression she was madly in love with him."

He shrugged, growing irritable with confusion. "It was none of my business why they got married. She never said much about Quent, and I didn't have anything to say about him, either. We never discussed their relationship."

Janine took a step backward. Her eyes widened. "You actually care about her."

"I care about a lot of people." As a dyed-in-the-wool feminist, his sister delighted in ragging him about his Neanderthal attitudes toward women. Usually he delighted in egging her on and teasing her with his false machismo. Her accusing manner now made him realize she actually believed at least some of his self-generated reputation.

"You *really* care about her."

"We're friends, nothing more."

"Look me straight in the eye," she ordered. "And tell me you aren't having an affair with her."

"I wouldn't lie about her."

"You lie to the Colonel all the time."

"That's different. He enjoys being disappointed in me. I'm just making him happy."

"Ross..."

He looked her squarely in the eyes. "Dawn and I aren't having an affair."

Janine crossed her arms. "So why did Quentin leave?"

He wished he knew.

Chapter Four

The Duke clan gathered in the resort's main office. Shunted off to the side, Dawn watched the family. The noise astonished her.

Elise Duke, looking too blond, elegant and young to have four adult children, hovered like an anxious hummingbird around Ross. She poked and prodded his head and peered into his eyes. In the universal maternal gesture, she pressed the back of her hand against his forehead. "Are you dizzy? Seeing double? Do you have a headache?"

The Colonel posted himself in front of the door. Shoulders back, chin up, he glowered at his son. "State the facts again," he ordered. "No embellishments. I want to know what you were doing in the honeymoon cabin."

Behind the desk, Janine sat on her chair. Arms crossed, she shifted her gaze between her brother and father. "He doesn't have a concussion, Mom," she said. "Go ahead, call his bluff. Call the paramedics."

On either side of the desk, Megan and Kara Duke traded stories about Ross as a teenager. Megan said, "Remember when he got caught skinny-dipping?"

Kara laughed and added, "Three girls! What were their names? Debbie Parsons—"

"Not Parsons," Megan interrupted. "She was Janine's friend. It was Debbie Calloway. Remember? She started dying her hair in the sixth grade."

In the middle of all this chaos Ross appeared resigned, as if this sort of fracas were business as usual. How this family functioned when everyone talked at once and nobody paid any attention to anyone else baffled Dawn. In her family communication had been simple: Father had spoken, Dawn and Mother had listened.

A wan, cold sensation gave her gooseflesh and she rubbed her arms. Except the chill came not from the room temperature, but from deep within her soul. Now that the initial shock of Quentin's disappearance had passed, she felt numb. Witnessing this crew in a free-for-all did nothing to clear her confusion or ease her fear.

She stepped away from a filing cabinet, clearing her throat with a loud, "Ahem."

"If you saw a prowler," the Colonel continued grilling Ross, "on the walkway, which is well-lighted, why can't you describe him? 'Some guy' is not a description."

"Pardon me," Dawn said.

"Nobody hit you. You tripped and banged your head," Janine said. "This whole story is fishy. Come clean, Ross. What really happened?"

Noticing a telephone book atop the filing cabinet, Dawn picked it up. Weighing it and her intended action, she decided desperate times called for desperate measures. She whomped the book against the filing cabinet. The resulting bang shut every mouth and turned every eye toward her. Embarrassed, but determined, she replaced the telephone book where she'd found it.

"Pardon me." She straightened her shoulders. "My husband has been kidnapped. I appreciate very much the way everyone helped me search the grounds for him. As you all can see, he is definitely missing. I should call the police now."

The Colonel harrumphed. The three sisters exchanged sheepish glances. Elise hurried forward and grasped Dawn's arm, urging her to sit. Ross gave her a look of unmistakable approval, so warm and focused that for a moment she forgot her situation. Everything centered on his slight smile.

"I agree your husband is MIA," the Colonel said. "But I do not agree he has been kidnapped. His vehicle is no longer parked in the POV lot. That suggests he is AWOL."

"Speak English, dear." Elise patted Dawn's arm. "Your acronyms are confusing her."

But Dawn understood the Colonel. Everyone believed Quentin had left on his own. "My car is missing, too." Her cheeks flushed. At Quentin's insistence, she had purchased the brand new Lincoln Mark VIII only three weeks ago as an early birthday present for him. It was his car rather than hers, but to have it stolen, leaving her stranded, added insult to injury. "If my husband left of his own volition, he could not have taken both cars."

"She has you there, Colonel," Ross said. "Call the sheriff. Let him figure it out."

"You are not given permission to speak."

Ross half rose from the chair. Muscles tightened in his jaw and his smile turned thin and tight. The Colonel tensed and his hands curled into fists. The enmity between father and son turned the air electric. Fearing she was about to see them start swinging at each other, Dawn pressed a hand to her mouth.

Ross glanced at her. He dropped back onto the chair.

For a moment the Colonel looked disappointed that Ross refused to fight. "Logistically, given the scenario you present, Mrs. Bayliss, I do not see how it is possible for kidnappers to have accomplished their mission.''

"But we'll call the sheriff anyway." Janine picked up the telephone. "This is way too strange, Colonel. Let the sheriff figure it out." Glaring at her brother as she dialed, she muttered, "If you need to come clean, you'd better do it before the cops arrive."

Elise took Dawn's hand. "Come to my office, dear. I have a couch. You can put your feet up. Megan, bring us some coffee." She looked to her husband again and spoke in a calm, somewhat dreamy voice. "Dear, perhaps it might be a good idea to take one more look around."

The couple exchanged a significant look, fraught with meaning. Dawn supposed the Dukes were as her parents had been, gifted with a type of mental telepathy developed over many years of marriage. A catch gripped her throat. She and Quentin might never have the chance to develop the art of reading each other's minds.

Numbly, she allowed Elise to escort her out of the business office, down the hall to the small office where Elise organized receptions, parties and conferences for the resort guests.

"Do forgive my family, dear," Elise said. "Despite the Colonel's insistence on strict discipline, my children tend to be willful." She sounded proud of them for it.

"They are...energetic." At Elise's urging, she sat on a camelback love seat.

Ross entered the office and joined Dawn on the love seat. "You've got a knack for crowd control. I'm impressed."

"Uh, dear, perhaps you should leave Mrs. Bayliss alone."

"Dawn needs me."

She did need him and that was reason enough to keep

as far away from him as possible. She'd come within seconds of committing adultery with him—intentional or not. Having him so near now reminded her of caressing his body and kissing him, and of the fun they'd had last week. The walks in the forest, the countless times he'd reduced her to helpless laughter with his silly tall tales...and how gazing into his eyes made her soul sing, as if with bells. If Quentin had left on his own, then he knew of her attraction to Ross. Accepting Ross's support now would do little toward soothing Quentin's jealousy.

Still, she could not make herself tell him to go away.

Kara poked her head into the office. "Mom, the Colonel wants to speak to you. He's in the kitchen." She avoided meeting Dawn's eyes.

Elise gave her son a warning look and left the office door standing open.

"How are you doing?" Ross asked quietly. He picked up her right hand and massaged it.

His touch distracted her. She stared at his long, muscular fingers. "I'm frightened. He must have been kidnapped, there's no other explanation."

"If this is a kidnapping, then the crooks took some weird risks. Does Quent have a habit of taking off?"

She shook her head, but couldn't put much conviction into the denial. "I suppose I don't know." She closed her eyes. "I don't know him as well as I should. We met only four months ago."

"Short engagement."

She pulled her hand away from his. "Everything happened so fast. He quite literally swept me off my feet. But I took every precaution. I followed my attorney's advice."

"What does that mean?"

"A woman in my position can't be too careful." She

stared at a window, but could not focus. "I have to be-
ware of predators. Father always assured me I'd make a
good marriage even though…I'm not pretty or interesting
or anything. He warned me that because of my inheritance, men might try to take advantage of me. I never
expected to find anyone who loves me as Quentin does."

He leaned close, his breathing deep and even, until her
awareness of him made her turn her head. "You don't
think you're pretty?"

"I hold no illusions about myself."

"You're beautiful, Dawn."

His words were sweet, but she knew better. Her mother
had been a beautiful woman. As her father had frequently
pointed out, Dawn could in no way, shape or form compare to Mother.

"This is not the time for flattery, Ross."

He snorted derisively and leaned back. Hooking his
hands behind his neck, he stared at the ceiling. "Try the
obvious. Call him."

She slid her pocketbook onto her lap and brought out
her Daytimer. She could not make herself open it. "He
never liked me calling him. If he's at home, it means
he's angry with me. Will you call? You know him better
than I do." The admission pained her and she had to
pause, breathing deeply until the hurt eased. "Has he
ever done anything like this before?"

He slid his hands off his neck. "I barely know him."

"But you've been friends since high school."

His expression turned incredulous. "I met him six
weeks ago, up in Cripple Creek." He clamped his mouth
shut and averted his gaze.

"I distinctly recall him saying you'd been friends since
high school." She also recalled Quentin saying Ross

owned Elk River resort. Thoroughly confused, she rubbed her temples. "He has no reason to lie."

"Neither do I."

"Then why were you his best man at the wedding?"

"I felt sorry for him." His brow lowered. He tapped his fingers against his knee. "He gave me a sob story about his brother dying. I thought, hey, what's the big deal? I already own a tux, so it doesn't cost me anything."

Uncertain what to believe, she opened her Daytimer and found Quentin's telephone number. "I'm sorry, Ross, but this doesn't make any sense. He told me we were to have the wedding here because you own the resort and you needed the business. It was a favor to you. Now I'm supposed to believe you barely know him."

"I'm starting to believe Quent likes to play games with the truth."

"He's my husband. He loves me. He has no reason to lie to me." Her chest tightened as if iron bands squeezed her ribs.

"And I do? The only connection I have to the resort is that my family owns it. Quent didn't know about it until a few weeks ago, when I mentioned I was taking a vacation. Then he got all excited and wanted to have the wedding here."

As the information sank in, Dawn clenched her fists. When Quentin had proposed, she'd wanted an August or September wedding date. Since her father had passed away the previous July, she'd wanted to wait at least a full year before marrying. Out of the blue, Quentin had insisted on changing the date and holding the wedding and honeymoon at Elk River. He'd been adamant about the early June date—just as he'd insisted she spend a week at the resort.

Ross touched her Daytimer. "I'll call."

She handed over the book. Lost in a fog of disturbing questions, she stared at her hands while Ross made the call.

"Phone's been disconnected," he said. "No forwarding number."

"Oh. Of course. He'll be living in my home. He was moving his belongings last week."

"Right."

His sarcasm cut her to the bone. "He did not desert me. He wouldn't do it. He loves me."

Ross sat on his mother's chair and lifted his feet to the desk. Rocking lightly, he stared off into space. "The sheriff is sure to have some ideas."

WHEN DEPUTY SHERIFF Mike Downes arrived at the resort he interviewed Dawn and Ross in an efficient, but sympathetic manner. A young man with sandy hair and quick green eyes that never left Dawn's face while she spoke, the deputy wrote without looking at the paper. Then, accompanied by the Colonel and Ross, he investigated the Honeymoon Hideaway cabin and he spoke to Stefan about the person seen carrying luggage at midnight.

Dawn waited in Elise's office. She drank coffee and nibbled a bagel, but had little appetite. She prayed the kidnappers had left a clue the deputy would find.

"Mrs. Bayliss?" the deputy asked from the doorway.

She prepared herself for the worst. "What have you found? What shall I do?"

He spoke softly to someone behind him before entering the office and closing the door. He sat on a chair. His empty hands heightened Dawn's fear. Shouldn't he be taking notes?

"The Colonel tells me there was a fight last night at the reception."

"It wasn't a fight, or even an argument. A friend of mine invited a society reporter to the reception. Quentin is publicity-shy. He didn't want the reporter there."

"Did you argue about it later?"

"Quentin never mentioned the incident again. Nor did I. It was forgotten as soon as it happened. You believe he left on his own, don't you? He didn't. I know he didn't. I'm a wealthy woman, deputy. My father was Edward Lovell, a prominent attorney. Quentin is also wealthy." She turned her worried gaze toward the window. "Father always worried about kidnappers. Especially those who kidnap for political purposes."

"Does Mr. Bayliss have political connections?"

Realizing she didn't even know the names of Quentin's friends, much less his political affiliations, embarrassment heated her face. "I don't believe so. He is, however, a real-estate developer. That could make him a target of environmental terrorists."

"Mrs. Bayliss, there's no evidence of a crime. No signs of a struggle. Nobody heard a disturbance. Even Ross can't swear he was actually assaulted. Every indication points to your husband leaving on his own. The bellboy swears he saw a person carrying luggage to the parking lot. Since Mr. Bayliss's luggage is missing, I'd say he was the person Stefan saw."

She began shaking her head and kept shaking it as the deputy reasonably explained why he could not investigate Quentin's disappearance as a crime. The most he could do was take a missing-persons report—after forty-eight hours had passed.

"He's been kidnapped!"

"Mrs. Bayliss." His voice was mellow and slow, as

if he were speaking to a rather stupid child. "How big is your husband?"

"Um, about six feet, two inches tall. Perhaps two hundred and twenty pounds."

"And you're what, about five foot four, maybe a hundred and ten? It would make sense for kidnappers to take the victim who'd give them the least problem."

"And if it's political? If the criminals are terrorists?"

"They wouldn't be interested in making sure he has clean jammies, ma'am. They wouldn't take his luggage. Besides, a big man like your husband would fight, but you didn't wake up. Housekeeping tells me Mr. Bayliss specifically requested they not unpack his luggage."

She kept shaking her head.

"I know you're upset, but this kind of thing happens all the time. A man gets angry and walks out. Then he gets embarrassed. The longer he's missing, the more embarrassed he gets. You live in Colorado Springs, right? He's probably at home right now, worrying about how you all will kiss and make up."

"What about the cars? Quentin could not have driven both cars."

"My guess is, he took one car and asked one of the wedding guests to drive the other. Being spiteful, you know? I'm not going to dig around for what you two were fighting about. It's none of my business, ma'am. My advice is, go home. I'm ninety-nine-percent certain you'll find him there." He gave her a reassuring smile. "I'm not married myself, but from what I understand there are bugs to work out in any marriage. Get some counseling. Learn how to argue without getting the cops involved."

Her face burned and her throat tightened, but she maintained a calm facade until the deputy left the room. She maintained it as she gathered her pocketbook and left the office. Ross awaited her. She couldn't face him; she couldn't face anybody.

"Do you want me to drive you home?" he asked.

She walked past him. "I must return to the cabin."

He tried to talk to her as she left the lodge and turned onto the gravel walkway leading to the Honeymoon Hideaway. Humiliation and fear blinded her to the sunny day and the columbine blooms peeking out of the shadows. Her dream romance had turned into a nightmare.

After she unlocked the cabin, Ross reached past her and opened the door. As she walked inside, she felt positive for a moment that Quentin would be there. Seated on a chair, perhaps, wearing a sheepish grin, launching into a rapid speech of apology and explanation.

But the cabin was empty, its rosy glow drained away into gloom.

A shuddering sob racked her, head to toe.

Ross gathered her into his arms. He splayed his large hand against her head and pressed her cheek to his shoulder. "I know this is awful, sweetheart. I know."

A single tear escaped her burning eyes. A wail rose in her throat, but stuck there, swelling until she thought she'd choke. Ross petted her hair and held her tight as he murmured soothing nonsense.

The spell passed and she grew aware of the wrongness of her situation. Quentin should be the man holding her. It should be his warm body her fear-chilled body sought for comfort. She worked her hands under Ross's arms and pushed against his chest.

He released her, but reached for her face. She turned away.

He shoved his hands in his pockets. "Pack your stuff. I'll have Kara check you out, then I'll drive you home."

"I must wait here. The kidnappers will call." She sat on the edge of the bed and stared at the telephone.

"Dawn, there aren't any kidnappers."

"It's the only reasonable explanation. They will make a ransom demand."

"You're in shock, you're upset. I understand."

"I am quite clearheaded, thank you very much."

He muttered a profanity. She slanted a sharp look at him.

"You're being stubborn." His gray eyes had darkened under lowered brows. "I should have never let you marry him."

"That's a ridiculous thing to say. You couldn't have stopped me, and you had no right to try."

Gone was the lighthearted playboy who'd been her companion. This Ross looked older, harder and very angry. He'd been victimized by the kidnappers, too, she reminded herself. Still, she sensed at least part of his anger was directed at her.

"The first time I met you, I knew Quent was a liar and a jerk. Seeing what he's doing to you now says he's cruel, too. He doesn't deserve to have you worrying yourself sick."

Aghast, she jumped to her feet. "How dare you?"

"Do you know how I met him? We double-dated a couple of blackjack dealers up in Cripple Creek. That was six weeks ago, Dawn. Quent never mentioned being engaged to you. I didn't know you existed until he wanted to hold the wedding here."

"Liar!"

"He told me it was going to be a marriage of convenience. He implied you were a dried-up old prune with a tax problem."

The tears she'd so painfully repressed now burst free.

Heartsick, unable to imagine why he was telling her this, all she could do was stare at him.

"Do you want proof? The woman he was dating is named Lucy and she works at the Imperial. My date's name is Carol. I'll give you their number. Call them."

"Liar," she whispered.

"He told me to entertain you. He said I'd probably be bored out of my skull since you're so lifeless."

She clamped her hands over her ears. "Liar!"

"Quent is the liar, not me. He lied to me and he lied to you. Nobody kidnapped him. He's pulling something."

"Get out. Go!"

"I know I'm stepping way out of line here. What I'm telling you hurts. But getting all worked up about kidnappers has to hurt even more. He's not worth the agony."

She pointed a quaking finger at the door. "Get out right now! You're cruel and vicious and I never want to speak to you again as long as I live."

"Dawn—"

"Get out!" she screamed, flailing about wildly for something to throw.

Ross walked out, slamming the door behind him.

She flopped full-length onto the bed and muffled her screams against a pillow. A nightmare, she told herself over and over. This was all a horrible nightmare and any moment now she was going to wake up. She had to.

ROSS KEPT a wary eye on the lodge windows as he plucked irises from the bed out front. Not that having Mom yelling at him for picking her flowers could make this situation any worse. Everybody was mad at him. The Colonel he could handle—the old man had been mad at him ever since Ross was fourteen and refused to join Junior R.O.T.C. The girls were mad at him, though, and that bothered him. He and Janine argued a lot, but Kara and Megan usually sided with him. Not this time. Everyone blamed him for Quentin's disappearance.

Dawn's anger made him sick and ashamed of himself. He'd told her the truth, but she hit the bull's-eye in calling him cruel. So, he'd spent most of the afternoon prowling the resort, beating himself up for saying what he had said. Now, bored with self-recrimination, he figured it was time to straighten out this mess.

Step number one: apologize to Dawn.

At the cabin, he paused before knocking. The sun had sunk to the mountaintops, and the trees around the Honeymoon Hideaway cast long purple shadows. No lights shined inside Dawn's cabin. He feared she might have found a ride back to the Springs.

When she answered his knock, relief filled him. Her face was drawn, and huge circles looked like bruises under her weary eyes. He wanted to sweep her into his arms and hold her until she slept. He offered her a white bag, which contained sandwiches and fruit, and the bundle of irises. A purple petal drifted from the bouquet to the ground.

"You must be hungry," he said. "Roast beef and cheddar sandwiches with the house-specialty horseradish sauce."

"I'm not speaking to you." She accepted the flowers and the bag. Her lower lip trembled.

"Too late. You spoke." He turned on his most winning smile. "I came to apologize. Please, Dawn, let me come in."

Chapter Five

Ross looked around the room. Except for a wastebasket overflowing with soggy, crumpled tissues, it looked exactly as it had when he'd left. He turned on lights.

Dawn's anger showed in her tight mouth and glowering eyes. Her narrow back was stiff enough to make the Colonel proud. Uncertain if he could charm his way out of this mess, he busied himself with tidying up the room.

"Have you heard anything?"

"No." Seated on a chair, she watched him carry the ice bucket to the bathroom. "You shouldn't be here. People will talk. Everyone thinks Quentin left me because of you."

"Eat a sandwich," he called from the bathroom. He rinsed the bucket and left it on the vanity to dry. To his relief, she opened the bag of food, pulled out a sandwich, and unwrapped its paper covering. He wanted to beg her to not be sad, but knew it wouldn't do any good. He couldn't imagine how he'd feel if someone he loved mysteriously disappeared—not that Quentin Bayliss deserved one ounce of her love.

He started a pot of hot water in the coffeemaker so Dawn could have some tea.

"You must leave, Ross. Can't you see what everyone thinks?"

He snorted in derision. "Who cares?"

"I have a reputation to maintain."

"Reputations are highly overrated. I know you're a good person, and you know it. We didn't do anything wrong." He approached her chair and dropped to one knee. She gave a start, drawing her hands high as if the sandwich offered protection. "You can't let what people think stop you from doing what you need to do. We're victims of…something. I don't know what happened, but I intend to find out." He stared until she looked at him. "I'm sorry for what I said. It was mean, thoughtless, and I'm ashamed of myself for hurting your feelings." He touched her knee with his fingertips. "Forgive me. Please."

She lowered the sandwich and her eyes. Color bloomed on her cheeks. "You're quite…persistent."

"That's me, Mr. Persistence. Friends?"

She nodded.

He rose. "Good, now eat up. I'll make you some tea."

"I must admit you're right about one thing." She dabbed at her lips with a paper napkin. "Quentin wasn't kidnapped for ransom."

He quelled his excitement over her finally coming to her senses. He busied himself making a pot of Earl Grey. "What makes you say that?"

"If kidnappers wanted money, they'd have asked for it already. If terrorists kidnapped Quentin, it does their cause no good whatsoever to remain silent." She nodded at the radio. "I've been listening to the news all day. Nothing. Whoever abducted Quentin—"

"Wait a minute. Abducted is the same as being kidnapped."

"I'm being quite reasonable, Ross. If Quentin had second thoughts about marrying me, why did he show up in the first place? Why marry me at all? He showed not the slightest reluctance the day before or the day of. He never expressed a single doubt or regret." She nibbled the sandwich. "He never mentioned you. I know he wasn't jealous."

"Delayed reaction?"

She shook her head. "I believe somebody is trying to make it look as if Quentin left on his own."

"Then why steal your Lincoln?"

"It isn't my car. I bought it for his birthday. It's registered in his name."

"You paid for it?" Ross's cheek twitched.

"It doesn't matter. What matters is how it *appears*. Quentin left me on his own. That tells me someone either wants to hurt him badly, or hurt me badly."

"Who would want to hurt you?"

She gazed evenly at him. Her tongue flicked across her upper lip, distracting him for a moment. He could almost taste her honeyed lips. All last week he'd been dying to kiss her, hold her...steal her away. Awakening to her tender kisses and hot little body had been the fulfillment of all his wishes.

"Wealth creates enemies."

Her utter conviction baffled him. "Who told you that?"

"People who know. All my life I've had to be cautious. The world is full of those who would harm me out of envy or greed."

Ross scratched his head. She made herself sound like a walking moneybag whose only redeeming quality was the size of her bank account. He'd already gathered from previous conversations that her parents had overprotected her. She'd never lived alone or traveled by herself. Ross suspected that when her parents died she'd been ripe for a manipulator like Quentin.

He poured a cup of tea and added a packet of creamer and two sugars while he considered the idea of a complicated plot. Fingering his shoulder, he found the sore spot he'd discovered earlier. "You might be right."

Her eyes widened.

"Maybe I'm crazy, but look at this." He pushed up his shirtsleeve on his left arm, working the stretchy fabric high on his shoulder. "I can't see it, so you tell me."

Warily, as if expecting him to do something dangerous, she eased to his side. Without touching him, she examined the spot, high toward the back of his shoulder.

"There's a spot like a bee sting." She brushed the tiny wound with her fingertip. "No, not a bee sting. It's bruised. Does it hurt?"

"Feels like a flu shot." Thoughtful, he pulled down the sleeve. Her claiming the wound looked bruised clarified his initial suspicion. "When I woke up I was definitely suffering from something. My eyes hurt. My head was stuffy and I was dizzy. I didn't drink, so it wasn't a hangover."

"Your eyes hurt?" She returned to her chair and absently picked up the remains of her sandwich. She frowned at him. "As if needles were pricking your eyes?"

"Exactly. I think I was drugged. What about you?"

Together they turned their gazes to the champagne bottle Ross had emptied and dropped into the waste can.

"Was the champagne already opened when you got here?"

Dawn's face scrunched in concentration. "I honestly do not recall. My eyes hurt, too, and I was dizzy and a little bit sick. I drank the champagne… I don't remember anything after that.''

Her complicated plot theory gained credibility. ''It makes sense to drug Quent. He's sloppy, but big. I wouldn't want to tangle with him. What doesn't make sense is somebody lurking around outside with a needle to jab me.''

''Unless,'' she said, ''it was for insurance. The kidnappers drugged the champagne, but had no way to make certain Quentin would drink it.''

He agreed with her reasoning, to a point.

''We must call the police.'' She set the remains of her sandwich aside and wrapped it up neatly.

''What for?''

''We have evidence of a crime.''

''We have an empty champagne bottle and what looks like a bee sting on my arm. By the time we can have blood tests done, any drugs will be out of our systems.''

''We can't do nothing.''

He felt positive he and Dawn had been drugged. He wasn't certain about Quent. ''I don't know anything about criminals. I do know about people in general. Some parts of this setup don't make any sense. In the first—''

''Wait.'' She fetched a small notebook and a pen.

''Taking notes?''

''It helps me think.''

''Okay, you and Quent left the reception around ten o'clock. I saw you leave the lodge.''

She wrote it down.

''The last people to show up at the reception came around nine-thirty. A man and a woman. An older woman, sharp-looking, wearing a stupid hat.''

''That would have been Desdemona Hunter and her photographer. Desdemona is a reporter. Quentin became upset because he didn't want any publicity. We left the reception soon afterward.''

It made him curious why a man as hungry for attention as Quent didn't want a newspaper write-up. "Your last guest left no later than eleven forty-five. After the reporter, no one else arrived at the lodge. And no one left unless either Stefan or I brought their car around.''

"You're assuming kidnappers would drive up to the lodge.'' She smiled. "And use valet parking.''

She had a pretty smile, strained though it was. His heart did a flip-flop. He'd have liked nothing better than to hold her and kiss her and make her forget Quentin Bayliss ever existed.

"Good point.''

"Then Stefan saw someone carrying luggage to the parking lot around midnight. You're sure about the time, right?''

Ross murmured agreement.

"So the kidnappers waited until the guests left the lodge. Quentin and I had been drugged, so we offered no resistance. When the coast was clear, they—''

"What about the prowler I saw on the walkway an hour after Stefan saw a man with luggage?''

She frowned at her notes.

"And why me? Why take the time to strip me down and put me in bed with you? Kidnapping is a major crime. If I were a kidnapper, I'd want to be in and out. No fooling around arranging bodies.''

Color rose on her cheeks; her mouth tightened. She cast a furtive glance at the bed and her blush turned hot. "They took pains to make it look as if Quentin left on his own. It's a distraction, a red herring.''

Ross vowed never to mention the bed incident again. Despite her innocence she was obviously embarrassed.

He also suspected a smart remark making light of the situation would get him tossed out on his ear. "Then who did I see peeking in the window? If you and Quent were already knocked out, why the handy-dandy hypodermic the prowler used on me?"

She hunched stubbornly and tapped her pen against the notebook. Ross longed to agree with her abduction theory, if only to make her happy. But he knew Quent was a liar and he knew kidnappers would never bother with taking luggage. "Get your stuff together. Let's go find Quent."

She blinked slowly, her mouth pinched small and tight.

"Don't look at me like I'm nuts. We can hash out the details for a week and it won't get us any closer to finding out what happened. It's time for action."

"But what if it is a kidnapping? This silence could be a ploy to prevent me from contacting the authorities."

Ross crossed his arms.

"I can't take the chance, Ross. Please don't be angry with me."

"If they were smart enough to follow you here, they must know your home number. Maybe they're calling your house."

She glanced between him and the telephone, her delicate face a palette of conflicting emotions. She pushed hair behind her ears and toyed with the neckline of her blouse.

Ross glanced at his watch. "Okay, let's give them until noon tomorrow. If nobody calls, we assume something is going on that doesn't involve ransom. Have you tried calling your house?"

"Yes. No one answers. I've tried his home again. Disconnected. I reached only voice mail at his office and on his cellular phone."

"What about anybody Quent might have spoken to recently? If he's in trouble, he might have told someone."

"What kind of trouble?"

Considering how Quent had cheated on Dawn and the lies he'd told, Ross figured either woman trouble or business trouble. "You're the one who thinks he's been abducted by an enemy. Who are his enemies?"

"I don't even know his friends," she muttered, pressing a hand to her head as if it ached. "I'm so confused. Quentin talked so much at times that he wearied me. Yet I know little about him." Her lower lip trembled and tears glazed her eyes. "I don't know if I should be angry, afraid, or just very, very ashamed of myself."

THE JANGLING TELEPHONE startled Dawn, bringing her from a fitful sleep into full alertness. She'd fallen asleep with the light on and now found herself staring up at the swirling plaster designs in the ceiling. The telephone rang again and she grabbed the handset. *Quentin, please be Quentin,* she prayed. "Hello? Hello? Who's there?"

"Where is that dirty double-crosser?"

The voice was low, slurred and female. Dawn peered at the bedside clock. It was a little past two o'clock in the morning. "Pardon me?"

"Where is he? We had a deal! You can't weasel out on me now. It isn't fair. I want my money!"

Dawn blinked rapidly. "Are you talking about Quentin? Did you kidnap my husband?"

Now the other end of the phone was silent except for odd background noises, and Dawn began believing she'd dreamed the ringing telephone and hysterical woman's voice. She sat up straighter on the bed, looking about.

No, the room was real, and so was her throbbing stress headache. No dream.

"Hello? Are you still there?" What did one say to a kidnapper? Her mind went blank.

"Look, just give me the check, okay? It's mine. He promised. I wasn't really going to hurt him. Okay? Just give me my money!"

The woman sounded drunk, or perhaps ill. In either case, she made no sense to Dawn. She listened a few moments to the woman's increasingly incoherent rambling, catching a few words now and then: "Double-crosser," "thief," "just debt." Finally the diatribe faded into a weepy mumble. Dawn grew certain the music, electronic pinging and laughter she heard in the background were from a bar.

Her confusion deepened. A drunken, remorseful kidnapper? A crank call? Wrong number? Panic tightened her chest.

"Look," Dawn said as calmly as she was able, "release my husband or tell me where to find him, and I'll give you anything you want. Okay? Just don't hurt him. Please."

The woman laughed. "You tell him something for me, sweetie. You tell him I'm not quitting. He can't hide. I won't give up until I get my money or he's dead. Got it?"

The icy words, without a trace of slurring, shocked Dawn. "No! No, don't hurt him!"

"How about I hurt you? I'll kill you!" the woman screeched, and hung up with a bang.

Dawn pushed the disconnect button and shook the handset, but the phone was dead. She leapt from the bed and raced to the door where she double-checked that the dead bolt and security latch were in place. Ordering herself to calm down, she called the front desk and spoke to the night clerk. The clerk said he'd transferred the call to Dawn's room, but hadn't identified the caller. Not knowing what else to do, Dawn called Ross. He promised to be there in three minutes.

By the time he arrived, she'd dressed in a warm-up suit, but her heart was still racing and her hands trembled. Ross grasped her by the shoulders.

"Hey, hey, it's okay, you're safe. Tell me what happened."

She clamped her hands over his, squeezing, absorbing his strength. She repeated what she remembered the voice saying, emphasizing how upset the woman had sounded. And how drunk. As her heart slowed and reason replaced fear, Dawn frowned and shook her head.

"She said I owe her a debt. She wants me to give her a check." She peered curiously at Ross's face. "I thought kidnappers demanded unmarked bills."

Ross guided her to a chair and urged her to sit. "Hmm. Quent likes to gamble. That time we were in Cripple Creek, he dropped a couple of grand in the slot machines."

"He's a respectable businessman," she said stiffly.

"Even businessmen can pick up bad habits."

She did not like the implication behind his words. "He didn't marry me in order to escape paying his debts. Besides, legitimate creditors do not call in the middle of the night, drunk, from a bar."

"I didn't say legitimate creditors. We better call the police—"

"No!" She reached out a hand to stop him. If Quentin was in debt to unsavory types, then involving the police meant announcing to the world she'd married, if not a criminal, then a man who associated with criminals. Nauseated, she pressed a fist to her mouth and swallowed hard. "Wait. I don't have anything to tell the police. I don't know her name or where she was calling from or why she thinks I should give her money. It could have been a crank call. Maybe she'll call back, and we can find out more. I can't bear to face the deputy again, especially if it appears Quentin ran away."

He flopped onto a chair and crossed his arms, sighing patiently. "All right, we'll wait."

Dawn fought falling asleep, but lost the battle. One moment she was trying to watch a movie, the next Ross was shaking her shoulder. She dropped her feet to the floor and sat up straight; her neck creaked and twinges shot through her back and shoulders. She groaned, pushing aside a blanket draped over her body.

"Breakfast is here," Ross said.

"Did she call back?" She rose creakily from the chair and arched her back, trying to work out the kinks. Disoriented, she stared at the windows, trying to judge from the light if it was day or night.

"No. I ordered breakfast. You need to eat."

Her appetite appalled her. A woman in her state shouldn't be thinking about food, but a tray held eggs Benedict and fresh fruit. The sight and smell made her mouth water and her belly grumble. A slim glass vase supported a single, perfect red rose.

"I suppose it was a crank caller," she said. When Ross failed to disagree, her depression deepened. She tasted the eggs Benedict. Perfection.

She'd finished the eggs and most of the fruit when someone knocked on the door. She envisioned sheriff's deputies bearing news of a tragedy. Or maybe the drunken woman had decided to confront her in person.

"I'll get it," Ross said.

She laid her napkin aside and rose. *Be brave,* she counseled herself. Lovells always showed a courageous face to the world. She straightened the hem of her sweatshirt. "It might be news of Quentin." Fingering her wedding ring, she walked slowly to the door.

Janine Duke waited outside the door.

Puzzled, Dawn invited the woman inside.

Even this early in the morning, Janine looked stunning. Tailored trousers and a sleeveless blouse showed off her curvy figure and finely muscled arms. Her hair curled luxuriously past her shoulders. Dawn surreptitiously tucked her hair behind her ears, wishing she owned even a smidgen of Janine's radiance. She knew it was shallow to care about her appearance while Quentin was missing, but as with her appetite, she couldn't seem to help herself.

Janine clamped a fist on one hip and glowered at her brother. "What are you doing here?"

He met her ire with a mischievous grin. "Can't have a sleazy affair long-distance."

"Smart aleck. Beat it. I have some business to discuss with Dawn."

He crossed his arms and smiled. From behind Janine, Dawn gaped at him in growing horror. He wore a white T-shirt, blue jeans and moccasins without socks. He was unshaven and his hair was tousled. He looked like a man who'd dressed hastily. Add to that her own disheveled appearance, the unmade bed and breakfast for two, and it looked exactly like a sleazy affair.

Dawn touched Janine's arm to get her attention. She nodded at the folder Janine held tucked under one arm. "What is it you wish to speak to me about?"

"It's better if you split, Ross," Janine said softly.

The damage had been done, Dawn knew. Catching

Ross once with his pants down—literally—might have been an accident as far as Janine was concerned, but this made twice. No amount of explanation would suffice. Dawn straightened her back and shoulders and settled her most coolly businesslike expression on her face.

"Please, finish your breakfast, Ross," she said. "Miss Duke, please state your business."

Janine's lips thinned and her eyes narrowed, her glare directed at Dawn. Crossing her arms to keep her shaky hands still, Dawn forced herself to meet Janine's eyes.

"Well..." Janine turned her back on her brother. "I know this is a bad time and you're feeling awful, but I've got a problem here. I apologize for having to bring this up." Janine opened the folder on the tabletop. "Your last two checks to us have bounced."

Dawn shook her head in reflexive denial. "I've never bounced a check in my life. There must be a mistake."

Janine handed over two checks, each covered with red ink proclaiming Insufficient Funds. One check was for the arrangements Elise had made for the wedding and reception; the other was for Dawn's stay in the lodge. Dawn puzzled over how such a thing could have happened. She'd maintained this checking account for twelve years and had never even incurred a service charge for allowing her balance to dip below one thousand dollars. She had overdraft protection, too, by keeping a savings account with the same bank.

"I'm so embarrassed, I don't quite know what to say."

Janine shoved her hands in her trouser pockets and rocked on her heels. "Your credit card was refused as well. I know the timing is terrible. Maybe it's a mix-up because of the wedding and everything."

"This isn't possible." She shook her head, unable to take her eyes off the red words—Insufficient Funds. "I'm very careful with my checking account." She brought out her checkbook and credit-card log. Her father had disliked credit cards, calling them funding for fools. So she kept one only for emergencies and always paid any bills in full as soon as she received them. She totted up in her head the amounts she'd charged this month. The total came nowhere near her credit limit. A quick check of her checking-account balance showed the same thing.

"Hey, come on, Janine, this is no big deal. You know Dawn is good for it." Ross rose from the table.

"Stay out of this," his sister snapped.

"I will call my accountant immediately," Dawn said. "I can't imagine what happened, but I promise you, I will straighten out this matter before close of business today."

Janine pulled her shoulders into an unyielding line and her face into an unreadable mask. "I'll have to ask for a money order or cash. It's policy."

"Get real, Ninny. You can't—"

Heat spread across Dawn's cheeks. Humiliation was bad enough, but then to be defended like a foolish child was more than she could bear. She waved a hand sharply to cut off his words. "I understand."

"I'll leave the checks and the bills here. Give me a call when you find out what the problem is."

Unable to speak for fear of deepening her humiliation, Dawn saw Janine out. She remained with her hands on the door. When Ross spoke, she jumped.

"I won't let her get away with talking to you like that," he said. He slammed a fist against his palm.

"She's only doing her job. I must call my accountant."

"Her job? She'd make a great prison guard. I'll make sure she apologizes—"

"My checks bounced," she said slowly, with emphasis. "This is a serious matter. She has a right to be upset."

"It's not the end of the world. Granted, the bad-check fees are criminal, but—"

"I have never bounced a check in my life! I cannot imagine what went wrong. This is humiliating."

He leaned on the back of a chair. "I know you're under a lot of stress right now, but bad checks are no big deal."

Without unblemished credit what was she? A deadbeat, a nothing. Armed with her checkbook and Daytimer she marched to the telephone. She called her accountant.

Georgia Vogle answered and as soon as Dawn identified herself, Georgia exclaimed, "Dawn! How is our happy bride today? I am so pleased for you. I have a gift for you and Quentin. I know I should have given it to you before, but I had to special-order it and it only arrived this morning. How—"

Dawn interrupted the woman. "I have a problem."

"Oh. I'm sorry. What can I do for you?"

Swallowing her embarrassment and stiffening her back, Dawn explained the bad checks. When she finished, the silence on the other end ran deep.

"Georgia?"

"I don't see how this happened. I'll contact the bank right away." Papers rustled in the background. "Can you put the bills on your credit card?"

"It's been refused."

"No way! Don't you worry about a thing. Once I finish with those idiots at the bank, they'll wish they'd never been born. Give me the number where you are. I promise to get back to you in fifteen minutes."

Much relieved by Georgia's confidence, Dawn gave

the accountant the telephone number of the resort and her cabin number. After she hung up, some of the tension drained away. Georgia had been her father's accountant and now she handled Dawn's books. She was competent, efficient and caring. She also had zero tolerance for sloppy bank errors, much less for so-called computer mix-ups. Georgia would put everything right.

Ross asked, "Does Quentin have access to your checking account?"

She folded her arms and watched the telephone, waiting for it to ring.

"Dawn?"

"Of course not. Even if he did, Quentin wouldn't use my accounts without my knowledge. Honestly, Ross, you're accusing him of a crime. It's merely a glitch in the computer. My accountant will have the entire matter straightened out within minutes."

Despite her confident words, his question gnawed at her. She had written a check to Quentin before. He'd been short of cash and his ATM card wouldn't work in the Colorado Springs machines. She'd thought nothing of it at the time, but as she replayed the incident in her head it seemed peculiar. She'd offered to go to the bank for him, or with him. He'd convinced her to wait at home while he ran the errand.

Ross sat beside her. "What are you thinking right now?"

"Nothing," she said quickly, breathlessly.

"You're wondering if he had access to your checking account. He did, didn't he?"

She opened her checkbook and pointed to her name printed on a check. "Quentin and I agreed to maintain separate accounts. He doesn't need or want my money."

"Okay, fine. Answer one question, and then I'll shut up."

"I don't want to answer any questions."

His smile disappeared and his eyes acquired blazing intensity. She leaned to the side, away from him, but could not make herself look away.

"Why did you buy him the car?"

"What?"

"The Lincoln. It's a nice set of wheels. Fully loaded. So what did you drop, forty-five, fifty grand? If Quent has the money, why did you buy it?"

"His birthday. And it's none of your business."

"Whether you like it or not, you are my business." He touched a finger to her chin. "It was his idea to buy the car, wasn't it?"

Emotion rose, hot and furious, threatening the fragile hold she kept on her composure. Though she wanted to move, desperately needed to move, all she could do was stare into his eyes as he caressed her chin and cheek.

"We've been had, sweetheart."

She slapped his hand away. "Don't you dare imply he deserted me or stole from me or is in any way responsible for the awful things happening to me. He's a good man. He loves me. He'd never do anything to hurt me."

"You keep saying how much he loves you. Do you love him?"

"He's the perfect man for me." She clutched her arms over her aching stomach. Breakfast sat there like a lump of wet sawdust. "My attorney checked his credentials most thoroughly. Father would have approved of Quentin."

"Father approves. What about Dawn?"

"You don't understand. You're very attractive and charming. You make friends easily, but I don't. I'm not pretty or smart or a good conversationalist. I don't have any talent or a career. All my life I've had to be very careful about people. The world is full of predators who only want to take advantage of me. Quentin loves me for myself. He doesn't need my money. He thinks I'm perfectly acceptable the way I am."

Cocking his head one way, he stroked his chin, then tilted his head in the other direction. His eyes narrowed contemplatively. "You don't think you're pretty?"

His stubborn refusal to understand annoyed her. "I know what I look like."

"I don't think you do." He grasped the side of her face, and when she tried to turn away, he stopped her. His hand was gentle, but firm, and much too hot against her skin. "You're beautiful. You're fascinating and interesting and a lot of fun."

During the week she'd spent with Ross, she'd felt interesting, she'd had fun, but she knew how she really was. Dull, routine and plain as mud. "You don't understand."

"You're the confused member of this little party. I don't know where you got the idea money is your only attractive asset, but it's nuts." He tucked hair behind her ear. "You're beautiful."

She longed to believe him, as she longed to believe the whispering of bells in her heart.

The ringing telephone startled her. She jerked away from him, banging her knee against the side table. Welcoming the pain, she rubbed the sore spot. To her relief, Ross strolled to the window. Hands in his pockets, he stood with his back to her.

Dawn snatched up the handset. "Hello?"

"Dawn?" Georgia Vogle sounded as if she'd been kicked in the belly.

"I'm here. Have you found the problem?"

"I don't know how to say this. It's *impossible!*"

Hair lifted on Dawn's nape and gooseflesh rose on her arms. A sick feeling of impending doom flowed through her like icy molasses. "Slow down. What's the problem?"

"It's gone. All the money is gone. Checking, savings, money-fund line of credit... It's...gone."

Chapter Six

"The bill is covered," Ross announced. "Get your bags packed. I'm taking you home."

He stood in the doorway of the cabin, outlined by golden rays from the morning sun. Dawn mused over how, though he wasn't an exceptionally large man, he still seemed to occupy the area fully. Wherever he went, he became the center of attention, turning the world into a mere backdrop for his glory. Watching him, observing the nuances, was as pleasurable as studying a fine piece of art.

"Dawn? Wake up, sweetheart. I know you're in shock, but you need to get moving."

She curled her fingers into the bedcovers. "My money is gone. It must be a mistake."

Mistake... Georgia Vogle had assured her it was all a mistake, but it would require further conversations with the bank officials in order to find the error.

Four days ago the money in her accounts had been electronically transferred via telephone, using her access code. The only things such transfers required were knowledge of her bank-account numbers and the code. How many times had she transferred funds from her savings to her checking account over the telephone while

Quentin stood nearby, distracting her with his chatter?
How easy it would have been for him to memorize the
four-digit code.

She closed her eyes and tightened her grip on the bedcovers as if somehow she could save herself from the
tidal wave of pain and betrayal.

Ross touched her shoulder. "I squared the bill with
Janine. You're covered. Let's go."

Confused, she peered intently at his face. Her thoughts
swirled, and at the center of the maelstrom was her husband, the man who loved her...who'd robbed her. Ross
made a questioning sound and she snapped back to the
present. "You paid my bill? Why? How?"

"Look, the only thing that makes the Colonel crazier
than dealing with me is getting stiffed on a bill. He'd
make Janine miserable over it and you don't want that.
So it's no problem. You can pay me back whenever."
He grasped her wrists and tugged until she released her
grip on the covers. He pulled her upright, then peered
closely into her eyes. "I'm really worried about you. Do
you need a doctor or something?"

"Quentin must have taken my money. Why would he
do that?" She bit her inner cheek to keep from blurting
out the words "robbed" and "stolen." A good wife
didn't accuse her husband of theft—she hated herself for
even thinking such a thing.

He held her by the shoulders and shook her lightly.
She stared wide-eyed at his face.

"Listen to me very carefully. You are checked out of
the resort. We will pack your bags and I will drive you
home."

"I didn't ask you to pay my bill."

He guided her away from the bed, aiming her toward
the closet where her luggage was stored. "Yeah, well,

I'm a presumptuous kind of guy. We'll worry about details later.''

Moving on autopilot, she packed her belongings. The fog broke slightly as she folded her rumpled wedding dress. So much hope had been contained in this length of silk, hope that now had turned into pain. Tears tried to escape, but she choked them down. When her belongings were packed, Ross handed her a car key. He gathered all her bags, informed her his car was parked in front of the lodge, then followed her out of the cabin.

Unable to bear the sight of the pretty hideaway where her dreams had been shattered, she walked quickly, head down. The only car in front of the lodge was a shiny black Lexus. Dawn envisioned Ross driving a little rattletrap sports car with a lot of flash and an unreliable engine. She looked around for another car.

"Hit the unlock-trunk button on the remote. My arms are going to sleep."

Bemused, she approached the Lexus, opened the trunk and stepped aside. "This is a very nice car." Every time she made an assumption about Ross something occurred to prove her wrong.

"It's a nice ride. I do a lot of driving." He took the keys from her. "Hop in."

"Gambling must be quite lucrative."

Over the top of the car, he gave her a puzzled look. Then he laughed. "Get in, sweetheart, and I'll tell you a little secret."

"Secret?" She opened the passenger door.

"I'm employed. Gainfully." He slid behind the wheel.

Staring at her hands so as not to see the lodge, she mulled over his odd comment as he drove off the grounds and turned onto the highway. He pressed a button on the

CD player and the rough, raw vocals of Bob Seger filled the car. He turned down the volume.

She peeked at her surroundings. Wide, rolling meadows melded into thick pine forests. Barbed-wire fencing kept red-and-white cattle from wandering onto the highway. She wondered if she'd ever be able to enjoy the mountains again. She hugged herself against a surge of loss, fear and loneliness, and focused instead on Ross. "Why is your being gainfully employed a secret?"

His laughter soothed her, offering a bright note to cut the gloom. Ross laughed a lot. He had a quirky sense of humor, and, unlike many men she knew, didn't mind laughing at himself.

"It's a game the Colonel and I play. A couple of years ago he got it into his head that I'm a hustler. He thinks I waste my time in casinos." He lifted his shoulders in a quick shrug. "I see no need to disabuse him of that notion."

"I don't understand."

"Come on, you saw the Colonel, ruler of his empire. There are only two ways to do anything. The wrong way or his way." He huffed a short laugh. "I appointed myself court jester."

"But he's your father. You should honor him."

"I do honor him and I love him. But I'm not jumping just because he barks an order." He gently nudged her shoulder with his knuckles. "As far as the Colonel is concerned, the only good son is one who follows exactly in daddy's footsteps. Attend West Point, get a commission, marry a pretty blonde with ambitions of someday being a general's wife, and have a lot of kids so I can drag them around the world while I climb the career ladder. No, thanks!"

Despite his flippancy, she caught an undercurrent of

defiant anger and realized the tension she'd seen between father and son was real. In many ways, her own father had been similar to the Colonel. Yet she never would have dreamed of defying, teasing, or arguing with her father.

"I served three years as an enlisted man and used the G.I. Bill to get my own college education. With no help from the old man, by the way, even when I had to work three jobs to pay the bills. When I have a family, my kids won't have to attend fifteen different schools and make new friends every eighteen months."

Dawn had lived all her life in the house her family had owned for three generations. Her travels had been limited to the two weeks of cultural holiday per year her father had allotted. She couldn't imagine being rootless—or striking out on her own, penniless while juggling three jobs.

"The Colonel decided a long time ago I was a major disappointment. Fine by me. I don't need him."

She tried to be appalled. She should have been appalled. His attitude toward his father was disrespectful, which was a terrible thing. Except, he appeared happy and at peace with himself. She, who always tried to do the right, sensible thing, felt as if ugly winds buffeted her inside a bottomless black hole.

"I respected my father and always did as he told me."

"Fathers aren't always right." He made an expansive gesture, indicating the mountain-ringed horizon. "There's a new dream around every corner and trying to follow someone else's vision is way too limiting."

Limiting...the perfect description of her narrow life. "So what do you do?"

"I'm a human-resources consultant. I do freelance work for big corporations. Employee morale, motivation.

Mostly it's rah-rah seminars and showing managers how to treat their employees like human beings. I travel a lot and set my own hours. I set my own fees, too. It's a great job."

She imagined he was very good at motivating people. "It sounds fascinating."

"The best part is, I'm paid to do what I like to do best—run my mouth."

She shuddered. "I'm terrified of public speaking."

"Most people are. That's how come I can charge outrageous fees and get away with it." The trilling of his telephone interrupted him. He flipped open the small unit and held it to his ear. He listened a moment and winced. "I'm on my way to the city now, sweetheart." He tapped his fingers on the steering wheel and nodded in response to whatever "sweetheart" was saying.

Dawn slumped on the seat, tuning out his conversation by concentrating on the music. She had no right to be jealous. She was a married woman and Ross was her friend. Still, she couldn't help envisioning "sweetheart" running her fingers through his thick, curly hair and staring deeply into his eyes and pressing her body against his hard, lean length.

A frisson of remembered desire slithered through her, startling her. Touching him, kissing him had been beautifully erotic, disturbingly perfect, as if he'd been created as her exact match. She shifted uncomfortably on the seat.

He deactivated the phone and placed it on the dashboard. "She's making me nuts."

Unable to resist the opening, Dawn asked, "Who?"

"Jennifer. I love her to death and she's the best, but I swear she wants a combination of Supergirl and Margaret Thatcher. A mere mortal won't do."

Dawn fixated on the "love her to death" part. "I'm certain she loves you, too."

He laughed. "Not likely. You'd think somebody in my business would have no trouble hiring a new secretary. But Jennifer is turning the search for her replacement into a quest for the Holy Grail."

"Secretary?"

He pulled a face. "Don't ever let her know I called her that. She's an administrative assistant. She's been with me since I opened the office, but her husband is in the military and he's being transferred overseas. Replacing her won't be easy. Especially since she hates everybody who's applied so far. Her organizational skills are beyond belief. She thinks everybody should be that good." He gave her a hopeful smile. "Know anybody who needs a job? She only has to be brilliant."

"I'm afraid not."

She lapsed into silence, deep in thought. She loved Quentin; it didn't matter how she felt about Ross. She wasn't supposed to feel anything at all. Not jealousy, and certainly not relief over Jennifer being an employee instead of a lover.

He patted her shoulder. "Hey, don't zone out on me again. It scares me when you go all blank. Need a picker-upper? We can stop at the Donut Mill in Woodland Park. Coffee and a sugar rush?"

"If that's what you'd like."

"I'm asking you."

Put on the spot, she eyed him warily. Did he actually need a cup of coffee, or was he merely being kind? Dividing his gaze between her and the road, he waited for her answer. She tried, very hard, to make a decision: coffee or no coffee. Buildings were cluttering the sides of the highway and business signs announced the town of Woodland Park. Ross slowed the car as the highway curved into town.

"Don't stop," she said breathlessly and hunched down on the seat. She braced for his disappointment or objection.

Ross maneuvered through the small-town traffic, passing the Donut Mill without so much as a glance. Once he reached the other side of town and picked up speed again, she breathed easier.

But her mind was once again preoccupied. She'd done everything right, but somehow, some way, everything had gone wrong. All her decisions had been wrong.

She stared at her wedding ring, pondering the permanence of gold and diamonds. She was going to have to live with what she'd done. She'd never felt so frightened in her life.

ROSS EASED the car through the boxwood-shaded gates and around the circular drive to the front of the house. He killed the engine, then leaned his forearms on the steering wheel, admiring the hand-cast brick Victorian-era home.

He hadn't been aware of this neighborhood, tucked behind Colorado College and flanked by Monument Creek Park. When he thought "rich," he imagined Broadmoor, to the south. These houses on fenced and hedged lots shaded by hundred-year-old trees qualified as estates.

Dawn held the door handle as she gazed pensively at the house. He wondered if she hoped Quentin would come bounding through the door, smiling and glad-handing and rattling off a perfectly reasonable explanation for why he'd deserted her and stripped her bank accounts. He wondered what his reaction would be if

Quentin showed his face. Could he watch him sweep Dawn into a passionate embrace and refrain from going out of his skull in a jealous rage? Punch first, ask questions later? He flexed his right hand. He'd been nine or ten years old the last time he'd used his fists in a fight—he seemed to recall bruised knuckles hurt like the devil. It'd be worth it.

Dawn turned her head slowly. She looked beaten and his heart ached.

"I don't know what's wrong. I'm afraid to go inside."

He touched her shoulder with his fingertips. She leaned slightly toward him. He trailed his hand over her linen sleeve and past the silky cotton of her blouse collar. Under her hair, the skin of her neck was cold. "Scared he's here or scared he's not?"

"Either way, I'm frightened. I can think of nothing—*nothing!*—to excuse what he's done. Just as I cannot understand why he would do it to me." She gave herself a shake and gripped her pocketbook firmly. She opened the car door, swung her legs out, then paused. With her back to him, her voice low and troubled, she said, "You told the truth, didn't you? About how you met him. He was dating another woman."

"I wish it wasn't. I'm sorry."

She left the car. Walking as one condemned, she climbed the brick porch steps. Ross fetched her luggage from the trunk and followed. On his way into the house he noticed the keypad for a security system.

Dawn stood inside the foyer. Two stories high, the foyer was colored by stained-glass windows set high in the walls and on either side of the door. The parquet flooring was too light for mahogany and too red for oak. Rosewood, he supposed, or some other exotic wood fashionable around the turn of the century.

"Where to with the bags, ma'am?" he asked cheerfully.

Her face had lost every trace of color and her enormous eyes seemed to float in the sockets. "The Wyeth is gone."

"Pardon?" He stooped, setting the bags on the floor.

She pointed a trembling finger at a wall. A small rectangle of paint was a slightly different shade of cream than the rest of the wall. "Mother's Andrew Wyeth painting. It's gone. I've been robbed."

He took a step, enabling him to see past the foyer. He gazed into a large room with oak wainscotting and plaster curlicues on the walls near the high ceiling. The curlicues looked as if they'd been formed with a pastry bag into ribbons and rosettes. He noticed off-colored rectangles on the parquet floor where he suspected rugs had recently been. He noticed, too, off-colored shapes on the walls, along with empty hooks and trailing wires.

Dawn dropped her pocketbook. It hit the floor with a thud. Stiff-legged, blank-faced, she moved like a sleepwalker through the empty room. Her footsteps echoed.

"I take it this room is supposed to have furniture," he said. His nose wrinkled against the dusty, stale air.

In the middle of the empty room, Dawn stopped. Feet apart, one arm crossed across her midsection, the other resting on it so she supported her chin on her hand, she had the look of an appraiser. "I never realized this room was so large."

Ross finally understood what Quentin had done. "Show the old lady a good time," Quentin had told him. "Keep her busy."

Busy for a week out of town while Quentin leisurely looted the house. It would have been easy as peeling a banana to hire a couple of day-workers and a moving van, then pull the van up to the front of the house where tall hedges offered privacy from the curiosity of neighbors and passersby on the street.

If he walked into his apartment and found it stripped, he'd be howling. Dawn's silence indicated shock. "Did Quentin have a key to the house?"

"Yes." Her tone was as dull as her eyes. "He was supposed to move his belongings in this week. He had a key and he knew how to disarm the security system." She gave him a frightening smile. "He was kind enough to reset the alarm. Why, I'm not certain. It would appear my husband operates on a level quite incomprehensible to me."

He followed her through the house. Except for the kitchen, the first floor had been stripped of all furniture, rugs and decorations, leaving only off-colored shapes on the floors and walls.

Dawn paused at the base of a wide staircase and looked up. A tangle of wires showed where some kind of light fixture had hung. Potted plants, looking forlorn and dried-out, sat at the edge of the steps. She plucked a brown leaf from some ivy, studied it a moment, then climbed the stairs.

The upper floor consisted of five bedrooms and a study. The octagonal-shaped study had built-in bookshelves from floor to ceiling. Dawn ran her hand over an interior wall and opened a hinged door, revealing an inset wall safe.

Ross peered at the combination dial and electronic keypad on the safe front. "I didn't know anybody used these anymore."

"Father did not trust bank safety-deposit boxes, and didn't approve of banker's hours, either. This was his office." She keyed in a combination and the light on the keypad turned from red to green. She turned the combination lock dial and opened the safe. It was empty.

She sighed.

The safe interior was surprisingly large. Ross stepped in closer for a better view. "What was in there?"

"Oh, the usual. Mother's jewels. Father's collection of gold coins. Stocks, bonds, some cash. Insurance papers. Household inventory. Father's memoirs."

"Did Quentin know how to get into the safe?"

"I had mentioned Father's coins and of course Quentin wanted to see them. He found the antiques in this house a subject of endless fascination. When I opened the safe, he was intrigued. A few days later, he asked me if I would keep some cash for him. He'd closed a real-estate deal and forgotten some kind of disclosure paper or something. So he needed to keep the cash safe until he could contact the buyer to sign the paperwork."

"You gave him the combination?"

She turned her head at an appealing angle. If not for her haunted eyes, the shadow of her thick eyelashes turning her eyes azure would have looked sexy. "He stood where you are right now." A shudder racked her body. "I always loved Quentin's eyes. They are so lively and quick, as if he sees everything. And he's very good with numbers, too. He never has to write down telephone numbers or addresses. He remembers."

She abruptly walked out of the study. Ross sensed a nervous breakdown in progress. Not one tear, not a single emotion was betrayed on her pale face.

In the smallest room on the second floor, a bed, chest of drawers, armoire and vanity remained. No art on the walls or carpets on the floor, but there was a bed.

"Is this your bedroom?" he asked.

"Yes." She opened a pair of folding doors, revealing

a closet. "Oh, look, he left my clothing. Wasn't that kind of him? Considerate? He left my bed and clothes for me to wear. Perhaps he loved me after all."

Unable to bear her quiet pain, Ross crossed the room in four long strides. He caught her by the shoulders and aimed her toward the bed. He pushed on her shoulders until she sat. He sat beside her and picked up her hand.

"If you don't show some kind of reaction, I'm taking you to the hospital."

"Reaction?"

"You look like a mannequin."

"You'd like me to be hysterical? To cry? Throw myself on the floor and wail?" She drew in a deep, shuddering breath then lifted her chin. "I'm a Lovell. Lovells do not succumb to hysterics."

"I'll settle for anything." He meant it. It caused him almost physical pain to see the woman with whom he'd spent the best week of his life reduced to this. He rubbed her limp hand briskly between his. "Your hand is ice-cold. There's no color in your face. You're scaring me."

"I'm sorry. It's not my intent."

"Stop with the politeness! Don't you feel anything? You've been robbed."

"Oh, I do feel something." She closed her eyes. When she opened them they burned with fierce light. "I am angry. I am furiously angry." With the words came a hint of color on her cheeks and a trembling in her chin. Her fingers tightened convulsively over his. She looked around and frowned, as if seeing the changes for the first time. *Really* seeing them.

"Anger is good," he said.

"I have been such a fool. He begged me to leave town for a week. I didn't want to. I didn't want a vacation, but I went anyway, because I thought he loved me." Her mouth twisted into a snarl and her voice dropped. "He *used* me."

"Looks like using people is the way he operates."

Color had returned to her face along with heated animation. With her head high and her eyes flashing, she was beautiful, dazzling. Ross hated Quentin Bayliss with a force and fury that shook him to his core. Quent had looked at Dawn and seen only a fat bank account and a house full of valuable antiques. He'd overlooked her gentle soul and tender heart; failed to appreciate the sweet curve of her cheek, the changing spectrum of her eyes, and the appealing self-consciousness of her laughter. For those crimes alone Quent would receive no forgiveness or hope of redemption.

She relaxed her fingers and extricated her hand from his. "I have so much to do. I suspect the damage Quentin has done goes even deeper than what I've seen so far. I can't express my gratitude to you for all you've done for me. I'll repay you as soon as I can."

"Are you giving me the brush-off?"

"You must have plenty—"

He shook his head firmly. "We're in this together, sweetheart. You and me. He didn't just rip you off, he used me to do it. Nobody does that to me and gets away with it."

"Taking on my problems is not reasonable." She lowered her face and eyelids. Even without cosmetics her eyelashes were long and lush, golden brown. "I don't quite understand why you feel such passion on my behalf. But I can't in good conscience involve you further than I already have."

"Passion" said it all. During the week they'd spent together, he'd walked the line between finding her wildly attractive and knowing she was strictly off-limits. Forced to ignore her sexually, he'd discovered a fine intelligence, quiet wit and a range of interests as eclectic as his own. He'd never met anyone he liked so much or on so many levels.

And he'd never desired a woman so much in his life.

"I got myself into this mess," she said, her voice pensive. "I must get myself out."

"Not without me."

"Your kindness—"

"Stop with the kindness crap. I'm kind to kittens and little kids. You're not either of those. You want to know why I'm really doing this? Fine." He caught her chin, forced her face up and kissed her.

At first she was wooden, unresponsive. Still he kissed her. He kissed her because she was beautiful and he desired her. Her lips softened. He peeked through narrowed lids and saw her eyelids slide closed like folding butterfly wings. He wrapped his arm around her shoulders and fitted her slender body against his chest and kept kissing her.

Her tender, tentative response fired his blood and her scent filled his head with clouds. He teased her with his tongue, tasting the softness of her lips and earned a tentative flick of her tongue. He fingered the silky skin of her cheek and the gentle line of her jaw. Sweet pain blossomed in his chest. He wanted her. All of her. In bed, out of it, he needed her as he'd never needed anyone before. He needed her smile and her approval.

Abruptly she twisted away. He buried his face against the side of her neck. She was silk and honey.

"Stop!" she cried breathlessly. "What are you doing?"

Her frightened tone alarmed him. She pushed at his hands and chest until he released her. She jumped to her feet. Her cheeks were flushed. Panting, wide-eyed, she backed away from the bed.

"I'm a married woman, Ross."

"What?" He turned his astonished gaze around the plundered room.

She twisted her wedding ring. "I'm married."

"After what he's done to you? Earth to Dawn. You've been had, sweetheart. Quent's a con artist."

"He's my husband. Even if he doesn't honor our wedding vows, I do. I must! As long as I'm married, I can't… we can't…it isn't possible." She hurried out of the room, her footsteps echoing off the bare walls.

Stunned, he watched her go. He shouldn't be surprised. If he'd learned nothing else about Dawn, he knew she comported herself within a strict code of honor. As much as he hated to admit it, he admired the depth of character it took to live up to the standards she set for herself.

The ache in his groin deepened his anger at Quent.

He found her in the kitchen. She spoke on the telephone and he caught enough of the conversation to know she was talking to the police.

After she hung up, she moved to a counter near a sink. "He took the silver and Mother's Wedgwood china, but he left everything else. I suppose mundane kitchen items don't have much resale value. Would you care for some coffee?"

Though she spoke calmly, anger seethed through the words. It gave him insight into how she'd grown up, probably with the constant reminder that a lady never raises her voice. Her rigid shoulders and wary, sideways glances told him to keep his distance. "If you want an apology for kissing you, it's not coming."

Her cheeks reddened.

"But I don't force myself where I'm not wanted. So I'm sorry for stepping out of line."

"If I've done something to encourage you then I am sorry." She pulled a can of coffee from the refrigerator. "I have nothing to offer you." She held up the can. "Other than coffee."

He sensed she had more to say. He murmured encouragement.

"I like you, Ross. I'm not certain why. I don't quite know what to make of you."

"I am what I am. And I think you have plenty to offer. You're funny and smart and I like being with you."

"I appear to be penniless."

He laughed. "Money comes and it goes. Didn't your dad ever tell you the easiest thing in the world to get your hands on is money?"

"That isn't true." She looked so horrified, he expected her to call him an infidel.

He laughed again, but she shot him a dirty look and he shut up. Assuming a posture of contrition, he watched her make coffee. Her slim back and graceful hips drew his gaze. She was as delicately put together as a fawn, but after a week of hiking, riding and tennis he knew her fragile appearance was deceptive. He rested his chin on his fist. Kissing her had definitely been a mistake—not because she was married, but because his concentration was shot.

"For the first three years when I started my business I was so broke I lived in a rented room in a friend's basement. I delivered pizzas at night just to have some cash. I'd go to Mom's and let her talk me into taking leftovers home so I'd have something besides free pizza to eat. Now I clear six figures annually. But I'm the same person. Even if Quent cleaned you out, you're still the same person, too.''

She frowned, but had no comment.

"In any case, I'm here for you." He crossed his arms over his chest and jutted his jaw. "You're not big enough to throw me out."

A single tear traced a silvery trail over her cheek. She dashed it away with an impatient hand.

He wanted to go to her, hold her, spill his heart to her, but he refrained. She was, after all, a married woman.

Chapter Seven

Dawn stood in the middle of the dining room. She spoke into her tape recorder, listing the items Quentin had stolen. "A William Gropper oil with a zebrawood frame, circa 1943 I believe. Um, the French chandelier with four, no, five tiers with lead-crystal prisms. A dining table, twelve feet long, made of English walnut—"

"Dawn? Won't your insurance company have an inventory list?" Ross asked. Hands in his pockets, he leaned a shoulder against the door frame.

Looking directly at him was impossible. He roused too many feelings. The sight of him dazzled her, blinded her, distracted her. She wanted so much to give in to the impulse to let him hold her, kiss her, pet her, shower her with the affection she'd always craved. If she met his eyes, if their gray sparkle touched her, she was lost.

She could not allow it. She was a married woman.

Even thinking those words pained her. Her mind refused to grasp the implications of what she'd done—of what Quentin had done. Even standing in the middle of a stripped-bare room, seeing with her own eyes the damage Quentin had wrought, she could not make herself face the depth of his betrayal. It hurt too much. Her own culpability hurt even more. In hindsight she could see how she'd allowed Quentin to sweep her off her feet. She'd been grieving, vulnerable, seeking something to fill the void caused by her parents' deaths. She'd latched on to Quentin as if he'd been a life preserver in a stormy sea. By ignoring the warnings of her heart she'd allowed him to take advantage of her.

She turned off the recorder, but reluctantly. "I suppose they do. What do you think is taking the police so long?"

"No emergency." He beckoned with a twitch of his fingers. "The coffee must be finished. Let's have a cup. You can call your insurance agent."

His kindness and understanding made her want to cringe. She hated his pity, hated being pitiful. She lifted her gaze to the high ceiling. Without furniture, the room was cavernous.

"The craftsmanship in here is awesome," Ross said. He trailed a hand over the ornate chair rail. "Hand-rubbed wood. The finish is like glass. Is that silk wall-paper? It looks antique."

He was trying so very hard to ease her mind. Resentment swelled within her, unnamed and without true focus.

"Mother was born in the wrong era. At heart, she belonged to the Victorian age." She lowered her gaze to the floor and envisioned the wood bleached to bring out the grain and brighten the effect.

Dawn turned, catching the concern on Ross's expressive face. The resentment bubbled over like overheated sugar candy, foaming and sputtering, shaking her from the inside out. "I *hated* eating in this room. It has the atmosphere of a catacomb. After Father died, I never ate in here. The adage about being careful what you wish for is quite true. I always wished for this room to disappear."

She strode to the window and jerked the velvet brocade

draperies. The heavy fabric resisted her efforts and she pulled and tugged until the carrier slides responded by moving along the tracks. Sunshine streamed into the room, highlighting dust on the floor.

Ross edged a shuffling step away from the door. "I didn't mean to upset you. Just making conversation."

After giving herself a shake, she strode out of the room and down the short hallway into the kitchen. The glare of afternoon sunshine streaming through the windows banished the chill from the dining room.

Ross ambled into the kitchen. His cautious expression heightened her shame and she wondered if she sounded as crazy as she felt.

"You can always redecorate." He searched through cabinets and found coffee cups. He added creamer and sugar to her coffee. "This kitchen is nice. The rest of the house could do with the same bright, white treatment."

She picked up her coffee and blew absently on the surface. She agreed with him about the kitchen. "I'm not certain if your optimism intrigues me or annoys me."

"Either one is better than feeling sorry for yourself."

The truth of his statement startled her into laughter. Fearing hysterics, she clamped a hand over her mouth.

"It's a lot easier to acquire material possessions than it is to get rid of them. Don't get me wrong, I don't condone what Quentin did and if it's up to me, he's not getting away with it. But, as long as everything is gone anyway, take advantage of it and do some decorating."

A responsive chord rang in her heart. She longed for bright rooms with wide-open draperies allowing in sunshine, and pale, comfortable furniture and shelves full of books people were allowed to handle. She wanted tables laden with lush, green plants and maybe a parrot to keep her company.

Troubled by such traitorous thoughts, she concentrated on her steaming coffee. "Impossible. I'm the third generation to live in this house. I have a responsibility to maintain it."

"To who?"

"What?"

"Who are you responsible to? Is this a museum or something?"

"Tradition is important."

"Not if it makes you miserable."

"I'm not miserable." The lie tasted lame. "Father worked hard all his life to maintain this house. It's my legacy." She gazed upon the empty, glass-enclosed shelves where the prized Wedgwood china had been stored. Dawn had been twenty-one years old before she'd been allowed to handle a plate.

The pealing of the doorbell ended the disturbing conversation. Dawn answered the door. A uniformed officer waited on the porch.

"Mrs. Lovell-Bayliss?" he read from a notebook. "You reported a burglary, ma'am?" He glanced at the security-system panel.

She invited the officer inside. "I was on vacation," she said. "When I came home, I found this." She indicated the empty living room with a sweep of her hand.

Ross moved to her side and rested a companionable hand on her shoulder.

The policeman roamed the house, examining it for vandalism and forced entry, before joining Dawn and Ross in the kitchen. He asked about the security system, the name of the company that operated it and whether she'd remembered to activate the system when she left.

"I activated it. There was no forced entry. My husband knew the system codes and had a key."

The officer looked expectantly at Ross. In the midst of freshening their coffee cups, Ross froze.

"Oh," Dawn said. "This isn't my husband. This is my friend, Ross Duke. My husband is the person who robbed the house." She rested her face against her hand for a moment until she found her composure. "He coerced me into taking a week's vacation in the mountains. While I was gone, he robbed me."

"Your husband." The officer stopped writing. He slipped his pen into a holder on the notepad. "Are you sure about that, ma'am?"

"Without a single doubt. He had keys to the house and he knew how to disarm the system. His name is Quentin Bayliss. Let me fetch my Daytimer and I'll give you—"

"I can't take a burglary report, ma'am."

Ross handed a cup of coffee to the officer. "Bayliss is a con artist."

The officer closed his note pad and murmured an absent thank-you for the coffee Ross handed him. "Are you and Mr. Bayliss legally married, ma'am?"

"Yes." She nervously twisted her wedding ring. It felt as if chewed her finger with little rat teeth.

"Then you need a lawyer, not a cop. It's a civil matter, not a criminal one."

"He robbed me! He stole everything. He took items that have been in my family for over a hundred years. That most certainly is a crime."

The officer shuffled nervously and gulped coffee, grimacing as if it burned him. He swiped at his mouth. "Do you have a court order forbidding him from taking items from this house?"

"No."

"Are you legally separated? Involved in divorce proceedings?"

She couldn't believe this was happening. How could a slip of paper and a wedding ring give Quentin carte blanche to rob her? "We're newlyweds."

"As far as the police are concerned, this is a domestic dispute. It's out of my jurisdiction unless you can show me some legal reason why your husband doesn't have a right to dispose of his property as he sees fit."

"It is not his property. It is mine."

"And since he's your husband, it's his, too." He reopened the notebook and made some more notes, darting pitying glances at her.

Dawn's cheeks warmed, as the shame fueled the rage simmering deep inside. If Quentin strolled through the doorway right now, she might very well do him physical harm.

She managed to remain calm until the policeman left the house. She closed the front door, using both hands to gently push until the latch clicked. She turned the twin dead bolts.

"I hate him," she said.

"The cop?"

"No! Quentin." She slammed a fist against the wall. The thud and rocket of pain through her arm to her shoulder satisfied her. She hit the wall again, and again.

Ross caught her wrist. "Save it for Quent, sweetheart."

"I hate him." She squeezed her eyes shut and quivered. "I never thought I held within me the capacity to hate anyone. But I hate *him*. He has lied to me and stolen from me and manipulated me. He used me! Why? Why is he doing this to me?"

"Come on." He tugged her hand, leading her toward

the kitchen. "I'm beginning to see Quentin knows what he's doing. I bet you aren't the first person he's done it to."

"Is that supposed to make me feel better?"

She trailed him to the kitchen, where she followed his orders automatically. She drank her coffee. She called her insurance agent and made an appointment for an adjustor to come to the house. She called Brandon Walters, her attorney. The attorney was unavailable, so Dawn left a message for him to contact her as soon as possible. She hung up the telephone and looked to Ross for further instructions.

With a narrowed eye he looked around the quiet kitchen and the mountain view outside the windows. He checked his watch. "I'm hungry. Put on your party clothes and let's go to dinner."

"Pardon?"

He grasped her hand and strode out of the kitchen. She trotted along behind him, wondering if he had snapped under the strain. He entered her bedroom and walked directly to the closet.

Rubbing her tingling hand, she eyed him warily. "What are you doing?"

"This house is bad news right now." He pushed hangers on the bar. They scraped and squeaked. Clothing rustled. "We need to eat. You need to get out of here." He shook his head and grimaced. Pulling out a beige cashmere suit, his grimace deepened, turning comical. "Pastels and neutrals are all wrong for you."

She snatched the suit out of his hand. "This is a classic."

He sorted through dresses and suits. "Who taught you how to dress? An undertaker? Where are your party clothes?"

She used both hands to push his shoulder. "Get out of my closet."

"Don't you have a cute little something in there?" Grinning, he allowed her to hustle him away from the closet. "You're way too pretty to dress like a Russian schoolteacher."

She gaped at him. When he scooped her pocketbook off the bed and thrust it at her, she took it. Talking cheerfully of attitude adjustments and clothes as an expression of self, he wrapped an arm around her shoulders and briskly swept her out of the house. Too tangled in emotions to argue—not that she suspected it would do any good to do so—she locked the door behind her and set the alarm. Ross helped her into the car.

Only when he was behind the wheel and had the engine started did she find her voice. "What do you think you're doing?"

He pulled the car around the driveway and turned onto the street, headed south. "There's an underlying theme to all my seminars. It is, you are not what people say you are, you are whatever you decide to be."

The basic truth she sensed subdued her urge to argue.

"Most people don't know what they're feeling most of the time." He held up a finger. "But everyone over the age of five can control his or her actions. There's an old saying, 'to know the artist, look at his art.' That's what I do in my seminars. I encourage people to concentrate on their actions, to find the artist inside by examining their art, and by taking stock of their accomplishments and creative potential. I tell them, I don't care how you feel, tell me what you've done. Show me, show yourself."

She squeezed her pocketbook. "I'm no artist."

His laughter filled the car. "Every word, every gesture

is an act of creation.'' He pointed at her. ''You pervert
the artist within by letting others shape your actions.''
His intense, gray eyes swept from her head to her toes.
''Or telling you how to dress. You're way too pretty for
those suits you wear.''

She fingered her blouse. ''I'm not certain I understand.''

''When we were at Elk River, I thoroughly enjoyed
the company of a vibrant, funny, lively woman. You
sparkled, sweetheart. You bubbled. You were Gracie to
my George, Nora to my Nick. And that, I am one-
thousand-percent certain, is the *real* you.''

Bubbled? Funny? She had sparkled? ''I still don't understand.''

''You're a smart cookie. You'll get it.''

How she was supposed to get it, he gave no clue. They
reached the Citadel Mall and he parked near the Dillard's
department store.

''What are we doing here?'' she asked.

''Party clothes.''

''But Ross—''

Heedless of her protests, he escorted her into the store
and aimed her toward the junior department. She stated
she was too old for junior clothing. He countered she was
as old as she felt. He planted her in front of a rack of
dresses.

''I don't have any money.'' She held her pocketbook
away from her body. Her checkbook was useless, as was
her credit card. She glanced about nervously, half expecting store security to throw her out for being a deadbeat.

''My treat.'' He looked her up and down. ''What are
you? A five, a seven?''

"A six. Ross, this is ridiculous. I don't need any clothes—"

He interrupted her by flashing an emerald-green slip dress in front of her face. It glittered under the fluorescent lighting. "Cute. Sexy."

She agreed, but shook her head. "I can't."

"Forget *can't*. What do you want?"

She wanted her money back and her sanity and to find her husband. "I—I don't…"

He cupped her chin with an insistent hand, forcing her to look at him. "Indulge me."

She couldn't resist his winning smile. At the very least he distracted her from her problems. She picked through the rack, unable to rouse much interest. Then she spotted a dress in dark red satin. The color was like the finest wine in candlelight, dark and rich and mysterious. She lifted it off the rack. It had a sleeveless bodice covered in matching lace and a straight skirt with a flirtatious walking slit in the back. "Okay, this is sort of cute." She held it up to her body. The skirt was above the knee.

He whistled appreciatively. "Go try it on."

"Ross, this is ridiculous. I can't—"

He waggled an admonishing finger in her face. "Uh-uh. No *can't*." He searched through the racks and found an electric-blue halter dress in stretchy panne velvet. Not only was it backless, it looked as if it would cling to every curve. She vetoed the blue and scooted away with the red before he talked her into something really outrageous.

Ridiculous, she told herself in the changing booth. Her life had been turned upside down and here she was, trying on a dress she'd never in a million years have the courage to buy, much less wear in public.

She zipped it up and faced the mirror. Not even the

harsh lighting detracted from the lush, red-wine color and how the scoop neckline flattered her thin neck.

"Ma'am?" the sales lady called. "Does it fit?"

Dawn opened the door and peeked out.

"Your husband would like to know your shoe size."

"My what?"

"Shoe size. We're having a wonderful sale on summer sandals."

"He's not my husband." She slipped her left hand behind her back.

A sunny smile brightened the woman's face. She handed over a package of sheer, black stockings. "In any case, he says if the dress fits, keep it on." She coaxed Dawn out of the booth. "I'd say that dress was made for you. It's adorable."

Dawn turned the package in her hands. They weren't panty hose, but elastic-topped stockings. She tried to hand the package back. "These aren't panty hose."

"It's too warm for panty hose. What do you think of the dress?"

Dawn peered into the bank of mirrors lining the wall. She tucked hair behind her ears. The lacy bodice made the most of her small bosom and the above-the-knee skirt flattered her legs.

The saleslady clapped her hands. "The color is perfect for you."

"Dawn?" Ross called. "Let me see."

"Go show him," the sales lady urged, shooing Dawn out of the dressing rooms.

She stepped into the open. Spreading her arms, she turned around slowly.

His gray eyes gleamed like jewels and his smile threatened to melt her joints. Bells whispered to her and her discomfort disappeared.

"We'll take it," Ross said. "The stockings, too. Leave on the dress, sweetheart. I found some shoes that'll be dynamite with it."

Why she obeyed, she wasn't certain. Except, and she scarcely dared think it, she was having fun. His good humor and determination were infectious. The weight of her grief and anger faded, so for long moments at a time Quentin never even crossed her mind.

By the time they left the department store, she wore the new dress, stockings and a pair of velvet-textured suede sandals with three-inch heels. She carried a chic little purse that contained the mascara and lipstick Ross had purchased after her makeover at the cosmetics counter. Her hair was swept up at the sides, held by clips decorated with glittering rhinestones.

As Ross held the door for her, a pair of teenage boys were entering the store. They both gave her a double take.

Dawn blushed. Ross chuckled and hooked his arm with hers.

"I don't know how I'll repay you for all this." She wanted to record the expenses in her Daytimer, but it was inside her pocketbook, which was inside the Dillard's bag Ross carried.

"All the repayment I need is for you to have a good time."

"Which makes me a bought woman. I can't go that far."

He opened the passenger door of his car for her. He loomed over her, looking handsome and relaxed and very pleased with himself. The setting sun crowned his hair with fire. He touched a finger to her chin. "Bought woman, huh? If we're talking cold, hard cash, I can't earn enough in this lifetime to afford you."

His mouth fascinated her. He had beautifully shaped,

perfectly proportioned lips, and memories of the taste of him chilled her skin and heated her insides. He was going to kiss her. He shouldn't kiss her. She shouldn't allow it.

Oh, but how she longed for his kiss.

He urged her into the car. When he got in, he divided his attention between the road and giving her warm looks. Sexy looks, filling her with awareness of the low neckline and of how the thigh-high stockings felt ultrafeminine. She tugged at the hem of the skirt, but could not pull it more than four inches above her knees.

As they cruised along Platte Avenue, she studied Pikes Peak and how unreal it looked with sunset outlining it in silver and gold. When Ross asked her where she felt like eating, she said the first thing that popped into her mind: "The Blue House." She regretted her impulsiveness. The Blue House catered to what Quentin called the tree-hugging crowd. House specialties tended to be vegetarian. She rubbed her throat, recalling how Quentin had always been insisting on something. Where and what they ate. The hours they spent together. She bristled. No more insisting, no more being bullied by a man. If Ross disparaged her choice, she fully intended to argue.

"Sounds good," Ross said. "Best pasta primavera in town."

Surprised, she gave a start. "You've eaten there?"

"Lots of times. The servers don't mind a lone diner who spreads papers all over the table."

"You eat alone?"

"It happens."

She fiddled with her new purse. The shiny, black leather was soft as face cream, seeming to melt under her fingers. Ross had selected it, as he had the shoes.

"I'm surprised," she said carefully, "you don't have a girlfriend."

"Why surprised?"

She lifted a shoulder, darting a glance and a smile at him. "You're very romantic." The words emerged in a rush and her cheeks warmed.

"Yeah, well, I also travel eight months out of the year and when I'm home, I generally work sixty or seventy hours a week. Not much time for romance." He clamped his mouth shut and his brow lowered. He stopped at an intersection and stared at the red light as if it might do something more interesting than turn green. "But things change. Priorities change."

He could be sounding so wistful about any of a hundred, or a thousand women. But her foolish heart dared hope he spoke of her. Hope that logic and reason—not to mention a marriage license—told her she had no right whatsoever to feel.

Chapter Eight

Dawn and Ross faced each other on her front porch. The day had begun horribly, but the evening ended on an almost musical note. It was a balmy night, with stars glittering overhead and the scent of lilacs floating on the breeze. Add to the mix an enchanting man with a smile to die for, and Dawn couldn't imagine life getting any better.

"Dinner was lovely," she said. "I needed it more than I realized. Thank you."

For the first time since awakening in her bridal bed with the best man rather than the groom, she felt relaxed and in control of herself. She almost felt clearheaded enough to consider her situation reasonably and notice her surroundings. A light breeze rustled the treetops, nearly drowning out traffic noise from nearby I-25. The glow of the twin porch lights cast strong shadows on Ross's face and she indulged in pleasurable study.

"Come to my place." He shoved his hands in his trouser pockets. Muscles worked in his forearms.

She backed up a step, striking the Dillard's bag with her foot and nearly turning her ankle in the unaccustomed high heel. Go to his place...forget being married, forget being a Lovell.

"I'm not putting the moves on you. I don't want you to stay alone, that's all. You can sleep in my spare bedroom. I won't bother you, I promise."

He bothered her by merely being. "I appreciate the offer, but I can't. It wouldn't be right." She turned for the door, her key ready.

He put a hand on her shoulder. His palm was cool against her bare skin. The skirt of her new dress ruffled against her legs. Uncomfortable awareness of the thigh-high stockings made her itch deep inside and her hand shook so the keys rattled.

"Don't, please." She stood rigid until he removed his hand. Only then could she breathe. She jammed the key in the lock.

"Let me stay here, then. I can sleep anywhere. I'll be quiet as a mouse."

Tempting. How very easy it would be to interpret *anywhere* as her bed. Allow him to hold her, kiss her, peel those ridiculous stockings from her legs...love her. Pretend Quentin didn't exist; pretend she was a normal woman with a normal life. Her chest tightened and every breath became a chore. When he moved closer to her, close enough to smell his healthy, woodsy scent and feel the heat of his body, it was with something akin to pain that she lifted her face to his.

He placed a hand over the side of her face, his fingers gentle in their demand. Her eyelids lowered in quiet rebellion against her skin's sensitivity. He feathered a kiss across her lips.

"It almost killed me watching you marry him," he whispered. He pressed a firmer kiss to her mouth, and her lips softened with languid hunger. "Spending a week with you was sweet hell."

Another kiss. She slid a hand around his waist and

touched with her fingertips the ridge formed by strong muscle along his spine. Her heartbeat pulsed against her eardrums, silencing the night.

"I want you, Dawn. I wanted you the first second I saw you. I know it's insane, but you were engaged and I thought you loved him, so all I could do was pretend I didn't care. I knew he didn't deserve you. I couldn't stand knowing you loved another man. I tried to be happy for you, but I couldn't. All I could do was pretend Quentin didn't exist." He inhaled raggedly. "It's ripping me apart, what he's done to you. I want you and I want to hold you and take away your pain."

What shock, anger and betrayal failed to do, his fervent words accomplished. Pain broke like a cracked egg in her chest. He kissed her deeply, the sweet taste of his tongue mingling with the salt of her tears. A deep quickening within was sweetly painful, sweeping her back to their unintentional lovemaking, and the feel of his hot, supple skin and sleek muscles and the hungry approving purr he'd made when she kissed him. She'd desired him so much then...she desired him desperately now.

"Don't cry," he whispered. "I don't want you to cry." He pressed hot kisses to her cheeks and eyelids. "I didn't want you to marry him. I wanted to stop you and it made me crazy. When I went to your room before the wedding, I seriously intended locking you in or tying you up or carrying you away or something, anything so I could make you listen."

"Ross, stop, please." She clutched his shirt, curling the fabric in her fingers. "I can't bear it."

"I want to kill him for what he's done to you." He slid both hands over her hips, down her thighs. He inched her skirt up until the light breeze caressed her skin above the stockings. She itched for his touch, for skin against skin. She ached for him.

One more second and she was lost. One more kiss, one more whispered word, and she'd throw away her self-respect and her pride. She pushed away, twisting and grabbing for the door. She found it and shoved the door open. She tugged frantically at her skirt.

"I can't do this, Ross! I *can't*. Don't you understand? What if this isn't Quentin's doing? What if this is some kind of horrible plot to make me think he's done it to me? What if he's been abducted? What if real burglars stole my property? What kind of wife would I be to start carrying on with another man while my husband is missing?"

"What if, what if," he said, a low growl thick with sarcasm. "He's a con artist and a thief. Wake up, Dawn, nobody abducted him. He planned all this from the very start. Getting you out of town, digging into your bank accounts, marrying you so he gains a legal right to your property."

"He's my *husband*." The words burned like acid on her tongue. "If I can't give him my loyalty, then I have nothing to give anybody. Not you, not even myself."

"You're crazy." He shook his head violently.

"I can't lower myself. What I want with you is—is—"
Adultery.

"It's wrong. His crimes don't give me license to commit crimes of my own." She wiped her hot, damp face. Her throat hurt so much even swallowing pained her. "Please understand, as long as I'm married, I have to comport myself as a wife. I can't have a romantic relationship with you."

Can't fall in love.

He threw his hands in the air and hopped down the steps, off the porch. "Fine, go inside. See you later."

She held out a hand, beseeching his stiff back, willing him to understand. "I don't want to hurt your feelings or make you angry."

He jerked open the car door. "I'm not angry."

He sounded angry, he looked angry, and the force with which he slammed the car door seemed very angry indeed. He gunned the engine and the headlights flared. The tires churned gravel and he barely slowed to maneuver between the gates and onto the street.

She picked up the Dillard's bag, which felt as heavy as a sack of bricks. She entered the house, losing both her will and her strength. In the empty foyer, she divided her gaze between the shopping bag and the skirt of her new dress.

With a sudden fierce cry, she flung the bag of clothing. It struck the wall with an echoing thud, as empty and lonesome as her weary heart.

ROSS SLAMMED his apartment door. He hit the light switch and glared at the living room. The place had grown dusty in his absence and the air smelled stale. Potted plants hanging from the ceiling and arranged on racks looked droopy.

He tossed his suitcase in the direction of the hall closet. Self-awareness, the characteristic allowing him success in the motivational field, plagued him now with brutal thoughts. The anger churning his gut had as much to do with the shock of being rejected as it did with Quentin Bayliss. He liked women, they liked him. He was careful in his affairs, choosing partners as committed to their single status as he was to his. Everybody always left smiling.

How the devil had he fallen so hard for a married woman?

Not that he considered Dawn's marriage a real marriage by a long shot. *What if Quentin is the victim of an elaborate plot?* Who was she trying to kid?

Grumbling, he checked his phone messages. A few friends wanted him to call when he was home from vacation and his mother asked if Dawn had learned anything new about Quent. He sorted through his mail. Nothing merited more than a cursory glance.

He filled a watering jug and tended the plants. He'd done a few things in his life he regretted. Over the years, he'd humbled himself for his share of apologies. Never once, however, had he conducted himself shabbily. He'd never chased a married woman or humiliated another person, and he wasn't about to start now.

Which left him with one option. Get Dawn unmarried.

First step, find Quentin Bayliss. He'd do the world a big favor if he could make Dawn a widow, he thought with a grim smile.

EARLY THE NEXT morning, he'd figured out the perfect solution. A quick telephone call and then a short drive downtown took him to the office of Hayes and Coplin, Private Investigations. Ross had met Rayne Coplin a little over a year ago at the health club. Despite his large size and laconic manner, the private eye played a wicked game of racquetball. Ross considered him a friend.

Ross entered the office and Rayne looked up from a glowing computer screen. The men shook hands. Rayne offered coffee. As he gave Ross a cup, Rayne yawned mightily and covered it with his hand. He had dark circles under his eyes.

"Sorry," he said. "My kid is teething and my wife

has a summer cold. Nobody in our house is getting any sleep.''

Uncertain what to say to a man with family problems, Ross merely nodded.

"So, what's up? You sounded urgent on the phone."

Ross told the story of Quentin Bayliss briefly, sticking to the facts. Nodding and taking notes, Rayne listened intently. His brow furrowed. When Ross finished, Rayne said, ''A con artist.''

"So how do I find him?"

"If he doesn't want to be found?" Rayne let out a disdainful snort. "You won't. Guy sounds like a pro. Ten bucks says Quentin Bayliss isn't his real name.''

Dismayed by the private eye's pessimism, Ross shrugged. "Dawn's attorney checked him out.''

"And he was probably real civilized about it," he said dryly. "My guess is, Quentin Bayliss exists, but he isn't your man. I'll snoop around. Shouldn't take much to find out if your man is an impersonator." He scanned his notes. "Tell me more about the woman who called your lady friend. You're sure she wanted a check? It definitely wasn't a ransom demand?''

"That's what Dawn said. She also said the woman was drunk, upset, threatening and calling from a bar. It sounds like Quent made some promises he expects Dawn to keep." Pondering the implications, he pulled at his chin. "You don't think anybody would hurt Dawn, do you? Because of Quent's debts?''

"It sounds as if Quent plays rough. Maybe.''

Fear tweaked him for having left Dawn alone in the huge, empty house. "I want to hire you, Rayne. I want to find this joker and I want him in jail.''

"No promises," Rayne said. He pulled some forms from a desk drawer. "I'll need to talk to Dawn." He gestured at Ross with a pen. "But one of the first things she needs to do is file a complaint with the cops. There's no telling how deeply Bayliss has injured her financially and without complaints on file she'll have a battle with the credit companies. I'd keep my eyes peeled for any lowlifes lurking around, too. He may have told more than one drunk that Dawn will cover his debts."

THE RINGING telephone made Dawn groan. After a long morning of nothing but bad news and worse news, she was tempted to unplug the phone and bury it in the backyard. Only the prospect of possibly hearing Ross's voice caused her to answer.

"Hello, my darling!" Connie Haxman said. "I finally found you. They told me you had checked out of the resort."

Dawn slumped on a stool and rested her face on her hand. "Connie, I'm so glad to hear from you."

A long pause preceded Connie's cautious reply. "My instincts are right, then. All is not well."

Every bit of pride remaining coiled tight and unyielding in Dawn's breast. She was broke, deserted, in debt and disgraced. As much as she treasured Connie, the idea of telling her about Quentin made her feel ill.

"What do you mean, instincts?"

"You cut short the honeymoon and—and—well—"

Dawn's nape and scalp prickled. Connie was usually blunt to a fault, and always outspoken. Hearing her stammer in search of words frightened Dawn.

"It's that witch Dizzy Hunter! I hate it when she starts acting like a reporter, especially when it's none of her darned business. My darling, one question and please do answer truthfully because it will ease my mind greatly and allow you to get back to wallowing in marital bliss."

Dawn caught her lower lip in her teeth. Connie knew. If not everything, then enough. "What question?"

"Is everything all right with you and Quentin?"

Other than shame, Dawn could not think of a single reason not to answer. Last night, she'd cried enough to last a lifetime. Which was good thing, for this morning she'd been able to speak to her attorney, accountant and insurance adjuster without breaking down. Now, however, a lump formed in her throat and her eyes began to burn. She choked back a sob. "Everything is so *not* right I don't know what to do."

"What happened?"

The story spilled out in a tumble of quavering words. She told Connie about Quentin's disappearance, Ross's appearance in the cabin, the possibility she and Ross had been drugged, how the police refused to help, the burglarized home, the plundered bank accounts and the insurance adjuster telling her he doubted if the claims people would consider the theft a burglary because, as her husband, Quentin had a right to dispose of items without reimbursement from the insurance company.

When she finished, she felt drained, weak and dry-mouthed. Her chest ached as if she'd run ten miles.

"Dizzy is right, then," Connie said quietly.

"What does Dizzy have to do with anything?"

"She thinks Quentin is a criminal. With what you've told me, I have to agree. Oh, my darling, stay right where you are. I'm throwing on my clothes as we speak. I'll be there in twenty minutes."

Connie rang off, leaving Dawn with a dead telephone and a million questions.

She'd barely hung up the phone when the doorbell rang. For a moment she imagined she'd blacked out or something, giving Connie time to make it from her home to Dawn's. She shook off the disassociated sensation and answered the door.

Laden with a pair of bulging plastic grocery sacks, Ross stood there, smiling at her. "Good morning. I figured you could use some groceries. Is there any coffee?"

If the anger he'd experienced last night still lingered, he hid it well. Wearing a pair of summer-weight tan slacks and a green knit shirt, he looked handsome and relaxed, his smile sunny and his eyes filled with pleasure as they stared into hers. The bleak emotion she'd been carrying all morning in her chest eased. With the weight lifted from her soul, wonder entered. She had nothing, not even a real chair to offer him, and yet his pleasure at seeing her was unmistakable.

"Come in."

He headed directly for the kitchen. "I brought you some fruit and salad fixings," he said. "The farmers' market is open over at Acacia Park. Strawberries to die for, sweetheart. They had melons, but they didn't look so hot. I always hold out for the Rocky Fords. They spoil me for any other kind."

Hands together in front of her, she cocked her head, watching him pull a basket of strawberries from a bag. He brought the fruit to his nose and inhaled, smiling dreamily.

Hyperaware of how she looked, she plucked at the neck of her T-shirt and finger-combed her hair. His mouth kept drawing her gaze. When she made herself stop looking at his mouth, she focused on his hands—graceful, gentle, clever hands.

"I thought you were angry with me, Ross."

"Yeah, well, I got over it. What about you?"

"I'm glad you're here." She put away the groceries. He'd brought milk and the brand of granola she liked.

The fruit he'd bought at the farmers' market looked and smelled just-picked fresh.

He slid onto a stool and folded his hands atop the breakfast counter. She poured him a cup of coffee.

"I hired a private eye."

She froze in the midst of pulling a tea bag from a box. "You did what?"

"He's a friend of mine. He needs to talk to you."

Her forehead tightened. She jerked the tea bag from the box and dropped it in a cup. "You're carrying presumptuousness a bit too far. I can't take your charity. I certainly can't afford a private investigator."

"Who says I'm doing it for you?"

Caught off guard by his rejoinder, she filled the cup with water and placed it in the microwave. "He's my husband, Ross."

"You should have told him not to jerk me around. I don't take kindly to being drugged and embarrassed." He waggled his eyebrows while flashing an unrepentant smile. "Rayne gave me the name of a detective in the Colorado Springs police department who works in the fraud division."

She slapped both hands on the counter. "Don't you understand? I've been on the telephone all morning. My accountant says everything is gone. Quentin got into every liquid asset I own and stripped it. He stole all the stocks and bonds." She marched to the counter next to the refrigerator and snatched up the bundle of mail delivered while she was out of town. She tossed the stack in front of him.

"Look at that! Credit-card bills. Thousands of dollars worth of bills, all in my name. Quentin used my name to open accounts. This is only from last week. What's coming this week? Or the next? Who knows what bills

Quentin prevented me from seeing?'' She snatched up a pale blue envelope. "This is a cellular telephone bill. There are almost two thousand dollars' worth of calls on it. It's in my name, but I don't even own a cellular phone. My checks have been bouncing all over town.''

His throat worked. "He couldn't steal the house. If all else fails, you can sell it. It must be worth—''

"I *can't* sell it. This house is included in the trust my father established. I can live in it for as long as I wish, but if I die or decide I don't want to live here, then the property is bequeathed to a charitable foundation my mother established. I cannot sell it. Nor can I borrow money by using the house as collateral. It isn't mine.''

"What about your trust fund?''

She hated herself for taking out her frustration on him, but her nerves were so frazzled she couldn't lower her voice or control her wildly gesturing hands. "My grand inheritance! The bulk of my father's estate was placed in trust. In five years, when I am thirty-five years old, I will be able to collect the interest, but I cannot touch the principal. When I turn forty, the trust will be disbanded and the money goes to charity. Father believed too much inherited wealth weakens character.''

She swiped at the bills, scattering them so some fell to the floor. The small act of violence soothed her somewhat. She panted, seeking her bearings.

"How bad is it?'' Ross asked gently. "How much debt did he run up?''

"I don't know yet. My accountant is contacting credit bureaus. My attorney is investigating my liability. It will take a week or so to figure out how much damage Quentin has done.''

She lightly touched her finger to an empty grocery bag. "I can't even buy groceries. I don't know how I'm going to pay you back for what you've done for me this far. I certainly can't afford a private eye.''

He maintained a calm demeanor, as if her ranting affected him not in the least. ''You can't afford not to hire one. It'll be worth it if you get your stuff back. If Quentin goes to jail, you can prove you aren't responsible for the bills he ran up.''

Despite his well-reasoned logic, it still felt like charity. She'd rather have Ross angry with her than feeling pity.

''Rayne's a nice guy. You'll like him.''

''This is all just so humiliating.'' The microwave dinged and she turned to retrieve her tea.

''Yeah, that's life. Humiliation and pain interspersed with bright little moments of bliss.''

Surprised into a smile as she added milk and sugar to her tea, all she could do was shake her head.

''By the way,'' he said. ''I like the shirt.''

She looked down at herself and blushed. She'd purchased the T-shirt three years ago on a whim and it had since been stuck in the back of a drawer, unworn. Made of hot-pink cotton, it bore a picture of a cat sprawled on its back with the caption Take No Prisoners. What it meant, she hadn't a clue; neither did she have a clue as to what little demon in her had caused her to wear it this morning.

With her cup of tea in hand, she joined Ross at the counter.

He placed a hand over hers and squeezed her fingers gently. ''Are you okay?''

''No.''

''If you want to yell at me some more, feel free.''

Abashed, she propped her face on her fists. ''I don't want to yell.''

''*I'd* yell.''

She moved her eyes to see him. "All I wanted was to get married and have kids. Nothing grand, nothing ambitious. Just a family. I couldn't even do that right."

She waited for his comments, but he remained silent. "I miss my parents. Mother's illness was a shock. She'd always been very healthy, very fit. She passed off the early symptoms of the cancer as signs of age. When the doctors found it, it was too late. She died three months after the diagnosis. Father never recovered."

"All this happened last year?"

"He died four months after she did. In those four months, I don't think he even knew I was alive. I tried to take care of him. He was depressed, but all he did was hide in his study. He wouldn't speak to me." Grief snuck up on her, catching her diaphragm in a tight grip and burning her eyes. "I'm rambling. I'm sorry."

"Ramble away. I'm listening."

"I acted like a romantic idiot over Quentin. I was lonely. I wanted to hear the bells."

"Bells?" he asked with a curious smile. "Wedding bells?"

Knowing she'd said way too much, she averted her face. "You know, hearing bells when you meet your soul mate. Bells whispering in your heart that everything is right. It's dumb. Life doesn't work that way."

"I don't think it's dumb. Ever heard the bells?"

Heat climbed from her throat over her cheeks. "Once," she whispered.

"What happened?"

She hopped off the stool, went to the window and looked out. Elms nearly blocked the view of the mountains.

"Dawn?"

"Nothing happened. Nothing at all." The lie choked

her throat and the bleak weight returned to her chest. "Quentin paid attention to me. He acted interested in everything I said or did. He told me everything I thought I wanted to hear."

"Did you hear bells when you met Quentin?"

His nearness startled her. He stood behind her, but she hadn't heard him move. When he placed a hand on her shoulder, she covered his hand with hers.

"I wanted to. I tried. I thought I could make myself love him...eventually. I had every logical reason in the world to love him."

"Love doesn't work that way, sweetheart. Reason doesn't have much to do with it."

She turned her head so she could see him. The warmth of his compassion melted her joints into jelly. "If logic has nothing to do with it, then how do you account for marriages that last fifty or sixty or seventy years?"

"I don't know. Sometimes I look at my folks and wonder what Mom possibly sees in the Colonel. At his best, he's a royal pain. But they're happy together." He rubbed her shoulder, his long fingers strong, kneading away the tension. "Maybe you fall in love, then figure out the reasons later. And because you're in love, any reason you come up with is good enough."

The doorbell rang. "It's Connie. I told her what happened. She said Desdemona Hunter found out something about Quentin." She didn't want to answer the door. Connie Haxman knew of Dawn's attraction to Ross. Seeing him here, Connie would, without a doubt, jump to the wrong conclusion.

Or the right conclusion, which was probably worse.

As soon as Dawn opened the front door, Connie swept into the house and enveloped Dawn in an embrace scented with White Diamonds. "Oh, my poor darling!"

Dawn struggled against having the air squeezed out of her. When she managed to step away, she gasped for breath.

Eyes wide, Connie wandered into the empty living room. "Good grief, now I know how my ex-husbands feel." She sniffed in the direction of the windows. "Too bad he didn't bother with the draperies. I've always thought those were better suited to an opera house." She dropped her alligator-skin portfolio on the floor and struggled with her suit jacket. Her jewelry clanked musically.

Ross stepped forward to help her with the garment. She flashed him a flirtatious smile. "What is your story, Ross dear? Rescuing our fair maiden, or seeking revenge against the dastardly Quentin?"

He exchanged an amused glance with Dawn. She couldn't help a smile.

"Both." Ross straightened the sleeves of the silk jacket. "Dawn said you've learned something from Desdemona Hunter."

"That woman! Every time I forget and begin thinking she's a friend, she pulls some kind of reporter shenanigan. I absolutely despise her. Come New Year's, my resolution shall be, I shall never invite her to another of my soirees." She scooped up the portfolio. "Is there any place to sit?"

"Stools in the kitchen." Dawn led the way. Curiosity about what the society reporter could have learned about Quentin was killing her, but she feared the information might do worse damage. Since Connie refused to drink tea brewed in the microwave, Dawn fetched the kettle.

Connie magnanimously allowed Ross to help settle her on a stool. She reached inside the portfolio, but rested her hand there. "I told Dizzy she was out of her mind.

That is, until I spoke to you. Now I believe she is on to something." She focused a comical scowl on Ross. "Women like her should be locked away."

Dawn placed the tea kettle on the stove. She tried not to look at the portfolio, but the glossy red leather drew her gaze like a beacon. "What did she find, Connie?"

Connie huffed and patted her bosom. Finally, she pulled a large newspaper photograph and a black-and-white print from the portfolio and laid them side by side on the counter. "Quentin raised her reporter's antennae, as she says. So she began snooping. I have no idea what she imagined she'd find. Some juicy scandal or a tidbit of embarrassing trivia."

The photograph was of Quentin, taken at the reception. He looked startled. The newspaper clipping showed several men walking down the outside steps of a large building. The heavyset man in the center of the activity had short, light-colored hair styled in a brush cut. He raised his handcuffed arms as if in protection against the photographer.

"Dizzy won't tell me anything except that this photograph is from a Salt Lake City newspaper dated three years ago. The man wearing handcuffs is named John Venetucci. Dizzy refused to tell me anything else. Nasty little twit. She's having a great deal of fun with this." Her voice dropped, turning small and worried. "I told her she's insane. This criminal most certainly isn't Quentin Bayliss. Please tell me it isn't him."

Dawn slumped on a stool and rested her cheek on her fist. She sighed, torn. Logic and reason told her to grasp at any explanation, take any excuse. Yet for better or worse, she'd committed her life to this marriage. Loyalty demanded she find her husband and listen to his side of the story.

Her heart refused to play along with the lie.

"Dizzy's right," she said wearily, looking at the photographs. "That's my Quentin."

Chapter Nine

Dawn left the kitchen to go upstairs and change her clothes. When the sound of her steps faded into the distance, Connie Haxman began sorting through bills.

"Awful," she muttered. As she tapped the tips of her long fingernails on the countertop, her bangle bracelets clinked. "Inexcusable. It appears Quentin has ruined her."

Ross sipped his coffee. He liked Connie Haxman, but he suspected, despite her fluffy, cute-li'l-ole-me appearance, she'd be a formidable opponent in any game she decided to play. "He did a number on her, but I believe there's a limit on how much she actually has to pay the credit-card companies."

"She shouldn't have to pay anything."

He pulled the photos of Quent near. His curiosity clamored to know why he—John Venetucci—had been arrested and why he wasn't in jail. He figured Rayne Coplin could put this information to good use. "In any case, she'll get a job and straighten everything out."

"A job? She has a job. She has volunteered as the business administrator for my Children's Betterment Society for years. She's invaluable. I can't lose her. This is all her parents' doing!" Heat colored her tone. "They treated her like some kind of exotic little pet. Whenever they were around she'd just fade away, too timid to speak her own name. It always infuriated me. Edward and Deborah convinced her ladies, *Lovell* ladies, don't lower themselves with careers. She earned a business degree in the hopes of assisting her father in his law practice. When she offered her services he told her she was too stupid to work for him."

"Her own father told her she was stupid?"

"He was wrong. She's brilliant. Organized, efficient, coolheaded in a crisis. I can't function without her."

Connie's hatred of Dawn's parents sounded old and well nourished. Realizing some of the woman's heat was now concentrated on him, Ross stilled.

"I should have listened to her." She reached inside the portfolio. "She told me of her doubts concerning Quentin."

"The more I see, the more I realize Quent is one smooth operator," Ross put in. "He knows exactly what he's doing."

"She knew there was a better choice available." She produced a leather-bound checkbook and a gold pen. "I may be utterly incapable of sustaining a romantic relationship, but that doesn't mean I don't know what's what. And *you!*"

He warily turned his head to face her.

"On the day of the wedding when you showed up in her room, what was that all about?"

"I didn't want her to marry Quent."

"Why?"

He lifted a shoulder. "I knew he'd lied to her and that he'd cheated with another woman. I wanted to tell her, but I didn't know how."

"And?"

This woman would be satisfied with nothing less than the naked truth. He lifted the coffee to his mouth. Over the rim, he said, "I was jealous."

"I thought so." She began filling out a check. "So, what are you going to do about it?"

"It's Dawn's call, ma'am."

She huffed a disgusted-sounding snort and ripped the check from the book. "You'll need to do a lot more than that. She's an innocent, totally at the mercy of the world. Her parents kept her a child, ill equipped to care for herself. She's defenseless."

Ross disagreed. Dawn certainly hadn't been defenseless against him. "She's a grown-up. She has a lot to learn, but—" At the sound of Dawn's footsteps, he cut off his speech.

Dawn had exchanged her bright T-shirt and denim jeans for a cream-colored cotton blouse with a prim Peter Pan collar and a slim skirt falling an inch past her knees. She carried her big pocketbook underneath one arm. Ross thought she looked like a cartoonist's version of the librarian from hell, and wished she'd left on the silly T-shirt.

Connie thrust out the check. Dawn hesitated, frowning at it.

"Take it," Connie said. "It will give you some breathing room until you catch that monster."

Dawn's forehead wrinkled and her chin quivered. Ross could almost smell her humiliation as well as see the way she struggled between needing the money and not wanting the handout. She pulled her pocketbook over her bosom. Her fingers dimpled the leather. "Connie…I can't. I appreciate it, but I can't take your money."

"Don't be absurd, my darling. I know all about that ridiculous trust your father created. How dare he beggar you? How dare he control you from the grave? I cannot stand by while you drive yourself into poverty for the sake of pride.''

Dawn lowered her gaze and accepted the check.

Swallowing his disappointment, Ross again focused on his coffee. Connie failed to see the damage her generosity wrought. Though she spouted hatred of Dawn's parents and their control of her, Connie appeared blind to the way she was now picking up the Lovells' banner. Guilt tightened his chest. He'd done the same thing when he paid her resort bill and hired a private eye. He and Connie were treating Dawn like a child, kissing her scrapes and patting her on the head while pretending not to see her wounded pride or shattered self-esteem.

That was no way to treat a grown woman.

Connie drank her tea and promised to give Desdemona Hunter the third degree. After Connie left the house, Dawn picked up the photographs of Quentin. She placed everything inside her oversized pocketbook.

''Dawn,'' Ross said. ''About last night. The dress is a gift. I bought it because you're pretty and it looks good on you and I'm a sucker for a great pair of legs.'' He met her gaze, uncertain whether he was apologizing, explaining, easing his guilt or hoping to win a smile. ''No strings. Not now, not ever. Do you understand?''

She lifted Connie's check to eye level. Ross caught a glimpse of an impressive number of zeros. ''I think I understand very well,'' she answered in a small, uncertain voice.

''I don't want you thinking I'm pushing you around or treating you like a kid. I'm not. I know you're strong. Man, oh, man, the way you handled my family was a stroke of pure genius.'' He held out a hand to her. ''I didn't buy the dress because I feel sorry for you.''

Ignoring his hand, she laid the check on the counter and used one finger to push it away. "I'm very confused. Every decision, large or small, seems difficult." She sighed. "I can't accept Connie's money, can I?"

"It's up to you."

"Wanting it makes me realize that if not for Quentin I'd have continued in the same way for the rest of my life. Making no decisions, always deferring to others, taking no responsibility." Her eyes widened and she recoiled from the check as if it might bite. She swiped her hand along her skirt. "I've always prided myself on doing the right thing, but it's always been what others have told me is the right thing. Now I don't know *what* to do."

He rubbed her shoulder, attempting to soothe the tension quivering under her skin.

"I don't want to be a charity case, Ross. Not yours, not Connie's, not anybody's. But I don't know if I can survive by myself. I'm terrified of being alone and penniless."

His head told him to keep his hands to himself, but his heart shouted louder. He gathered her into his arms and held her slim body close. She stiffened in his embrace, her folded arms creating a barrier. Still he stroked her back and kissed her flower-scented hair.

"You've got me, sweetheart," he whispered. "I have faith in you. You'll make it."

She pushed against him. "I can't give you what you want. That much I know is right."

He kissed her again. "The married thing, huh?"

She twisted in his grasp and he let her go. She stood with her back to him, her head hanging.

"Nothing worth having is easy." He envisioned Quentin's heavy face and fleshy smile, and his knuckles fairly itched with the urge to smash that smile into never-never land.

"I'm not playing hard to get."

"I'm not playing."

She raised her head, but remained so he couldn't see her face. "Every indicator points to Quentin's guilt. But appearances can be deceptive, so as long as he's my husband, I have to give him the benefit of doubt. It's painful. I may be foolish in thinking this way, but it's what I must do."

Ross raked his fingers through his hair. He let loose a heavy breath. "I understand." Saying so made his stomach ache.

She turned around. The pure gratitude shining in her eyes made the discomfort worthwhile. He shoved his hands into his pockets and forced a smile.

"I need your help, but I cannot bear your charity."

"That's cool."

"It's not my intention to hurt your feelings. I fear if you keep helping me for—" She blushed and covered her mouth with a hand. "I have nothing to offer you until I know the truth about Quentin."

Quaintly spoken, but her meaning came through loud and clear. She warned him that she was fully prepared to accept whatever troubles Quentin piled at her feet—he was her husband, after all. Common sense said cut his losses and walk away. The sweet curve of her cheek and the halting lilt of her voice drove common sense out the back door. "Hey, don't worry about me. My feelings can handle it. I'm a macho kind of guy."

She lowered her eyelids. "You're such a good person."

Good, kind...a real chump. The only thing preventing him from saying something stupid was knowing Quentin

Bayliss could never, in a million years, talk his way back into her good graces. In time she'd accept the truth: her husband was no husband at all and she owed him nothing.

He hoped.

DAWN GINGERLY sat upon the chair in Detective Sergeant Billy Goldenberg's office. Back straight, feet together, she clutched her pocketbook on her lap, hoping her nervousness did not show. She watched Ross and the detective shake hands. When Ross said they'd been referred by Rayne Coplin, the detective brightened.

In his mid-to-late forties, Detective Goldenberg was a small man, not much taller than Dawn. He exuded an air of confidence Dawn found assuring. Even better, he displayed numerous photographs of children on his desk. It seemed to her a family man would understand the reasons she'd married Quentin. He wouldn't consider her an utter fool.

The detective scanned the photographs of Quentin. Ross had made copies and he urged the detective to keep a set for reference.

Setting the pictures aside, Goldenberg said, "Tell me what happened, ma'am. Start from the beginning, when you first met this man."

In hindsight, the story of her courtship sounded ludicrous. What sane woman would have trusted in love at first sight and allowed herself bullied into a hasty marriage? Ross touched her arm and nodded. His steadfastness warmed her, giving her courage. She drew a deep breath and began. As she explained how she'd met Quentin at a charity Valentine's Day ball, then described the whirlwind courtship and Quentin's proposal, the detective scribbled notes on a legal pad.

He interrupted. "I've heard of your parents, ma'am. Prominent folks. Your father was involved in several high-profile civil cases, right?"

"Yes, sir. Is that important?"

"Bayliss probably saw the publicity following your father's death, then orchestrated meeting you. Go on."

She spoke for over an hour. Memories crystallized: how Quentin had been fascinated by the quality and value of her belongings; his careful questioning about her relatives, of which she had none living; his interest in her trust fund and his failed attempts to get her to file a suit to break the terms of the trust. When she spoke of the honeymoon and Quentin's disappearance, her composure slipped. The detective offered a box of tissues and a cup of water. She declined the tissues, drank the water, and finished her story.

Drained, she slumped on the chair while Ross gave his version of recent events. He included the information about being stripped naked and placed in the bed with Dawn. Cringing inside, Dawn couldn't bear to watch the detective's reaction.

"Weird," Goldenberg said. "Sounds typical, except for that."

"What do you mean?" Ross asked.

"This clown is obviously a pro. The slick way he pulled off the thefts tells me he's had plenty of practice. He set this up right down to the last detail. But involving you that way, Mr. Duke." He shook his head and pursed his lips. "That's got a nasty ring to it. Out of character."

Dawn widened her eyes. "After what he's done?"

"You see, ma'am, these guys don't think of themselves as bad guys. They don't physically hurt people. No guns, no weapons, no strong-arming. It's all mouthwork. Quentin here thinks he's a businessman. He provides a service. In your case, it was hearts and flowers. Your money is his paycheck.''

He was an experienced detective and no doubt had pursued and captured many men such as Quentin. Still, if he meant to reassure her, he failed. Bad enough—humiliating enough—to have believed Quentin's lies, but knowing she was but one of many victims was disheartening.

''A partner is out of character, too. A con artist doesn't get this slick by trusting anybody. I need to do some checking around, run some data requests. Who did you talk to with the sheriff's department over in Elk River?''

Ross gave him Mike Downes's name.

''Even though I married him, he had no right to my property.'' Dawn nodded earnestly. ''The police refused to take a burglary report. My insurance company refuses to pay for the items I lost. I can't lose everything because of a loophole. You will make him give me my belongings back, won't you?''

The detective's face tightened in an apologetic smile. ''Straight up, ma'am. If this John Venetucci in Utah proves to be one and the same as your Quentin Bayliss, then the chances of catching him are slim. He's probably out of state by now, and your money is locked up in an offshore account.'' He slid open a desk drawer and rummaged around inside. He handed over a business card. ''Talk to victim services. They can explain your options.''

Dawn tucked the card, unread, in her pocketbook. *Victim.* Anger boiled through her veins, fresher and hotter than before. ''Am I legally married?''

''If you can prove he married you illegally, then you can get the marriage annulled. Speak to your attorney. He can tell you more than I can.''

In a strange way his lack of pity helped, making her feel strong enough to bear the truth. She stood, taking a moment to straighten her clothing and tuck her hair behind her ears. "Thank you for your time, detective."

"I'll do what I can, ma'am. You're welcome to call any time if you have more information, or I'll call you with any updates." He offered a handshake.

If he expected her to wait by the telephone for news from him, he'd best think again. Not only did she intend to find Quentin, she intended to retrieve her property, too. She shook hands.

She and Ross left the police station. Clouds had built up, shrouding the mountains in wispy gray, and streaks of rain angled across the far southern sky. A brisk wind swirled leaves and dust in the street. The wind ruffled Dawn's hair and cooled her skin, but simmering anger warmed her from within.

"Looks like we'll get some rain." Ross's voice held a flat note Dawn found curious. He took her elbow, steering her toward his car.

Once inside the Lexus, she continued to puzzle over his demeanor. He'd seemed all right while they spoke to the detective. Now, unsmiling, he appeared preoccupied.

"You're neglecting your business because of me," she said. "You must have pressing matters to attend to."

"I'm still officially on vacation." He made a minute adjustment to the rearview mirror.

"Did I say something to upset you?"

"No." He flashed an absentminded smile, then started the engine.

She didn't believe him. "Did the detective say something I missed?"

"He didn't say a single thing that surprised me. What

about you? How are you feeling about Quent right now?''

She plucked at her skirt, smoothing the fabric over her knees. ''I—I'm angry.''

''Angry enough to file for divorce?'' He pointed with his chin in the direction of the county courthouse, which was only a few blocks away.

She drew away from him, pressing against the car door. On the surface his question appeared no more than concerned, but she sensed a deeper meaning.

''I didn't think so.'' He checked the street before pulling out of the parking space. At the corner, he turned north, headed for her house.

With each passing second she turned his comment, and his tone of voice, over in her mind. She kept returning to the same conclusion: Ross was jealous. The knowledge added to her general unease. He wanted her divorced— he wanted her free. Why he wanted it so much baffled her.

Just as her wanting him made no sense. Wanting him was proving a source of deep guilt and deeper pleasure that had nothing to do with sense or logic, and everything to do with the comfort of his presence, the sound of his voice and the mushy, off-balance feeling aroused when he stared into her eyes.

She wondered if Ross would want her when she was available. A challenge always piqued his interest. Whether in a game of tennis or a hand of cards, the game mattered most.

Even if she meant more than a challenge to him, she doubted if she could live with the guilt of not doing everything humanly possible and exploring every option to save her marriage. She took her vows seriously, even if

Quentin did not. Because of those vows, she could allow herself no shortcuts, no easy paths.

She was a Lovell, after all.

When they pulled through the gates of her home, Dawn spotted a Rocky Mountain Security Systems car parked in front of her door. She and Ross simultaneously said, "What?"

She looked at him. He looked at her. His wide-eyed surprise matched her own.

"Looks like trouble." Ross parked behind the white sedan marked with a red logo.

When she emerged from the car, a man wearing a Rocky Mountain Security uniform walked around the corner of the house. He slapped a hand against the walkie-talkie unit hooked on his belt.

She raised a hand. "I'm Dawn Lovell-Bayliss, the owner. Is there a problem?"

"Todd Sams." He presented identification. "Your alarm activated, ma'am. No one answered our telephone call. I've notified the police."

She sighed. "It's not as if I have anything left to steal." Catching Ross's smirk and swift aversion of his gaze, she felt laughter rising. She struggled against the urge.

Sams pointed toward the back of the house. "You've got a broken window, ma'am. Looks like forced entry. The perpetrator may still be inside."

That was not the least bit funny. She edged a step closer to Ross, and he wrapped an arm around her shoulders.

A patrol car drove between the gates, driven by the same officer who'd come before. Sams trotted to the patrol car. He and the officer conferred in voices too low for Dawn to hear what was said.

"Do you think it's Quentin?" Dawn whispered to Ross.

"He wouldn't have set off the alarm."

The officer asked Dawn for her house keys, then requested she and Ross wait inside the Lexus. Dawn obeyed without comment.

Ross locked the car doors. A few drops of rain spattered against the windshield. "Maybe kids playing in the park popped a baseball through the window."

"The back fence is quite high. I doubt it." Her calm astonished her, but the worst had happened already. She couldn't rouse enough fear or excitability to feel shaken.

When the policeman gave the all clear, Dawn entered her house. The way things were going, she half expected to find her furniture returned. None of it was.

"A window is broken and the latch is undone, ma'am. It looks like someone crawled inside, then left by the back door. Check around and see if anything is missing."

She turned him an incredulous gaze. Didn't he realize he stood in the middle of an empty room inside a stripped-bare house? The absurdity of the situation did not escape her.

The officer and the security man finished their reports. When they left the house, Dawn slumped on a stool in the kitchen, laid her head on her arms and tried very hard to not cry.

Ross touched her back.

She jumped and nearly fell off the stool. Gasping, she clutched her blouse over her pounding heart.

"Sorry," he said, his face wrinkled in worry.

"No, I'm sorry. I just realized how very frightened I am." She warily studied the broken windowpane. "Crime is unheard of in this neighborhood. I feel like...like a target."

"I'll fix you some tea."

"You're the expert on human behavior," she said. "Why would a burglar risk daylight and alarms to break into this house? Even if he missed the alarm-control boxes on the doors, he must have seen the decals on the windows."

"Good question." He placed a mug of water inside the microwave. "Something has been bugging me. What Detective Goldenberg said about con artists not trusting a partner makes it bug me even more."

"What's that?"

He tapped himself high on the left shoulder. "Knocking me out. I'm convinced Quentin drugged you. I'm also convinced he was the one Stefan saw carrying luggage to the parking lot. That makes sense. He tucks you in bed and makes a clean getaway."

Dawn followed his line of reasoning. "So you think the person you saw outside the cabin wasn't working with Quentin? He *was* abducted?"

He shook his head. "Two cars, remember? I think Quent took the Lincoln. Which means somebody else followed in the other car." He frowned at the broken window. "Suppose Quent was working with someone, but that someone sensed a double cross in the making." He mimed depressing the plunger on a hypodermic. "The shot was for Quent."

"But you got in the way."

"Exactly. I caused a little change of plans. Only now, Quent has given his partner the slip."

"Even if that were true, why would he break into my house?" Remembering the call from the drunken woman, Dawn amended her comment to, "Or she?"

Ross shrugged and showed his palms. "Looking for

Quent? Maybe the partner thinks you two are working together.''

"How could he possibly think that?"

"You married the man."

Stung, she crossed her arms tightly over her chest.

Ross's cellular telephone rang. He gave it a baleful glare before unhooking it from his belt and flipping it open. "Hello." His eyebrows lifted. "I see."

Tuning out his conversation, Dawn turned her gaze on the pile of bills. She sorted through it until she found the cellular-phone bill. Every single telephone call had been logged and charged, both incoming and outgoing. Most of the outgoing calls included a telephone number. The majority of calls were long distance, with a northern-Colorado area code.

She had asked to see Quentin's offices, but the timing had always been poor. He had not liked it when she called him at work, either, though he generally answered the telephone. She scanned the telephone bill, seeking any familiar numbers. He'd made a lot of calls to this house and to the Children's Betterment Society during the four days a week she volunteered there. She didn't recognize any other numbers.

"What's up?" Ross asked. He folded his small telephone and hooked it on his belt.

"This bill. Quentin may have erred in leaving it for me to find." She tucked the entire bill into her purse. "He spent a lot of time on the phone discussing business. But there aren't any calls to the number I used to call to reach him. Connie is always diverting her telephone number to wherever she is. Quentin could have done the same. He could have given me a phony Denver number and when I called, had it diverted to his mobile phone. I want to visit Palone Developments, Quentin's business.

My attorney assured me it's a viable company. Somebody must be there.''

"The odds of Quent being there are a million to one."

She laid a hand flat on the telephone bill. "He knew enough about the business to tell me he at least knows the true owners. They might have a clue as to where he's gone."

Ross shook his head. "Odds are—"

"If I have to look in a million places, then that is exactly what I will do."

Chapter Ten

Dawn entered the office of Palone Developments Incorporated in the Denver suburb of Aurora. Quentin had overwhelmed her with a blizzard of information about building shopping malls and developing subdivisions of single-family homes. She'd wanted to see his offices and meet his employees, but he always put her off and delayed.

Now here she was, standing inside the tastefully appointed reception area, decorated with framed photographs of houses and aerial shots of subdivisions. A door behind the receptionist's desk had a brass nameplate: Quentin Bayliss, President.

She glanced at Ross. He wore a neutral expression.

"May I help you?" the receptionist asked.

"I'd like to see Mr. Bayliss, please. Is he in?"

"Do you have an appointment?"

"I don't need one. I'm his wife."

The receptionist raised an eyebrow. Her right hand slid along the desk and rested atop a telephone. "Pardon me?"

"I am Dawn Lovell-Bayliss. Is Quentin in?"

"He got married? But he's only been back one day."

She picked up the telephone and punched a button. After

a moment, she said, "Q.B., your wife is here to see you." The other eyebrow lifted, completing her expression of utter confusion. "I see. Very well." She hung up. "He'll be—"

The office door opened. A man with a round face and hair falling in bangs over his forehead, wearing a neatly tailored suit, peered at Dawn. He looked about twenty years old. "Well, here I am." He laughed uneasily.

Uncertain what to say, Dawn tapped her fingers on her pocketbook.

"Quentin Bayliss?" Ross asked.

He held up his hands in a gesture of surrender. "You got me. Go for it. I'm ready."

Dawn looked at Ross, he returned the look.

"Go ahead, wifey. Sing, dance, smack me with a rubber rolling pin. Come on, I'm in the mood for a bit of public humiliation. Do your thing." Grinning, he strode across the office. He jerked open the door and called, "Ollie ollie, oxen free!"

Dawn sidled a nervous step closer to Ross. Bayliss's behavior went beyond odd. The man was downright bizarre.

Bayliss stepped out the door and looked up and down the corridor. "Where is everybody? Where's the party, Ruth?"

The receptionist mouthed silently, "I don't know."

"Excuse me," Ross said. "We aren't here for a party."

"But it's my birthday," Bayliss said. "Didn't Tony send you?" He nodded eagerly, looking very much like a man ready for a good joke. "Isn't this a payback for the male stripper I sent to his office?"

His birthday...of course. The Lincoln had been an early birthday present. She pulled the marriage license from her pocketbook. "Mr. Bayliss, I'm Dawn Lovell-Bayliss. A few days ago I married a man who is using your identity. Your name, your social security number, your birth date. I need to talk to you, sir."

Bayliss shut the door. "Is this a joke?"

"I wish it were." She gazed upon an artist's rendition of a shopping mall, recognizing both the design and the name. Quentin had boasted about it. "Apparently he knows you and this business. He claimed he owned the company."

"That's not possible. Ever since Dad retired, I'm the sole owner of Palone." He crossed his arms and jutted his chin.

Right hand outstretched, Ross stepped forward. "Ross Duke, Mr. Bayliss. The man we're looking for has committed fraud."

Bayliss shook hands, reluctantly. He glanced at the office door as if uncertain whether or not to believe this wasn't part of the hoped-for birthday joke. "I don't see how that's possible." He crossed his arms again. "I've been out of town."

"All the better for our man. Can we talk?"

Bayliss invited them into his office. He told his receptionist to hold his calls. He took a seat behind a large, black-lacquered desk that was completely bare except for a striking crystal sculpture. Dawn noticed the graying hair at his temples and crow's-feet etched into the corners of his eyes. He was much older than she'd assumed.

Dawn again offered the marriage license and Bayliss took it. He stared at it for almost a minute before handing it back. "What's this all about?"

Dawn balked at telling a stranger about her troubles. The tale wasn't getting any easier with time. "Before I married Quentin—the man calling himself Quentin—my attorney conducted a background check. I insisted upon discretion and that he not speak to anybody, because…because I didn't want my fiancé thinking I didn't trust him. My attorney searched public records and assured me this business was legitimate, well-established and profitable.''

"He told you right.'' Bayliss's voice was low and angry. "He said he was me?''

"That's what it looks like, Mr. Bayliss,'' Ross said. "In order to impersonate you so well, he had to have known you. He had access to your personal records. He speaks knowledgeably about real estate and investments.'' He nodded at Dawn and pointed at her purse.

She handed over copies of the photographs. "Do you know him?''

Color darkened Bayliss's rounded cheeks. He clenched and unclenched a fist atop the shiny surface of the desk. "I knew he was a crook. I smelled trouble the minute I met him.''

Dawn leaned forward on her chair. "Then you do know him.''

"Tim Wiley.'' He closed his eyes and muttered an obscenity. "He blew in here last November. From Boston. He represented a big group of major investors wanting to build a shopping mall. Bigger than Cherry Creek, he says. Bigger than anything else this side of St. Louis. Man, what an operator. I even let him stay in my house for a couple of weeks so he wouldn't have to live in a hotel. But it was all talk. I gave him the boot when he kept pressuring me for good-faith money. He wanted half a million to show his back-east investors.''

"You let him stay in your house?'' Ross asked.

He clenched and unclenched his fist even faster. His knuckles whitened. "When I went skiing. It was a mistake. He ran up over a grand in telephone charges, emptied my liquor cabinet and trashed the place. What a pig. I still don't know how he talked me into it. I even let him use my car.'' He frowned and lifted his gaze to the ceiling. "The last time I saw him was in January. None of the contact numbers or addresses he gave me are any good.''

Dawn debated telling him how lucky he was to have come home without finding all his furniture gone.

"Did you give him any money?"

"Other than the telephone bill he stiffed me with, no.''

His youthful appearance notwithstanding, this man was astute. Dawn wished she'd listened to her instincts, as he had obviously done.

"What a character,'' Bayliss said. "For a while there I really liked him. He seemed to have a lot on the ball. He could sure talk a good line. But that's all it was, talk, and lots of it. Too much. I don't trust anyone who can't keep his mouth shut.''

"Any hard information you can give us would be appreciated,'' Ross said.

"I don't have any. Like I said, everything he told me was bogus.'' He cocked an eyebrow and grinned unpleasantly at Dawn. "So you're his wife. I guess I can talk to you about that phone bill.''

Ross stiffened, his shoulders seeming to swell. His eyes acquired a dangerous gleam.

Dawn glanced at the marriage license and the irony struck her again. With it came strength from remembering she was her father's daughter. Her days of being manipulated were over—a harsh lesson, but she'd learned it. "Actually, sir, as far as the law is concerned, I'm married to you.'' She cocked her head, mimicking his expression. "Perhaps we can discuss my debts. Or should I say, *our* debts?"

Ross shot her an incredulous look. Bayliss gave a start and for a moment looked stunned. Then he laughed. "I was only kidding."

She smiled sweetly.

Ross stood. "Mr. Bayliss, here is the name and number of a fraud detective in Colorado Springs. Please call him. I also advise filing a complaint here in Aurora."

"Yeah, yeah."

Intuition told Dawn that Bayliss wasn't particularly concerned about her plight. He'd been inconvenienced, but not particularly harmed, so to his way of thinking, why embarrass himself by linking his name with a con artist? "Since he had your personal information, you might want to check with the credit bureaus to see if he obtained credit cards or loans in your name."

Bayliss's eyes widened.

"He could have arranged for the bills to go to a post-office box." Dawn shrugged. "He's very clever. I do hope you will speak to the police and root out whatever damage he's done to you. Good day."

On the way to the parking lot, they walked fast, hunched against a rising wind. "Married to you...credit cards," Ross muttered, and laughed. "You're too much, sweetheart. Did you see his face?"

Basking in the glow of his approval, Dawn felt a stirring of hope that everything might turn out well after all.

"WHY ARE WE stopping here?" Dawn asked when Ross turned off the engine. She watched traffic trundling down Cascade.

He pointed to the second floor of a brownstone building. "Rayne's office."

"You heard what Detective Goldenberg said. Probably Quentin is out of state and my money has vanished. You said yourself that the name Tim Wiley is most likely as phony as Quentin. I can't imagine what a private investigator can do for me."

"If it was only money, I'd agree. But how many moving vans do you think it would take to haul all your furniture away?"

She pondered the question. "Even spring cleaning required weeks of moving things about to reach the floors and walls. Two or three full-sized vans? I honestly do not know."

"It was definitely more than one. If it was local, using a rented van and day labor, then maybe he stored your stuff someplace. In any case, there will be records. It's a lead."

"I didn't consider that." She opened the car door.

Ross led the way up a narrow stairwell and entered an office. A dark-haired man bent over a filing cabinet. He straightened and smiled.

The private eye's office wasn't at all what Dawn expected. Sunny and bright, it contained several desks and a lot of computer equipment. Potted plants offered touches of color. A playpen set up in a corner was occupied by a sleeping baby.

The man offered a hand. "Sorry about the kid. My wife had to take her grandfather to a doctor's appointment and the sitter had an emergency." He shook hands with Ross and nodded a greeting to Dawn. "You must be Dawn. I'm Rayne. Nice to meet you. Have a seat." He indicated a chair.

Wearing blue jeans and a cotton shirt with rolled sleeves, he appeared quite ordinary. An attractive, powerful-looking man, he could have been a construction worker rather than a private eye.

Ross edged closer to the playpen and peered warily inside. "Cute kid."

"Looks like his mom," Rayne said with a note of pride. "So, where do we start?"

Ross settled on a chair and filled in the private eye with all they'd learned so far. He ended with, "This joker is too good."

While Ross was speaking, Rayne had been taking notes. He studied what he'd written. "Creeps like this count on their victims being embarrassed. He may get cocky, thinking you won't attempt to run him down, and if he does, we'll nail him. Let me see what the reporter gave you."

Dawn found the private eye's demeanor encouraging. Her father had often used investigators to help his cases, but he'd always talked about them as if they engaged in not-quite-savory practices. Rayne Coplin appeared wholesome. The baby proved he was quite human, as well. Feeling better about Ross taking the initiative to hire the private eye, Dawn also produced the phone bill.

"He stuck me with this bill. Will the numbers help you?"

"You bet." He whistled appreciatively. "Andi says *I* run up big bills. Incredible." He rose and pointed to a door. "Give me a minute to make a copy. If possible, have your insurance adjuster send me an inventory. I'll check with auction houses and pawnbrokers to see if Quent is selling anything locally."

"Certainly."

"Chances are, he won't," the private eye said. "But he might get cocky. In any case, I can check with authorities in Salt Lake City to find out the story on John

Venetucci. If this joker has active warrants out on him, we might be able to coax some big guns onto our side.''

On that hopeful note, Ross and Dawn made their farewells. All the way back to her house, she contemplated exactly what she'd like to say to her errant husband. Or do to him. Images of boiling oil tickled her fancy.

After parking in front of her home, Ross touched her arm. ''I know it sounds like Quent is too many steps ahead of us to catch him, but it's not hopeless.''

''Huh?''

He caressed her cheek with his fingertips. ''You look so sad.''

She forced a smile. ''I'm not sad, I'm angry.'' She pushed open the car door.

He joined her on the porch as she punched in the code to deactivate the alarm. ''The offer of my spare bedroom is still open. No strings.'' He waggled his fingers. ''I promise, my hands will never leave my arms.''

She lowered her face to hide a genuine smile, and the eagerness to accept which must be as plain as her nose. ''It wouldn't be wise. But do come in. May I fix you dinner? It's the least I can do.''

He twisted his mouth in comic suspicion. ''I didn't know you could cook.''

''I'll leave it up to you to decide.'' She didn't want him to go; it was wrong begging him to stay. When he accepted her offer, her heart sang and she could almost ignore the still shocking sight of the plundered house.

Ambling after her, with his hands in his pockets, Ross said, ''This would be a great place to hold a dance.''

How horrified her parents would have been about Ross. His flippant comments bordered on blasphemy.

Chuckling, she entered the kitchen. A small puddle of rainwater had pooled beneath the broken window. She mopped it up with a towel and made a mental note to call someone in for repairs—then realized she had no money to pay a repair man.

The doorbell rang. Doubting it was anyone with good news, she sighed. Wondering if it might be the police, hoping it might be Connie—though the woman never dropped in unexpectedly—she went to the front door.

A strange woman stood on the porch. About Dawn's height, she was heavier, curvier, and her huge mane of dark blond hair was impressive. Dawn touched her straight hair, wishing she'd been blessed with thick curls.

"Hello, may I help you?"

The woman smiled, but didn't look happy. "Dawn?"

"Yes." A prickling sensation crawled over her scalp. Suddenly she wanted to slam the door and lock it. She swallowed the impulse. "May I help you?"

"Sure." She raised her right hand. She held a small pistol, blue and plastic-looking, like a toy. "Tell me where I can find that no-good, cheating crook."

Dawn's heart seemed to lodge in her throat. She stared at the little gun, knowing it was not a toy and this woman was not kidding. The woman advanced; Dawn backed up. The woman closed the door behind her and backed Dawn out of the foyer, into the living room.

"I don't like being double-crossed. Trust me, honey, the same thing will happen to you if you don't tell me where Brad is."

"Excuse me?" Dawn's voice squeaked. She'd never touched a firearm in her life, much less had one pointed at her. The longer she stared at it, the bigger it seemed.

"Dawn, is there—?" Ross stopped short in the doorway. He stared wide-eyed at the woman's gun. Color drained from his face. He suddenly darted for the front door.

If Dawn could have found her voice, she'd have screamed at him to run. Even when the woman turned toward Ross, Dawn couldn't make herself move. She tensed, certain she was about to hear firsthand what a gunshot sounded like.

"What are you doing here?" the woman demanded. "Who else is in the house?"

Hands high, Ross edged toward Dawn. "In about three minutes, the cops will be here. I hit the alarm, lady." As if in confirmation, the tinny ringing of the telephone burred in the distance.

She gestured sharply with the gun. "Idiot! Get over there. Move!" She ordered them to sit on the floor. Unable to take her eyes off the gun, Dawn obeyed. Hands locked on her head, her skirt cutting off the circulation in her folded knees, she focused on staying calm.

The woman paced to the window, her heels thudding on the wooden floor. Her agitation frightened Dawn more than anything. Obviously, this woman was mentally unbalanced.

She stopped pacing and glowered at Ross. "You're in on it," she said, her voice low and hateful. "I knew it! I never should have trusted him. Not for a minute."

Ross smiled, his expression queasy. "In on...*it?*"

"Shut up!" She eased draperies aside to peer out the window. "All right, all right, I don't care. I just want what's mine. You promised."

"You're the woman who called me! I don't even know who you are and I certainly didn't promise you anything." Dawn pulled her hands away from her head, fully intending to get to the bottom of this right now.

The woman snorted a short, humorless laugh. She leveled the pistol, pointing it directly, without a quiver, at Dawn's face. Ross inhaled sharply.

"I have had enough. Do you understand? All I want is my money. It's mine. Give it to me, then you can keep him. I don't care. Good riddance."

Dawn swallowed hard. Her mouth was dust-dry. "How much money did he say I would give you?"

"Only what he took from me. Not even that, considering the interest. I'll settle for one-fifty."

Ross cleared his throat. "Do you honestly think you can point a gun at someone and have her write you a check? I'm fairly sure this is illegal." He cocked his head as if listening. "I think I hear a siren."

"Shut up! I am not a criminal! *He* is."

Dawn's arms began to ache. "I know he is. He's committed crimes against me. Look around you. He took everything. He stole all my money, all my belongings. He used me and lied to me. I don't know why he told you I would give you money. I don't have any to give."

The woman lowered the gun a few inches. A single fat tear leaked from the corner of her eye. She dashed it away. "You were supposed to make everything right."

"You were the one peeking into the honeymoon cabin," Ross said, his tone indignant. "You shot me up with something to knock me out."

The woman lowered her face and a heavy fall of hair grazed her flushed cheek. "You surprised me. You shouldn't have been snooping around. It was none of your business." She backed up another step and gasped. "He sent you to stop me! I should have known. I knew he was going to try something!"

"Try what?"

"He told me to wait. He said he'd bring me the check, but he never showed and I found the drugs. He lied from the very beginning."

Calm, calm, be calm, Dawn told herself. "He never

told me I was supposed to give you any money. Honest. We want to find him as much as you do. What's his real name? Did you say Brad?''

Ross nodded earnestly. ''Pointing a gun at us doesn't help.''

''Nothing helps! Don't you understand? The cops won't help, lawyers can't help! The only thing that'll stop him is killing him! He's like some kind of—of—*disease!* He's gotta be burned off the face of the earth. He's gotta be exorcised. He lies and lies and *lies!*''

Five minutes ago if anyone had asked Dawn if she'd ever sympathize with a person threatening her with a gun, she'd have laughed. Now she understood, and she sympathized. Her heart went out to this woman.

''What's your name?'' Dawn asked. In this position her legs were going to sleep. She shifted, trying to hike her skirt without using her hands.

She pinched the bridge of her nose and squinted anxiously out the window. ''Galena. I am not a criminal. If you didn't know about me, why did you give him a car? Why did you help him get away?''

''Everything he told me was a lie. His name, where he's from, what he does. All lies.'' Dawn eased her hands off her head. When the woman made no objection, she lowered them. ''Believe me, I know what you're going through. But violence isn't going to help anything. Please, let's go have a cup of tea and discuss this. Okay? I'll be more than happy to share all the information I've learned so far.''

''Listen to her, Galena,'' Ross said. He, too, eased his hands off his head, but he kept them away from his body and gentle in their movements. ''We can help each other.''

Another tear leaked from the woman's eye. She inhaled a long snuffling breath that shook her shoulders.

Dawn began to rise. The sound of tires crunching gravel announced a car turning into the driveway. Galena gasped and pointed the gun at her again. Dawn hit the floor with a thud. Ross slapped his hands back on his head.

"No!" she shouted, her voice echoing through the house. Her lips drew back over her teeth in a wolfish snarl. "It took me five years to find him, but I made the mistake of listening to him. I'm not making that mistake again." She glanced out the window, then dropped her hold on the draperies. "Don't move. Don't you dare move." She backed toward the door, neither the gun or her eyes leaving Dawn's face. "You've got twenty-four hours. I'll be back and there won't be any talking. Do you understand? I'll kill you. I'll kill both of you. All of you!"

She whirled about and ran through the foyer, running toward the back of the house. The doorbell rang.

Terrified of a potential shoot-out between Galena and the police, Dawn sat frozen. Ross shoved off the floor and scrambled to his feet. "Get the door!" he whispered harshly, and ran after Galena.

Dawn opened her mouth to scream at him to stop, but realized in time Galena might hear. She struggled to her feet, made clumsy by pins and needles in her lower legs. Footsteps pounded. A door slammed in the back of the house. Dawn stumbled to the front door and jerked it open, but no one stood on the porch. A red-marked security-company car was parked in the drive.

Not knowing what to do, Dawn clutched the door and listened intently for shouts, screams or gun-shots. Her fluttering heart ached in her chest.

Ross shouted, "She went over the fence!"

Dawn ran to the kitchen. Ross stood in the doorway, directing the security man to call the police. Dawn groaned and pressed a hand to her pounding heart. Nausea churned her belly.

"She's gone." Ross caught her shoulders in both strong hands. "She went over the fence."

Her knees wobbled and she clutched his arm for support. "She means it, Ross. She'll be back. I don't have any money. She'll kill me!" The world swam before her eyes and she blinked hard until she could focus. A vinegary scent tickled her nose, increasing her nausea. She smelled her own fear.

"Shh, shh, sweetheart. She's gone, it's okay." He wiped his brow with the back of one hand. "Wait here, I'm going to see if I can find her—"

"No!" Dawn grabbed his arm and held on with every ounce of strength she possessed. "You aren't going anywhere! Lock the doors. Call the police!"

"It's okay, sweetheart. The police are coming. She's gone." Ross stroked her hair and made soothing noises.

Gone...for now. But Dawn knew without a doubt that Galena—enraged and armed—would be back.

Chapter Eleven

The police officer did not believe her or Ross.

Dawn suspected the officer was as sick of seeing her as she was sick of seeing him. He'd arrived promptly enough, and listened attentively, but the security-company man had not seen Galena nor had he noticed any strange vehicles in the area. He had nothing to add to the story except that he'd answered an alarm call by following standard procedure. When Ross mentioned Detective Goldenberg, the policeman said, "Sure, it's probably best to call him." His attitude was one of complete indifference. His expression had been resigned, as if he fully expected to make many such trips to Dawn's home in the future.

Before he departed, he'd slipped a business card to Dawn. While doing so, he'd given Ross a pointed look. Dawn stared at the card: a domestic-abuse hot line.

Alone with Ross, Dawn stared at the card and chuckled bitterly. "He thinks we're nuts, Ross. I can't say I blame him. Every time I complain, you're here. It must look like some kind of perverted love triangle. If someone else was telling me this kind of story, I'd find it all difficult to swallow."

"What's so hard to believe?"

His testy tone subdued her. She turned her attention to the refrigerator. As she studied its scant contents, the idea of cooking, much less actually eating, repulsed her.

"I hate being played for a chump, and I *really* hate a crazy woman wagging a gun at my face." He snatched up the telephone and began punching in numbers. "I don't care what that cop thinks or what it looks like."

Dawn closed the refrigerator door. "Who are you calling?"

"Rayne. He takes us seriously." Plopping onto a stool, he tapped his fingers in a rapid tattoo atop the counter, then he clutched the telephone receiver so tightly his knuckles whitened. He tapped the counter again, and raked a hand through his hair. His chin was thrust out at a pugnacious angle, and his eyebrows nearly knitted together.

Appreciation curled through Dawn, warming her from the inside out. His outrage was for her benefit as much as for his. Though they were different in background, education and life-style, she felt close to him, as if their souls were in sync. He actually cared about her. At least, he cared enough to be angry on her behalf.

A whistling gust of wind made her tangled nerves jump. She doubted if she'd ever feel safe in this house again. She went in search of a piece of cardboard to cover the still-broken windowpane. While she made repairs, she thought about what Galena had said. Somebody had helped Quentin get away.... Whatever could that mean? He had a brand-new car and all her money. All he'd had to do was drive off into the sunset.

Ross finished his telephone call. He'd calmed down considerably. "Rayne advises we get out of the house. And he's right. Galena wants Quent and her money, but getting you might be the next best thing."

She wanted to believe Galena was bluffing, but knew better. "Did what she said about helping Quentin escape strike you as odd?"

"Everything she said was odd."

"No, I mean, why would Quentin need help to escape? That is what she accused us of, right?" She tapped her chin, thinking. "Stefan described a large man, so it must have been Quentin. Not even in the dark could anyone mistake that woman for a large man."

"You get no argument from me."

"So what was Quentin doing in the hour between when Stefan saw him and you saw the prowler?"

Ross frowned and cocked his head. "Waiting to make sure nobody was around to see him leave, I guess."

She fetched a notepad and a pencil. She wrote: Q. carries luggage to Lincoln—midnight. She looked up at Ross. "She admitted knocking you out."

Ross nodded solemnly. "She says she found drugs. Which means they belonged to Quent. Which means he drugged you, then was waiting to drug her. Only I messed up the plan."

Having never done a devious thing in her life, Dawn found it all confusing, and morbidly amusing. "Let me get this straight. Quentin owes her money and tells her I will give her a check."

"But she doesn't trust him."

She held up a finger. "Right. So she goes to Elk River to make sure she gets the money."

Ross laughed, a dark sound to match his angry eyes. "She waits in his car, thinking he can't slip away, but she doesn't know about the Lincoln. He sneaks his luggage into his car, but she gets tired of waiting, so she investigates the honeymoon cabin."

"And there you are! If she saw the wedding party, then

she knows you're the best man. No wonder she thinks you're helping Quentin. She must be as confused as we are.''

He nodded eagerly. "So Quent has you passed out on the bed, me passed out in the bushes and Galena knowing he's pulling a fast one. So what does he do?''

"He talks,'' she answered promptly. "Either he convinced her that I reneged on that so-called 'just debt,' or else you and I were conspiring to…?'' There her imagination failed her.

"Right. He gets her worked up, involved. Who knows what he said or how he convinced her to help arrange bodies. Maybe he told her we were having an affair and were double-crossing *him*. In any case, he kept her busy enough for him to slip out of the cabin.''

"Right again. She has the keys to his car, so thinks he can't go anywhere. But he drives off in the Lincoln.''

"Right.'' Ross threw his hands in the air. "Sticking us with the job of convincing Galena not to blow our heads off. Let's get out of here. Pack a bag. You're staying at my place.''

She considered his offer carefully. "I'll stay with Connie. She has live-in help, and her house is even more secure than this one.''

His smile softened and turned a little sad. "Don't you trust me?''

She couldn't resist. Fluttering her eyelashes, she murmured, "Perhaps I don't trust myself.''

He appeared pleased. "Oh, yeah?'' He raked a finger diagonally across his chest. "I solemnly promise to be trustworthy enough for both of us.''

"I'll be more comfortable at Connie's.'' She reached for the telephone. She expected Ross to argue, but he didn't. Instead he washed and polished a pair of apples while she called her friend.

On hearing Dawn's request, Connie didn't demand explanations. "Come anytime," she said. "The green suite is yours as long as you want it."

Ross handed her an apple. "Let's grab some dinner, then I'll take you to Connie's." He bit into his apple.

His white teeth and the juice glistening on his lips caught her attention. His every touch, the way her body fit against his, made him seem as if he were custom-made for her. She'd heard every person had a soul mate, a perfect someone somewhere. The bells in her heart whispered Ross was hers.

But it was wrong to feel this way, and she knew it.

"My father's daughter," she muttered.

The non sequitur brought his attention to her. He eyed her quizzically.

Heat caressed her cheeks. She smiled sheepishly and set the apple on the counter. "I think I'll just go to Connie's. I don't have much of an appetite." Except for his kisses and smiles.

"Oh, okay. Get your stuff, I'll drive you."

One step closer to him and he'd kiss her. She felt it, she knew it—she wanted it. She twisted her wedding ring, and resentment bubbled up. What a fool she'd been to marry Quentin! All along he'd told her everything she wanted to hear, made promises to fulfill her desires, and because of her foolishness, she'd believed what she so desperately wanted to believe.

Ross deserved better. He was too good a man to have to settle for half her attention, less than her complete devotion. Once she settled the matter of Quentin and her marriage, then and only then could she offer any encouragement to Ross.

DAWN ROSE EARLY, as usual, surprising herself by how soundly she'd slept and how clearheaded she felt. She stood in the kitchen of Connie's home, sipping from a cup of vanilla-flavored coffee, watching birds in the scrub oaks growing between the rocks behind the house. Sunrise gilded the oak leaves and flashed iridescent colors off the glossy wings of a magpie. The view was all the more lovely since she knew Galena couldn't touch her here.

"Would you care for some breakfast, Dawn?" the housekeeper asked.

She inhaled the rich, sweet aroma of the coffee. Her stomach grumbled. She couldn't remember her last meal. "I don't want to put you out, Ada. I'll wait until Connie gets up."

The housekeeper barked a laugh. "It'll be lunchtime by then. You aren't putting me out any. Be my pleasure."

Connie staggered into the kitchen doorway and sagged against the frame. Her flowing silk robe trimmed in marabou and her dramatic grasp of the door frame was in the manner of Bette Davis at her campy best. An entourage of four Yorkshire terriers dragged about as if begrudging having to rise so early.

"Oh, my darling, this is a wretched hour, but I knew you'd be up and about. It's that peasant blood your late mother so heartily denied."

"You didn't get up just for me, did you?"

"Of course I did. How dare that witch threaten you with a pistol? I barely slept a wink last night." She waggled her fingers at the housekeeper. "Ada, hurry! I must have coffee or I shall perish." Sighing, moaning, but managing to make every gesture quite pretty, she glided to the breakfast table and sat down on a chair. The Yorkies gathered at her feet, snuggling into the feathery excesses of her robe.

Dawn exchanged a smile with Ada.

"If the authorities won't take you seriously because that beast of man is your husband, then you should begin divorce proceedings."

Dawn's smile faded. Divorce—such an ugly word. She joined Connie at the table. "I suppose, all along, I've been hoping for some kind of reasonable explanation. Some miracle where Quentin would return and make me understand he had no choice. I hoped he wasn't a criminal. Wishful thinking. He *is* a criminal."

"We'll find that rotten so-and-so and make him pay for what he's done."

Ada brought the coffee. Connie cooed in gratitude.

"Truth is," Dawn said, "I don't know if I'll ever find him. He's so clever, and everything points to him being very experienced, too. Ross tells me I should look for the good in what's happened, but that's hard to do."

"Easy for him to say." Connie nodded firmly. "His money didn't vanish into thin air. Although—and you may slap me if I'm too impertinent—cleaning out that museum of a house was quite a good thing. Your mother had macabre taste. Count Dracula would have felt right at home there."

Dawn couldn't decide if Connie's words annoyed her or if she annoyed herself by agreeing. "You cannot know how guilty I feel. I couldn't feel worse if I'd lost everything in a poker game. What hurts the most is knowing how very stupid I was."

"Quentin fooled me, too." Connie clucked her tongue. "I hate to admit how very taken I was with him. I thought him charming. I don't think you were stupid at all."

"Oh, but I was." She tapped herself between her breasts. "I felt the wrongness right here, but I ignored it. I wanted so much to be married, so much to have a family and children, I completely ignored every doubt. I talked myself into loving him. I convinced myself it was the logical, reasonable thing to do. I'm less Quentin's victim than a victim of my own idiocy."

Connie lifted a Yorkie onto her lap. The little dog yawned, showing all its tiny teeth, then settled sleepily in the crook of her arm. "You know what love is supposed to feel like?"

Dawn let hair fall over her face to hide her blush.

"It's Ross, isn't it? You've fallen in love. For real."

Lifting a shoulder, Dawn toyed with her coffee cup. "I don't know. All I know is, everything feels right when he's around. I don't know how to explain it. When I'm with him I feel...bigger. Smarter. As if I can do things I was too scared to try before. He's smart and funny and very gentle. I trust him. Not because I want to or have to, but because it feels right."

"Sounds like love to me," Ada said as she placed a plate of French toast in front of Dawn.

Steam curled off the fat triangles of golden bread dusted with powdered sugar, carrying the egg-heavy scent to Dawn's nose. Her stomach growled so loudly all four dogs pricked up their ears.

Connie pointed a finger at the housekeeper. "For once, old girl, I agree with you. Sounds like love to me, too. All the more reason to shed that nasty Quentin like a snake's skin."

Dawn spooned raspberry sauce over the toast. "I'm not at all certain how Ross feels about me. I know he's angry at Quentin, but..."

"But what?" Connie and Ada asked in unison.

Sorry she'd started this conversation in the first place, Dawn ate a piece of toast and chewed slowly. Unable to procrastinate with both women watching her so intently, she sighed and dabbed at her mouth with a napkin. "Ross loves a good game. If you'd ever played tennis with him, you'd know exactly what I mean. He has the same single-minded quality that made Father such a wonderful attorney. The game is everything." She chewed over her thoughts. "Ross is...different. I don't quite understand him. He's a successful businessman, but he allows his father to believe he's a bum. He thinks it's funny. And I think he's enjoying the challenge of playing Quentin's game."

"Ridiculous!" Connie exclaimed.

"Pshaw!" Ada said.

"A world record. We agree twice in one day, Ada. Now be a dear and bring me more of that lovely caffeine." Connie held her cup up for a refill. "And as for you, my darling, I think you are thinking far too much. Ross is smitten with you. Just because Quentin has proven untrustworthy, doesn't mean you must read nefarious intentions into Ross's actions. Play your cards right and you may very well win that longed-for wedded bliss after all."

The telephone rang. Drying her hands on a towel, Ada answered. She brought the cordless unit to the table, bypassing Connie and handing the phone to Dawn. "It's Mr. Duke."

Curious, and wary about why Ross would call her this early in the morning, Dawn took the telephone. She turned her back on Connie. "Hello?"

"We've got trouble," Ross said.

"What's the matter?"

"Janine called me. The cops found the Lincoln and now they're looking for us."

She clutched the telephone with both hands, squeezing the plastic until her fingers ached. "They found Quentin?"

"No, only the car. Janine says there's trouble, but she doesn't know exactly what it is. I think we'd better follow her advice and get back to Elk River before we're dragged there."

"You're scaring me, Ross. What exactly did Janine say?"

He drew in a long, audible breath. "She said Deputy Downes showed up at the resort at the crack of dawn. Janine pumped him for information, but all he would tell her was that forest rangers found the Lincoln and now the cops want to talk to us. He refused to tell her anything else."

Images of Galena and her gun filled Dawn's mind. She knew with every fiber of her being that something very bad had happened to Quentin—and the police believed she and Ross were involved.

"I CALLED Detective Goldenberg," Dawn said. "He's very interested in the Lincoln being found. He said he's learned some information about Quentin, too. He told me to come see him this afternoon."

Ross stared distantly for a moment, frowning, then nodded. He'd arrived at Connie's home twenty minutes after he and Dawn had spoken on the telephone. Though he'd sounded urgent and upset on the telephone, he now sipped the coffee Ada had brought him, apparently in no real hurry to hit the road.

He also looked handsome in a pair of cream-colored linen slacks and a matching jacket. Gorgeous, actually,

Dawn thought, with his light clothing setting off his striking coloring. She kept finding excuses to touch him—straightening a lapel, placing her fingertips on his forearm, brushing his shoulder as she passed his chair.

Connie still wore the flamboyant dressing gown, but had made up her face. Her lipstick gleamed. She asked Ross exactly the same questions Dawn had asked, and received the same answers.

"Why does anyone believe you're involved in foul play?" Connie asked.

"Who knows?"

Dawn caught her lower lip in her teeth, uncertain if she wanted to ask what had to be the next logical question. "Ross, do you think Quentin is dead?"

"No," he answered without hesitation. "If he'd died in a car wreck, Mike Downes would have told Janine. If Galena had murdered him, she wouldn't be looking for him." He drained the coffee, set down the cup, and smiled his gratitude at Ada. "Have you heard anything else from your reporter friend, Mrs. Haxman?"

Connie checked her diamond-encrusted wristwatch. "I'll call her."

"If she knows anything, ask her to get in touch with Detective Goldenberg. Dawn, we better go."

Connie caught Dawn in a perfume scented embrace. "Promise to call as soon as you hear anything."

Dawn promised solemnly, then she and Ross left the house. Once they were in his Lexus and headed for Highway 24, he said, "The cops are overreacting. Quentin probably ran out of gas or had engine problems, and abandoned the Lincoln."

"Do you believe that?"

He considered for a moment. "No." He flashed a broad smile. "But, hey, this gives me a good excuse to see you this morning. I like what you did with your hair. You look pretty.''

On impulse, she'd moussed her hair and clipped up the sides, drawing it away from her face. Discomfited, but pleased, she turned to look out the side window.

"Everything will be all right, sweetheart, trust me. I don't like the idea of the cops chasing me, but if it gets us closer to finding Quent, then I can live with it.''

Morning rush-hour traffic was heavy, especially when they reached Highway 24 through Old Colorado City and into Manitou Springs. Road construction caused bottlenecks at intersections. His attention fixed on traffic, Ross drove in silence. Dawn sank into her own thoughts. She wondered how she'd feel if Quentin were in truth dead, or what she would say to him if he turned up alive.

Mostly she wondered if she were in love with Ross Duke and what her life would be like if she were free to openly pursue a relationship with him.

They passed through Manitou Springs and the highway wound through the mountains between towering, red-rock cliffs. Traffic lessened on the road going west and Ross speeded up. Dawn stared at the passing scenery, admiring the thick stands of trees and majestic rocks.

"I have a proposition for you," Ross said.

She lifted her eyebrows. "What kind of proposition?"

"You need a job and I need an administrative assistant. We might be able to work something out.''

His offer both excited and dismayed her. "No charity, Ross. I can't—''

"What charity? According to Connie, you've got more than enough experience in running an office. I might have to fight her for you. Can you operate a computer?''

"Well, yes. I don't do programming, but I'm proficient in word processing and spreadsheet programs.''

"There you go. You sound more than qualified. Think about it. I've got exactly thirteen working days to find a replacement for Jennifer. So don't think too long."

She saw his sincerity and heard it in his voice. He offered more than employment and an opportunity to pay her bills without accepting Connie's—or his—charity. He offered trust.

The bells in her heart rang like a symphony.

Chapter Twelve

Ross didn't like this situation one little bit. He and Dawn had arrived at the resort over an hour ago. Deputy Mike Downes had been present, along with a gentleman wearing an olive-green gabardine suit and a dour expression. The deputy had seemed pleased to see Ross and Dawn, but the other man had given no indication at all how he felt about them. He'd asked—ordered—Ross to wait in his mother's office, then he'd asked Dawn to accompany him to another part of the lodge.

So Ross had been cooling his heels, his instincts twitching in anticipation of impending trouble.

The deputy and the man in the cheap suit entered the office. "Ross Duke, this is Deputy Investigator Artie Longbow," Mike said. "He'd like to ask you some questions."

"Sure, as long as you guys give up some answers. What's this all about? Did you find Quent?"

The investigator placed a tape recorder on the desk. He moved a few stacks of papers and magazines out of the way. Without looking at Ross, he asked, "Should we have found him?"

"Come on, Mike, what's the deal? Am I under arrest?"

"No." The investigator fiddled with the controls on the tape recorder. "You're under no obligation to speak to me, Mr. Duke. You may leave if you so desire. Do you wish to leave?"

"I want to know what's going on." His scalp prickled with nerves and he shifted uneasily on the chair. He had no reason to feel guilty about anything, but the investigator's glowering stare made him feel as if he'd just been caught robbing a bank. He took a few steadying breaths.

"Do you mind if I record this session? It's more accurate than notes." Longbow settled on a chair and nodded at Mike Downes.

"Go ahead," Ross said.

"I'll leave you two alone." Mike slipped out of the office, closing the door behind him.

The investigator pushed the Record button. He spoke the time, date and Ross's full name into the microphone. "Tell me about your relationship with the man you know as Quentin Bayliss. How and when did you meet?"

Ross told how he'd met Quentin in a casino in Cripple Creek and provided the names of the blackjack dealers they'd double-dated. The investigator prompted him to continue, so Ross explained about how the wedding came to be held at Elk River and why he'd stood in as Quentin's best man. Then he dredged up every detail he could recall about Quentin and Dawn and Galena. While Ross talked, making no attempt to evade anything, the investigator relaxed. When Ross provided the names and telephone numbers of Detective Goldenberg and Rayne Coplin, a faint smile cracked his stony expression.

"Okay, let me see if I have this straight," Longbow said. "You told the man you know as Bayliss that you were going to vacation here, and then he asked about holding the wedding at the resort."

"That's right. He also said Dawn wanted a vacation and asked me to pal around with her."

"You didn't find that strange."

"Not at the time, no. It only struck me as strange when I met Dawn. She wasn't what Quent led me to believe." He glanced at his watch, amazed to see an hour had passed. "Will you tell me what's going on now?"

"Forest rangers found the Lincoln in a ditch, disabled. There are signs the car had been forced off the road. We've been unable to find Mrs. Bayliss's husband."

"She did catch him then." Ross nodded earnestly. "Galena chased him, caught him, but he got away from her. Did you find his luggage in the car?"

"I'm not going to discuss case particulars, Mr. Duke." He shut off the tape recorder.

Ross heaved a sigh of relief. His mouth was dry from talking and nerves. Then the investigator replaced the cassette tape with a fresh one and reactivated the machine. Ross scowled. "I thought we were finished."

"A few more questions. My understanding from your father is that you, how shall I say it, have a rather loose life-style. Your mother, on the other hand claims you're a businessman. Which is it?"

"I have a human-resources consulting business. I conduct seminars and personnel-relation studies for corporations." He fished in his wallet for a business card and handed it over the desk. "I apprenticed with Jack Morgan, working for him during my senior year of college and for two years after that. I have an office in Colorado Springs."

The investigator appeared disappointed as he read the card. "So the first time you met Dawn Lovell-Bayliss was here, at the lodge. At Bayliss's request."

"That's right."

"How would you describe your relationship with her?"

Insight flashed: everything up to this point was merely testing the waters. This was what Longbow really wanted to know. "We're friends."

"Good friends?"

"I'd say so."

"Romantically good friends?"

"We're not having an affair." He looked away. "Dawn's a victim. Quent ripped her off, took everything. His disappearance has nothing to do with me. The person you should be looking for is Galena."

"Ah yes, the mystery blonde." The corners of his mouth tipped in an unpleasant smile.

Ross felt, heard, saw, and practically smelled his skepticism. He sat up straighter. "If I'd run him off the road, why would be I going through so much trouble trying to find him?"

"Good question. Why *are* you going through so much trouble to find him?"

Ross intuited any answer would be the wrong answer. If he said he wanted revenge, then it gave him a motive to run Quent off the road; if he said he wanted to help Dawn, then it sounded as if they were lovers, and he had an even greater motive to get rid of Quent. He lowered his gaze to his hands.

"I'm not accusing you of anything, Mr. Duke."

"Then what's this all about?" He waved a hand toward the recorder. "If I'm not a suspect, why are you treating me like one?"

"Look at it from my point of view. I've got a potential crime scene, a missing person, and a wife and her...friend on very friendly terms. Said friend being the missing man's best man. Oh yeah, and a mystery blonde with a gun. Can't forget her. Except, you and Dawn are the only ones who've seen her. If you were in my shoes, what would you be thinking?''

Ross pulled at his jaw. "I'd be thinking about what kind of enemies a scam artist has. Including former wives he's pushed over the edge. I'd be wondering what happened to Dawn's money. And why she's been talking to cops and private eyes all over the state of Colorado. If she wanted to do Quent in, wouldn't she at least get her money back first?''

"I stopped being surprised a long time ago by why people do what they do.''

Dawn was definitely the target of this investigation, then. Chills ran up and down Ross's spine. "What about Quent's other car? The Buick he arrived here in. Did you find it?''

"Not yet.''

Ross sensed this was the real reason the investigator couldn't openly treat Dawn as a suspect. The logistics didn't add up. If this clown thought for a minute Ross was going to sit here and chat until something did add up, he was out of his mind. Boldly, he turned off the tape recorder. Longbow quirked an eyebrow, but said nothing.

"If you want to accuse me of something, go ahead. But you'll have a hell of a time proving it.'' He stood and stretched his tension-filled, stiff muscles. "Have a nice day.''

Fully expecting the investigator to order him to sit down, fully prepared to tell him to go pound sand, Ross stalked out of the office. When Longbow let him go, he wondered if that were a good sign or a bad sign.

He found Dawn seated in the lounge area off the lobby. She stared pensively at the view out the bank of tall windows. Clouds curled down the mountains, wreathing the trees in mist. Her quiet elegance and wistful expression caused a pang in his heart. Ever since the wedding, she'd suffered shock after shock, and the strain showed in her haunted eyes.

A heated rush of protectiveness washed through him. Nobody would hurt her anymore—not if he could help it.

He sat beside her. "How are you doing?"

Anger glittered in her eyes. "They believe I've harmed Quentin. Mr. Longbow never said so directly, but you wouldn't believe the questions he asked me. I've never been so insulted in my life."

"If Quent turns up dead somewhere, we're both in hot water." An idea occurred to him and he laughed. In response to Dawn's frown, he explained, "It wouldn't surprise me for a minute if Quent faked his own death to get you off his trail."

"Is that possible?"

"Can you think of any other reason he'd ditch a fifty-thousand-dollar car?"

"What about Galena?"

"Faking his death would get her off his case, too. Unless, she's part of the setup. All that hair, the heavy make-up—I bet it was a disguise. We run to the cops, then the car is found, and two and two gets added up to murder."

Dawn shook her head. "She accused us of helping him get away from her. If he wants us thinking him dead, then why hint about the possibility of his escape?"

Ross opened his mouth to rebut; no argument occurred to him. He heaved a sigh. "So maybe she isn't in on it." He noticed his father marching across the lobby.

Terrific. No doubt the Colonel was on the warpath. Ross crossed his arms and leaned back against the fat sofa cushion. He vowed he wasn't taking any of the

Colonel's insults, but he wasn't going to agitate him, either.

The Colonel stopped before Dawn and Ross. He planted his feet at shoulder width and locked his hands behind his back—parade rest position. He cleared his throat gruffly.

"Morning, Colonel," Ross said. From this angle, and with the sun shining through the windows and highlighting the deep seams on his face, the old man looked his age. Ross totted up the numbers, and it shocked him to realize his father was almost seventy years old. He was in excellent health and as vigorous as ever, but still...

"Good morning, Ross, Mrs. Bayliss. Explain what it is the deputies want."

A smart-aleck retort rose in Ross's throat, but he squashed it. Now was not the time to jab at the old man. He relaxed his arms and stood to face his father. "I'm afraid you know as much as we do, sir. They suspect foul play and want to know if Dawn or I have anything to do with it."

The Colonel looked Ross up and down. His eyes narrowed. "Is that what this is all about? They suspect you of maleficence? Well! We'll see about that."

Ross gave a start. His father was on his side? "They have to suspect somebody. But considering all we know so far, it looks like Quent set it all up."

"His strategy being?"

Stunned at having his father taking his side, all Ross could do for several seconds was stare. Ever since he'd been old enough to talk, he and the Colonel had disagreed about everything from foreign policy to sports teams to what kind of clothing Ross should wear and the length of his hair. Whenever something went wrong, his father blamed him. During his teenage years the fighting had escalated into a war—Ross had escaped at seventeen to join the army. Which had the added benefit of driving the Colonel crazy because he'd enlisted instead of earning an officer's commission.

"Don't stand there like a dolt, son, what is Bayliss's strategy?"

Ross gave himself a shake. "What do you figure he got away with, Dawn? Two million?"

"It depends on the worth of the furniture he stole, but well over a million in liquid assets. Father's coin collection alone is worth nearly half a million dollars."

"That's grand larceny, plus there's a crazy woman on his trail. I'm betting he set it up to look like he's dead."

The Colonel nodded thoughtfully. "How would he account for the lack of a body?"

"Maybe he's counting on the terrain. Longbow wouldn't tell me any details, but Quent could have made it look as if he was hurt in the crash, then wandered into the mountains to die."

"Hmm," the Colonel murmured.

Dawn touched Ross's hand. "When people are lost, Search and Rescue goes out."

"Right. Searchers on foot and on horseback. They bring in dogs. Sometimes they use helicopters. And ninety percent of the time, there's front-page coverage in the news. Colonel, remember the first year you owned this place and that seventeen-year-old kid disappeared? What was that, ten miles from here?"

Nodding, the Colonel frowned contemplatively. "His remains were found this spring."

"It made all the papers. We know Quent does his research. He could have seen the story."

Dawn sighed. "I remember reading about that. Such a tragedy. Unfortunately, it's not all that unusual."

The more Ross considered the possibility, the angrier he grew. Quentin had probably never considered Dawn might be implicated in his disappearance—but if he had, he must figure it was a cost of doing business.

"This calls for a recon mission," the Colonel announced. He snapped to attention. "Son, join us in the private dining facility at twelve hundred hours. Deputy Downes has a few questions to answer. Mrs. Bayliss, you shall join us, too." He executed a crisp about-face and marched away.

After three paces, he stopped and looked over his shoulder. He lifted an eyebrow and a smile softened his craggy features. "That is, unless you have pressing business matters to attend at your office?"

All those years of fun and games down the drain. The old man not only knew the truth about Ross's life style, he approved. Ross grinned sheepishly. "We'll be there, sir."

Ross sat on the sofa. He noticed Dawn fighting a smile. "Go ahead, laugh. Looks like my days as the family black sheep are over."

"I'm so sorry you're respectable now." She laughed into her hand. Some of the strain left her features. "What did he mean by a recon mission?"

Ross lifted both shoulders and his hands in a shrug. "Not a clue. Uh-oh, there's Longbow." Watching the investigator cross the lobby, Ross folded his arms. Softly, he said to Dawn, "No more questions and answers. Make him talk to your lawyer."

She lifted her chin, her expression taut with anger. "I have nothing to hide."

Longbow reached the lounge, and set a large briefcase on a chair. His heavy, sloped shoulders made him appear larger than he actually was. Ross didn't like the man hovering over him, but he refused to stand.

"When will you be returning to Colorado Springs?"

"After lunch," Ross answered.

"I may have some more questions for you. I'd appreciate it if you'd stick around." His tone of voice made it sound like an order.

"We'll stick around until after lunch. After that, you can talk to our attorneys."

"This isn't a game, Mr. Duke. It's an investigation. Your cooperation is necessary."

Dawn stiffened and her eyes flashed with rebellious fire. "We *have* cooperated, Mr. Longbow. If the sheriff had taken me seriously when I first reported my husband missing, perhaps we wouldn't be having this conversation at all. I am sick to death of being victimized, first by Quentin and then by the very law-enforcement officials who are supposed to help me."

Longbow backed off a step. Dawn stood up and gave her skirt a brisk tug. "I will not accept your bullying, sir."

Dawn's angry assertiveness had an oddly erotic effect on Ross, rousing memories—uncomfortably, considering the circumstances—of her small, silken body pressed against him while her sweet lips worked their magic. She was the sexiest woman he'd ever known and indignation made her downright luscious.

"Look, Mrs. Bayliss—"

"Do not call me that. Quentin, whoever he is, married me under false pretenses, using another man's name, and I will no longer use the name Bayliss. You may call me Ms. Lovell."

"Fine." He raked a hand through his thinning hair. "*Ms.* Lovell, I—"

"And furthermore, I will thank you to remember who I am. I have been a productive, useful member of Colorado Springs society all my life."

Longbow backed another step, striking a chair and having to fling out a hand for balance. "Now you—"

"I have been robbed and betrayed and humiliated. I will no longer, under any circumstances, accept this kind of abuse from you or anyone else."

"Yes, ma'am," he muttered, his face growing dark.

"If you insist upon treating me as some kind of criminal, then I will insist you speak to my attorney. I assure you, you will not find Mr. Brandon Walters a pleasant individual to deal with."

"Whatever," he snapped and snatched up the briefcase. Shoulders rolled so his neck seemed to disappear, he stalked out of the lodge.

Amazed, amused and far more aroused than he knew was wise, Ross whistled softly. Dawn suddenly clutched at her chest and staggered backward. She sank gracelessly onto the sofa. She gave herself a shake before turning wide eyes on him. "I can't believe I actually spoke to him like that." She patted her breast.

"I'm impressed," Ross said.

"It would seem I learned more of my father's tactics than I realized. And Mother's. She said a true lady is a first-rate actress. I never understood what she meant by that—but now I do. My goodness, but he's a scary man." She smiled wanly. "But I fear we're in more trouble than we know. Father always claimed the police are only rude when they believe they are right. Mr. Longbow was quite rude, don't you think?"

"Yep."

"I wish we had some evidence to prove Galena exists."

"Maybe we can find some." He jumped up and caught her hand, hauling her to her feet. Holding her hand, he headed to the main desk. "We checked out the honeymoon cabin, but we didn't look around outside."

"Do you think she grew bored and carved her initials on the wall?"

"Ha, ha, she makes a joke." He stopped to wait for his sister to finish with a couple who were checking in. "She could have dropped something, or left footprints."

"It's rained since we were here."

"We can't know for sure until we look."

When Kara finished registering the couple and directing them to their room, she nodded at Ross. "Did they find Mrs. Bayliss's husband? Mike Downes won't tell me anything, the big jerk."

"I'll tell you all about it at lunch. Is there anyone in Honeymoon Hideaway C?"

"It's booked and the people should be checking in any time." She cast a suspicious glance at Dawn. "Why?"

"Don't worry your pretty little head, sweetheart."

Outside, on the graveled pathway to the Hideaway, Dawn sighed loudly. "Your family does not approve of me. I see how they look at me. It's as if I'm corrupting you."

"Get real. They all like you." He stopped where paths intersected and a lamppost lit up the area at night. He looked back toward the parking lot behind the lodge. "This is where I first noticed the person that night." He closed his eyes, trying to recall details. Distance and poor lighting had made details impossible. All he'd seen was a shape. It could have been male, female or gorilla for all he knew.

"They think we're having an affair. That I'm the type

of woman who'd shed a husband and immediately take
up with another man.''

"Don't worry about it." He strode up the path.

"I do worry about it. My reputation has never been
called into question."

He looped an arm around her shoulders, urging her
toward the Hideaway. She balked and shoved at his arm,
so he dropped it. She moved to a tree and lightly fingered
the rough bark.

"I like you, Ross. Lord knows how many times I've
wished I'd met you instead of Quentin. Even more so, I
wish I had something to offer you."

He glanced around. A few people were in the parking
lot. Up ahead, a housekeeper wheeled her cart out of a
honeymoon cabin. He folded his hand around Dawn's
and drew her off the path into the trees. She eyed him
with question, but without suspicion.

In the green-tinged shadows, he backed her against a
tree. She stared into his eyes and he wanted to stare forever. "You're worth waiting for, sweetheart. You're
worth seeing this thing through to the end."

"Oh, Ross…"

"Careful. You get all breathy like that, and I might
lose control." He stroked her soft cheek and her eyelids
lowered, those pretty lashes like golden fans. "You're a
sexy woman. You're making me nuts. And you're also
making me wait, which is pretty much a first for me."

"No one ever called me sexy before."

The breathless huskiness of her voice made his head
swirl. He looked around again, then snatched a kiss. A
mistake; it only made him hungry for more. When she
slid a hand around his neck, he lost all strength in his
knees.

"I'm going to make love to you all over the place,''

he promised. "Not now, not for as long as you wear that wedding ring. But we will, and my top priority will be making you regret every second you made me wait."

A shivering shudder racked her body. Her pupils swelled, turning her blue eyes dark and hot. She toyed with the hair at the nape of his neck. Exquisite agony flooded through him, heightened by the light floral scent of her perfume. Knowing one more second of this would send him over the edge, he sprang backward.

Gasping, she held the tree behind her. Her mouth had never looked so kissable.

He bowed from the waist. "Your most honorable servant, ma'am. And don't worry about my family. I'll straighten them out. Now come on, let's go play Sherlock Holmes."

To Ross's surprise, they found Deputy Mike Downes outside the cabin, on his hands and knees beneath an chokecherry bush. He picked through leaf debris and small stones.

"What are you doing?" Ross hunkered into a crouch.

"Hey, Ross." The deputy scrambled to his feet and swiped at his polyester trousers. Damp leaf mold had stained his knees. "I've been thinking about the lady with the gun." He nodded graciously at Dawn. "The bit about two cars being missing keeps bugging me. And what's the deal with Timothy James Wiley?"

Dawn gasped. Ross's mouth dropped open and he nearly fell over.

The deputy shifted his gaze from one to the other. Slowly his features tightened, giving him a trapped expression. "Longbow didn't tell you?"

Ross picked through a pile of pine straw, not knowing what to look for, but needing to occupy his hands. Longbow had never mentioned Tim Wiley to him or to Dawn.

He couldn't begin to imagine what was going through the investigator's suspicious little brain. "Tim Wiley is the name Quent used to scam the real Quentin Bayliss. How'd you know about it?"

"That's the name the car is registered in. The plate number matched the info you gave me, Mrs. Bayliss, but the name threw us for a loop. Longbow is going crazy trying to figure out what's going on." He bent over to reach his lower trouser legs and brushed at them briskly. "So is Tim Wiley his real—?" He suddenly froze.

"Drop a contact lens?"

Mike straightened, holding carefully a small piece of clear plastic. Tube-shaped, it was open on one end, rounded on the other.

"What is that?" Ross asked.

Dawn moved in closer for a better look. "I know. It's a protector cap for a hypodermic needle."

Chapter Thirteen

The discovery of the cap for the hypodermic, which bolstered Ross's story about being drugged, changed the atmosphere at Elk River resort. Dawn noticed the subtle shifts in attitude when she joined the Dukes for lunch. The Colonel had insisted Mike Downes also join them in the sunny private dining room off the kitchen. The patriarch ordered Ross to tell again what had happened in the honeymoon cabin.

Afterward, the Colonel called her "Dawn" rather than "Mrs. Bayliss." Janine stopped shooting her brother skeptical glares. Instead of snickering, Megan and Kara pumped Ross and Mike Downes for juicy details concerning scam artists. Their artless curiosity about Quentin's crimes disconcerted Dawn, but at least she no longer felt like a fallen woman. The quickness with which the Dukes forgave and forgot astonished her, but as lunch progressed it stopped making her uneasy.

"Okay," Megan said, "Galena was in on it with Quentin, right? Only he was going to double-cross her, so she was going to double-cross him first, but then you interfered and she had to knock you out. This is confusing, Ross."

"There was no 'in on it' at first," Ross explained.

"Apparently, Quent ripped off Galena several years ago. When she hunted him down, he convinced her Dawn would give her a check. Things went bad when Galena figured out Quent had lied again."

"It's all speculation," Mike said. He smiled in gratitude as Elise ladled venison stew into his bowl. He'd removed his Smokey the Bear hat and tucked his brown tie into his shirtfront. The small radio hooked on his belt crackled with soft static. "We're only guessing until we can get all the players together."

Dawn took a square of warm corn bread then passed the basket to Ross. Beneath the table, he touched his knee against hers. His accompanying smile was more than playful.

"Speculation or not, finding the needle cap supports my story, right?" Ross said to the deputy.

"Your story is not in question," the Colonel announced. He looked to his wife. "Sit down, dear, we're capable of serving ourselves."

"Let me fetch the iced tea." Elise disappeared through a swinging door.

"Deputy Downes." The Colonel rapped a spoon against the table. "What are the exact coordinates where the Lincoln was found?"

"Longbow's the primary, sir. I can't release any information until he gives me the go-ahead." He glanced at Dawn, then quickly averted his eyes. Dawn guessed he'd released too much information already because of his friendship with the family, and probably wondered how much he was going to regret.

The Colonel's silvery glare was capable of peeling paint off a wall. Red-faced, Mike focused on his stew.

"Wait for the six-thirty news, Colonel," Janine said. "There's nothing you can find that the sheriff hasn't.

Besides, I agree with Ross. Quentin didn't get hurt and wander off in a daze to die. He set it up to look like it. Do you agree, Mike?''

In spite of the circumstances, Dawn enjoyed the gathering. The Colonel made a good effort at playing despot, but his family cheerfully, if respectfully, ignored him. He obviously desired discipline and order, but unlike Dawn's father, he lacked the streak of ruthlessness necessary to a true autocrat. The only person who appeared the least bit cowed by his ringing voice was Mike.

A trilling noise came from beneath the table. Conversation hushed as Ross brought out his cellular phone. "It's for me." He flipped the unit open.

"That's exactly the kind of contraption that will be the ruination of civilization," the Colonel said to no one in particular.

Dawn ate a bite of stew, watching Ross's eyes widen and his smile grow pleased.

"You're kidding!" He slapped at his shirt pocket, then gestured wildly for a pen.

Mike handed him a ballpoint. Janine produced an envelope to write on. Murmuring, "Uh-huh," Ross scribbled on the envelope. "Call Goldenberg and tell him what you found. I'll be back in the Springs in a couple hours. You are too good, man. Thanks." He shut the phone with a flourish.

"Who was it?" Dawn asked.

Everyone watched Ross and he smiled smugly, sitting up straighter on his chair. "Rayne tracked down the movers who cleaned out your house."

Dawn dropped her spoon. It hit the bowl with a clatter. She dabbed a napkin absently at her mouth.

Ross waved the envelope at her. "Quent stored the items in a facility in Fountain."

"We can get my belongings back?" She clutched her blouse over her pounding heart. She'd never wanted to hug and kiss a man so badly in her life. If not for the presence of his family, she'd have done exactly that.

"Quent rented a van and a day-labor crew, and he used the name Tim Wiley." He flashed a knowing smile at Mike. "That could be the mistake that trips him up. The good thing is, the van-rental place recorded the license number of his Buick." He handed the envelope to Mike. "I bet the Buick is registered to Tim Wiley, too. The bad thing is, Rayne says we can't get into the storage units without a warrant."

"But it's mine!"

Ross laid a hand on her knee and squeezed. "As far as the storage company is concerned, it's Tim Wiley's. Rayne says we still have to prove Wiley and Bayliss are one and the same."

"Your friend knows what he's talking about," Mike said. He'd recorded the information in his notebook before handing the envelope back to Ross.

"Rayne's got a deal going with the storage people. They'll let him know if Quent shows up. More bad news—the one day-laborer he found has a record of burglary. He told Rayne he'd been to your house, but he won't talk to the cops. So Rayne is hunting down the other members of the crew to see if he can convince any of them to talk to the police. If only one will testify to cleaning out your house, Rayne thinks we can get the warrant."

"You sure know some interesting people." Kara eyed her brother speculatively. "This private eye sounds pretty smart. What does he look like?"

"He's married, sweetheart."

Dawn noticed a pained expression on Mike's face as

he excused himself from the table. The way the look cut to Kara made her wonder if the deputy had a crush on Ross's youngest sister. She also wondered if her own emotions were as transparent as the deputy's. Keeping a straight face while Ross played with her knee under the table was a chore.

"I'll call this in to Longbow."

"Use the phone in my office, Mike," Elise said. "Ross, dear, surely you can convince the owner of the storage facility about Dawn's right to her own belongings."

"Afraid not, Mom." He gave Dawn an apologetic smile. "It's either get a warrant or wait until he shows up."

"That's not fair." Elise's comment brought nods around the table.

Dawn agreed wholeheartedly. The way her luck was running, they'd never get a warrant and her belongings would rot inside the storage units. Although, she mused, if she never recovered her dining room furniture, she wouldn't mind. This bright room with solid, well-used furniture, colorful curtains and arrangements of photographs on the walls was exactly the kind of decor she'd like to have in her home.

"You should get a crowbar and break into the storage unit." Megan suggested, gesturing vigorously. "It's your stuff. Technically, you can't steal your own belongings, so it isn't as if you'd be committing a crime."

Kara chimed in with impassioned agreement.

"Hey, Colonel," Megan said. "Let's put together a raid. Black clothes, masks, the works. We'll be just like Delta Force. How about it?"

The elder Duke harrumphed.

Mike appeared in the doorway and gestured at Ross

and Dawn. They excused themselves from the developing strategy session concerning a raid on the storage facility. Dawn followed Ross and Mike to Elise's office.

Mike shut the office door. "I'll be straight. Longbow isn't willing to drop his suspicions about you two. He found blood in the Lincoln and in the vicinity. The car was hit by a bullet."

Dawn gasped. "He never said that!"

"I shouldn't be saying it, either. You have to know it's serious."

Dawn exchanged a look with Ross.

Mike eyed the door uneasily, as if expecting Longbow to come bursting through. "The man from Utah using the name John Venetucci is also known as Bradley Ellis Carter. He skipped bail in Utah and there's a warrant out for him. Bradley Ellis Carter is also wanted by the feds because of some kind of securities fraud he committed in California."

"Bradley, Brad," Dawn whispered. "Galena called him Brad." How many identities had her husband possessed, and how in the world was she going to straighten them all out?

"I know I'm being vague," the deputy said.

Ross gave him a friendly punch to the shoulder. "Just doing your job, man. What's your advice? What do we do?"

"Talk to Goldenberg in the Springs. Ask him to get an artist to put together a sketch of Galena. Maybe Goldenberg will stake out the storage facility, too. If we can prove conclusively Carter, Wiley and Bayliss are the same guy, the FBI might provide the manpower."

Mike had to return to the sheriff's station, but he promised to call Ross as soon as he had any news he could divulge.

Ross made his farewells to his family. Dawn watched with amusement as the Colonel gave Ross a friendly pat on the shoulder. Ross grumbled on the way out of the lodge.

"The least he can do is pretend he's upset about me scamming him."

"You're so funny, Ross. I thought reputations didn't matter."

"*Good* reputations don't matter. But it takes a lot of time and effort to build up a great bad reputation." He opened the passenger door of the Lexus. "Next thing you know, he'll be bragging about me to his friends."

WHEN SHE AND ROSS returned to Colorado Springs, they went directly to the police department downtown. During the drive from Elk River, Dawn had reached the conclusion that Quentin had *not* staged his own disappearance and death. Blood and bullet holes meant Galena had caught him. Quentin may have escaped from her, but he was hurt, possibly dying.

Detective Goldenberg shook hands with both Ross and Dawn. "Your husband appears to be a heavy hitter, Mrs. Bayliss. I ran down that lead you gave me. John Venetucci, also known as Bradley Ellis Carter, is wanted by the state of Utah for bigamy, grand larceny, fraud and conspiracy to commit fraud. He jumped bail, so he's a fugitive. The feds have open warrants out for him, too. Securities fraud. Turns out his specialty, besides stealing from women, is manipulating money transfers. He's a high-tech bank robber."

"That's all well and good, detective, but what about Galena? She's the one with the gun." Ross reached for Dawn's hand and gave her a squeeze of assurance. "Dawn is afraid to go home."

"Have you some place safe to stay, ma'am?"

"With a friend who lives in Broadmoor." Dawn instinctively shuddered when remembering Galena. She pitied the woman, but was frightened, too. "Could we trap Galena? She wants money and has it fixed in her head that I'm the one who is supposed to give it to her."

"Does she contact you by telephone?"

"Once." In despair, she closed her eyes. In order for Galena to contact her by telephone, Dawn would have to wait at home. The woman had proven herself adept at bypassing security.

"I'll go to work on it. Give me the address where you're staying and I'll make sure local patrols keep an eye out."

"Can't you assign an officer to protect her?"

"No. Do you want a lecture about why I can't? We can start with the city budget—"

"Never mind," Ross grumbled.

Dawn and Ross worked with the police artist to compile a portrait of the mystery woman. The process fascinated Dawn. A computer program contained thousands of facial features the artist could combine into an infinite number of faces. Dawn felt convinced the face they eventually came up with bore a photographic likeness to the woman with the gun.

Goldenberg asked Dawn for a list of her wedding guests.

She balked at his request. If the police questioned the people who'd attended the wedding, the telephone calls and gossip sessions over lunch would begin. Before long everyone would be aware of how she'd lost her inheritance. She shunned gossip about others, but she doubted if she'd be able to avoid the gossip about herself.

Ross drew her aside. "What's the matter?" His voice was low and concerned.

"Why didn't I listen to Quentin? He didn't want any guests at all. Now everyone will learn what happened. They'll be so ashamed of me."

"I'm not ashamed of you. Connie's not ashamed. We're the ones who count, right?"

She knew what she had to do, but it didn't make this any easier. Quentin couldn't be allowed to escape with his crimes. Galena had to be apprehended. Though she ached inside, she gave Goldenberg the list of her wedding guests.

When the ordeal was over, she and Ross drove to Connie's house.

"I feel trapped in a nightmare," Dawn said. She peered suspiciously at the thick brambles of scrub oaks lining the driveway. Security lights lit up the house as bright as day, but made the shadows very dark. She had to force her hand to open the car door.

"We'll catch him. He got greedy, and it'll trip him up. You watch and see."

"What do you mean?"

"If I was Quent, I'd have gone for the bank accounts and the stuff in your dad's safe."

As his meaning sank in, she nodded. "Liquid assets and easily pawned items. So why take heavy furniture and valuable paintings anybody with sense would know are stolen?"

"Exactly. He's arrogant enough to think he can get away with it. Now that he has it, he's not giving it up."

"So why hasn't he emptied out the storage units already?"

Ross's smile turned calculating. "Maybe he's lying

low until Galena gets bored." He snapped his fingers. "You're brilliant!"

Startled, she clapped a hand to her throat. "What did I do?"

"He thinks you're a chump, but he knows darn well that Galena is dangerous. If we get her out of the way, he'll come out of hiding."

"I am most certainly not going home to wait for that—"

"Rayne used the cell-phone bill to find the storage facility. We can use it find Galena." He checked his watch. "It's too late to call Rayne to find out if he's identified all the numbers. But you have the bill with you, right?"

She patted her pocketbook. "What if she recognizes my voice?"

"Then you tell her you have her money. We set up a sting, the cops arrest her, Quent sees the story in the paper and we nab him when he goes for the stuff he stole. Case closed."

Her nerves were too frazzled to think logically about flaws in his plan. "There are hundreds of numbers."

"You have other plans?"

His optimism coaxed a laugh from her. She eyed the distance to Connie's front door and felt like a frightened child judging how far it was from the light switch to the safety of her bed. "It's worth a try."

She scampered to the door and fumbled the key in the lock. It took only thirty seconds, but it was the longest thirty seconds of her life. Ada appeared and Dawn almost screamed, but managed to choke it back in time. Ada informed them Connie was attending a committee meeting for her upcoming Fourth of July charity picnic. The housekeeper then invited them to help themselves to anything they fancied in the kitchen. She retired to her own room, leaving them alone.

Bolstered by cold chicken sandwiches and fruit salad, Dawn produced the telephone bill from her purse. The thick package consisted of thirty-eight pages, front and back, of telephone calls.

"It's awfully late to be calling people."

"Pretend you're selling soap." He frowned at the bill. "Hmm, too bad they don't list incoming numbers. I bet she called him a lot more than he called her."

Flustered about calling strangers, and afraid of hearing Galena's voice, Dawn called the first number. She reached a recording for a real-estate company. Ross wrote the number on a separate sheet of paper so Dawn wouldn't call it again. She called number after number, reaching recordings for businesses and voice mail for individuals. She'd worked through three pages and hadn't spoken to a single live person when Connie arrived home.

Dawn gave her a welcoming smile. When she noticed her friend's taut features and flashing eyes, her smile faded.

Connie flung her portfolio onto a kitchen counter. Her little dogs raced, yipping and stumpy tails wagging, to their mistress. Connie barely glanced at them.

Ross asked, "What's wrong, Mrs. Haxman?"

"That little witch!" Connie kicked off her shoes, nearly striking a Yorkie. "She is dead in this town. I swear to God, she'll find nothing but slammed doors from this day forward."

"Sit down." Dawn pulled a chair from the table. "What happened at your meeting?"

"It wasn't the meeting. It was afterward." She flopped onto a chair. "Dizzy Hunter. Has she contacted you?"

Dawn's chest tightened. She knew what was coming. "She's writing a story about Quentin, isn't she?"

"That horrid little woman. I can't believe I ever trusted her. According to her, Quentin is wanted by the FBI. If she wasn't so stingy about grabbing all the glory for herself, she'd have given the information to a real reporter and you'd be ruined already."

Dawn rested her face on her hands. All hope of saving herself from public humiliation had vanished. If the reporter knew about the FBI, then she knew about California and the real Quentin Bayliss. And who knew what else she had dug up?

"She had the audacity to ask me to arrange an interview with you." She fluttered a hand over her breast. Ross brought her a glass of sparkling water and she managed a wan smile of thanks.

"Maybe it isn't such a bad idea."

Connie and Dawn turned astonished gazes on Ross. He slid onto a chair and folded his arms on the table. His expression was neutral, but Dawn had known him long enough to realize the gleam in his eyes meant he was up to something.

"It's an awful idea," Connie said. "It's criminal exposing my darling that way. I won't allow it."

"Quent gets away with his crimes because his victims are embarrassed. For every person who goes to the police, there are probably twenty who don't. Or can't, because it's too humiliating. Remember the real Quentin, Dawn? I bet he still hasn't filed a complaint."

"I don't see why Dawn must suffer because Dizzy has ambitions." Connie placed a hand over Dawn's.

"Desdemona Hunter is going to write her story with or without Dawn's cooperation. We can't stop her, but we may be able to use her."

She'd suffered so much humiliation already, Dawn figured she'd developed an immunity. "How?"

"You grant an interview, but every time she asks a question, you tell her you can't answer because of the police investigation. It'll sound as if you know a lot more than you do. It might work to get Galena off your back."

"Then Quentin leaves town. What good will that do?"

"Don't forget the stuff in the storage units."

Dawn rolled her eyes heavenward. "He won't risk going to jail because of furniture."

"Why not? He's eluded the FBI for years. He's skipped bail. He probably runs around singing, 'Can't catch me, I'm the gingerbread man.' Remember what Goldenberg said. Quent believes he's earned what he took from you. Yeah, if the heat is on, he'll run. But I bet he tries for the storage units first."

"Ross, dear," Connie said slowly. "Dizzy Hunter is a malicious little twit. She likes nothing better than slinging mud, and she'll consider dragging Dawn through the dirt the highlight of her year."

"Have to take the bad with the good. Besides, she'll write her story with or without Dawn's cooperation. It's up to you, sweetheart."

Dawn met his gray eyes, now solemn with concern. She twisted her rings, fingering the large stone in her engagement ring. It occurred to her that since Quentin hadn't stolen it, it was probably a fake. "Let's do it."

Connie gasped.

"I have to, Connie. If for no other reason than to prove Quentin didn't pick the perfect victim."

"That's my girl."

Connie shook a finger at him. "Young man, you're a bad influence. I can't believe you're coercing Dawn to subject herself—"

Dawn interrupted. "It's *my* decision. Besides, you're the one who always said the best way to get out of an embarrassing situation is to hold your head high and walk proud."

"I did not," Connie muttered.

"Did too." Dawn wrapped an arm around Connie's shoulders and gave her a hug. "I may never get my money back, but Quentin is not stealing my self-respect. If public humiliation is what it takes to catch him, then that's what I'll do. What difference will it make, anyway? The police intend to interview everyone who attended the wedding."

"Ross, dear, you're worse than a bad influence. You're horrid." Connie clamped her arms over her bosom and glowered at a spot beyond Ross's head. "Dawn has a reputation to maintain. She is a Lovell."

Cringing inside, Dawn had an insight: Connie and her mother had disliked each other so intensely because they had in more in common than either cared to admit. At this moment, in expression and tone of voice, Connie could be Deborah Lovell's twin.

"I will help you through your time of trouble, my darling, but I will not be a party to your self-destruction. I will certainly not stand by idly while you further Dizzy Hunter's ridiculous ambitions!"

"Mrs. Haxman," Ross said patiently, "we have to catch Quent."

"You stay out of this!" she snapped. She caught Dawn in a painful hug. "You had your chance to save her, but you blew it. So you stay out of it now."

Dawn squirmed, trying to escape. "Connie, please—"

Connie dropped her arm. She slapped the table with both hands and stood. "You are an innocent adrift in a sea of sharks. Dizzy is the worst of the lot. She will eat you for breakfast and enjoy every morsel. I forbid you to speak to her." On that note, she flounced out of the kitchen, trailed by scampering Yorkies.

Stunned and embarrassed, but worse, feeling as if both her parents had somehow materialized in the room, Dawn sank onto the chair. What if Connie was right? A story by Dizzy could make Dawn a social outcast, or worse, hurt her charity work, tainting worthy causes by association.

"She feels guilty." Ross's face was solemn and his voice was soft.

"Connie?"

"She's the one who brought Dizzy to the reception. But you can't let her influence your decision."

"She's my friend. I love her. I can't hurt her."

"Dizzy is going to write her story with or without you. The damage is already done."

Dawn closed her eyes as her chest ached with the weight of indecision. She envisioned life as a social outcast, ridiculed by the important and self-important, blackballed from prestigious parties and events. Having never been a fan of such events anyway, she couldn't rouse much concern at that prospect. Connie, though, concerned her very much. The possibility of losing Connie's love, affection and support scared her to death.

Ross touched her hand. She opened her eyes. He half turned on the chair and patted his thigh. "Come here, sweetheart."

Too weary to consider right or wrong, she sat on his lap. Sighing, she laid her head against his shoulder. He draped his arms loosely around her. For a long time they sat still. She grew aware of the mingling of his shampoo and his natural masculine scent—an erotic fragrance she'd always associate with pleasure. She listened to his breathing and the rustling of windblown branches against the windows.

At last, he murmured, "Feel better?"

She nodded against his shoulder. With his interlocked hands, he massaged the small of her back. He kissed her forehead, and she felt safe, warm and relaxed. She wished life could always be like this.

"I'm feeling too good. You better get up."

She raised her head. His smile had a mischievous cant and his eyes were smoky-dark. She wanted to fling her arms about his neck and kiss him senseless, letting nature take its course. She touched his face, tracing the strong line of his cheekbone. She knew this was wrong, she told herself it was wrong, but it felt right. He felt right. She rubbed a strand of his soft, heavy hair between her fingers and thumb.

Her wedding ring gleamed.

She sighed. "I'm so confused." She left the comfort of his lap. At the window, she stared out into the night. Clouds concealed the stars and moon, and shrouded the mountaintops. Far below, the city glittered with thousands of lights.

"What feels right to you?"

Loving you... "Catching Quentin, making him pay for his crimes." She clenched her fists. "But Connie is my best friend. I'd rather throw myself off a cliff than have her angry with me."

"She won't stay mad long."

"What if she does?" She shivered and hugged herself.

His reflection in the window behind her was cast in silver, looming over her, strong and beautiful. She lowered her eyelids, leaning back slightly, enough for him to cup her elbows in a gentle embrace. In her mind, she glided through the week they'd spent at the resort. The laughter, the closeness, the conversations and sense of belonging. Maybe he was right, the woman she'd been at Elk River was the real her, the genuine Dawn, relaxed, fun-loving and carefree.

She wanted to be that woman again. She didn't need money in order to laugh. Or a fancy pedigree in order to enjoy popcorn while watching old movies.

"Ross?"

He rocked her gently from side to side and nuzzled her hair. "Uh-huh?"

The bittersweet pain of arousal was centered low in her belly. Attempting to ignore it made her knees feel liquid. "Did you mean what you said about offering me a job?"

"Sure did."

"I've never held a paying position before."

"You're in for a treat when you see what the IRS snatches out of your paycheck."

She laughed softly. "Do you really think I can do it?"

"Does this mean you'll say yes?"

His smile reflected in the mirror melted her heart. For that smile alone, she could accomplish miracles. "I'd like to see your office and speak to your sec—administrative assistant." She swallowed hard. "But first thing tomorrow I'm calling Desdemona Hunter. Will you go with me to speak to her? She's very pushy."

"Let her push. Our every answer will be, no comment. My hunch is, she'll make it sound as if the cops are minutes away from an arrest."

Now that she'd committed to a course of action, her nervousness increased tenfold. "What about Connie? She'll be furious."

"You can stay at my place." He kissed her ear, tickling her. "But as much as I'd like to have you all to myself, sweetheart, I don't think she'll throw you out."

"I feel like a little girl rebelling against my parents. Isn't that silly?"

"Nope." He kissed her again. "Rebellion is a good thing. As long as you don't start piercing body parts."

She tried to picture herself with studs in her nose or eyebrows. The imagery made her shudder. "A tattoo perhaps, but nothing pierced."

"I *heart* Ross." He rubbed her shoulder, slowly, sensually, his fingertips teasing the sensitive ridge along her collarbone. "Right here, bright red. I'd like that."

"You would." She leaned fully against him and sighed. He filled her with her courage. For that alone, she could love him forever.

Chapter Fourteen

"What in the world?"

At the sound of Connie's voice, Dawn hunched her shoulders and prickles ran up and down her spine. She'd had the cowardly hope of escaping before Connie awakened this morning. Ross was late, however, and since she didn't have his cellular-phone number, she didn't know how to reach him. For twenty minutes she'd been pacing across Connie's living room, watching for him.

Connie's gaze swept over Dawn. "Where did you get that dress?"

Dawn covered a sheepish smile with a hand. On impulse she had put on the wine-red dress this morning. It was a bit dressy for day wear, so she wore nude stockings, a pair of pumps, and a cream-colored silk jacket.

Dawn walked to a wall mirror and fussed with her hair. She'd swept it up this morning into a loose knot on the back of her head. She barely recognized herself, but she liked how she looked. As she studied the way the dark color set off her complexion, she hoped Ross would think she was pretty.

"You're going to speak to Dizzy, aren't you?"

Dawn gave her hair a final pat before facing her friend.

"I have to. It'll take me days to call all the numbers on the phone bill. I don't think Galena will give me days."

"Dizzy will hurt you."

"A bit of embarrassment won't even sting." Her stomach clenched in a tight knot, but she kept her head high. Humiliation did hurt, and the prospect of talking to Dizzy Hunter held about as much appeal as sticking her head in a hot oven. She had to forcibly remind herself of Quentin's crimes—her empty bank accounts and house, and the horror of awakening in her bridal bed and finding her husband missing. Not to mention the terror of meeting the business end of Galena's gun. "I don't want you mad at me. And I certainly don't want to hurt your feelings, but I *have* to do this. Please understand."

Connie sank onto a sofa and rested her forehead on a hand. She sighed dramatically. One by one her little dogs hopped onto the sofa beside her. "You don't know Dizzy the way I do."

"This has nothing to do with her."

"I don't see why humiliating yourself—"

"I'm already humiliated." She joined Connie on the sofa. "But I don't want to lose you, Connie. You're my best friend in the whole wide world. But, don't you see? If I don't do everything in my power to find Quentin and bring him to justice, then he wins."

Connie lifted her eyes. Without cosmetics, she looked her age. The strain of conflict showed in her downturned mouth. The knots in Dawn's belly jerked tighter, but she had to continue.

"You're right about Mother and Father. Every time I said 'I will,' they told me 'you won't.' They thought money could protect them. Protect me. It's time I learned how to take care of myself. I have to start with Quentin."

"But Dizzy—"

"The very worst thing she can do is tell the truth, and that's going to come out anyway. Did you see this morning's paper? There's a big story about how the park rangers found the Lincoln and now Search and Rescue are looking for Quentin." She covered Connie's hand with her own. She wished she'd been able to speak to her mother in this way. "Since the car is registered in another name, the reporters haven't connected me to it, but it's only a matter of time."

"This is Ross's doing." The fire had gone out of Connie's words.

"Ross Duke is the best thing to ever happen to me. He's fearless." She lifted a shoulder. "I'm learning how to be fearless, too. So please don't hate me."

"I don't hate you. Don't ever say that." She sniffed and entwined her fingers with Dawn's. "But I don't agree with what you're doing." Her eyes narrowed. "You haven't cashed my check yet."

"I may not have to. Ross has offered me a job. He's losing his administrative assistant, and needs another to start right away."

"Oh, for pity's sake!"

"I'll have to adhere to a strict budget, and I may have to find roommates, but I'll pay my debts."

"Who's going to run the office at the Society? I need you." She slammed a fist against her palm. "I can convince the board to turn the office-manager position into a paid position. I'll top whatever Ross offers as salary."

Dawn laughed in astonishment. "I thought you were angry with me?"

"I am. I'm furious. But I need you." She pressed the back of one hand over her eyes. "I shall recover. Eventually." She peeked between her fingers. "Will you at least promise to keep your options open until I can speak to the board?''

The doorbell rang before Dawn could answer. She and Connie watched Ada cross the foyer. Dawn's calf muscles bunched in apprehension even though she knew it must be Ross and not Galena.

Ross strode into the living room wearing a dark red cotton shirt under a light linen jacket. His eyes were grim and his mouth was set. Yet, he seemed excited. She slowly rose.

"I think we've found Quent," he said. "For real."

ROSS WATCHED Dawn's eyes widen and her mouth turn slack. He knew exactly how she felt. He'd felt the same way when Rayne gave him the news.

"How? Where?"

"Rayne called before I left my place. That's why I'm late. After he heard about the Lincoln, he started checking around the local hospitals and clinics. A Tim Wiley was admitted last night to Memorial Hospital."

Dawn wrung her hands. "How do we know it's Quentin?"

"We don't. We better get over there. There's no telling why he's in the hospital or for how long."

Connie Haxman waved a hand. "Have you called the police?"

"Not yet. If it's Quent, we will. Come on, sweetheart." A scared look tightened her features and he grew scared himself. After all she'd been through, no way could she believe she might salvage her marriage. Even so, without a direct line to her heart, he had no way of knowing exactly how she'd react when she faced her husband.

Dawn's slender throat worked with a hard swallow. "I don't know what to say to him."

"Say whatever is on your mind. Come on."

"What about Dizzy?" Connie nudged Yorkies out of the way and stood. "She'll call looking for you."

"She can wait, but whatever you do, don't tell her about the hospital or Tim Wiley." Ross picked up Dawn's pocketbook from a small table and handed it to her. She clutched it over her breast as he grasped her elbow and steered her out the door.

Dawn sat silent during the short ride to the hospital. Looking dazed, her breathing shallow through parted lips, she twisted her wedding ring round and round her finger. Ross kept glancing at her, curious about why she'd chosen this morning to wear the new dress. The wine-red color made her complexion glow. Upswept hair emphasized her delicate bone structure and graceful neck. He wished she didn't look so pretty for her meeting with Quent.

Once at the hospital, Ross went directly to the elevators. He hadn't asked the private eye how he'd obtained the information about Tim Wiley's admission or room number. He supposed Rayne made it his business to win contacts where it counted.

The door to Wiley's room stood open.

Dawn stopped in the hallway. She trained a worried look on the nursing station. At this time of the morning the hallway bustled with orderlies carrying cleaning supplies, nurses making rounds and uniformed men and women pushing food-service carts. None of the hospital workers paid them the slightest bit of attention.

Ross grasped her elbow. "Let's see if it's him."

"Tim Wiley isn't that uncommon a name."

"Dawn..."

She patted the base of her throat and fussed with the neckline of her dress. Her feet shifted restlessly, soundlessly on the tiled floor. "I don't know what to say to him."

He knew what he wanted to say to Quent, most of it crude, lewd and unfit for the ears of women and children. "You don't need to say anything. If it's him, we call the cops." He tugged gently on her arm. She lurched a step toward the door.

She suddenly gave herself a shake, straightened her shoulders and marched into the room.

Of the four beds in the sunny room, only one was occupied. The man on the bed sat up with his back to the door. His bare, beefy shoulders and broad back were covered with bruises and healing scrapes. Stiff bandaging was wrapped around his ribs. He struggled to slide an arm into a shirt, but in slow motion, as if every movement agonized him. Black hair was matted on one side of his head as if he'd lain still in one position for a long time.

A young woman was helping him with the shirt. She winced every time he did and her eyes glistened on the verge of tears.

"This is crazy," she said. "You should stay at least one more night, honey. The doctor said—"

"I don't care what the doctor said!" he snapped, then groaned loudly. The arm he'd raised for the shirt quivered and flopped. He leaned to the side, pressing an arm against his ribs, and groaned again.

Dawn's chin trembled. She clutched her pocketbook so tightly the leather squeaked. She whispered, "Quentin."

The young woman noticed them and gave a start. She glanced at the empty beds, then smiled. About twenty-

five, she was a big woman, probably five feet, ten inches
in her stocking feet with broad shoulders and an Ama-
zonian figure. Wild, blond hair and dimples in her deeply
suntanned cheeks made her look like an ad for a camp-
ing-supplies catalog.

Quentin creakily turned his head. Another groan
slipped through his clenched teeth. He squeezed his eyelids shut.

"Hi," the blonde said, uncertainly. "Are you looking
for someone? The other guy in here went home already—"

"We found him." Ross strode to the foot of Quentin's
bed.

The man looked as if someone had used him for bat-
ting practice. The black-blue-green-and-yellow bruises on
his shoulders extended down both arms. Some of the
scabbed-over scrapes on his arms were surrounded by
angry-looking red flesh. Butterfly bandages closed gashes
on his forehead and cheeks. Both eyes were blackened
and his lips were scabbed. Underneath the bruising, his
complexion was gray.

Dawn stared into her husband's eyes. Her face was
blank.

"I didn't know you had friends in the Springs, honey.
Oh! You must have come from Boston. You didn't tell
me your friends were coming—"

"Angie," Quent growled. "Shut up."

"He broke a rib and didn't know it. Last night it punc-
tured his lung and I had to bring him to the emergency
room. It was awful, he couldn't breathe. I thought he was
going to die! I know I should have brought him in sooner,
but—"

"Shut up!"

"What happened?" Dawn asked, now looking at the younger woman.

"Poor thing. He was on a wilderness trek up in Pike National Forest. The outfitters dropped him off and were going to pick him up in a week, but then he crashed." She swept her hands before her. "Total wipeout. He lost all his gear, even his phone. Good thing I found him or he'd have died." Oblivious of his murderous glare, she gazed at him with adoring eyes. "He's a total mess and I wanted to bring him to the hospital, but he wouldn't go. Silly, macho man. But last night...oh, it was horrible!" She suddenly thrust out her hand. "I'm Angie, by the way. Did you fly in from Boston to take Timmy home?"

Ross peered closely at Quent, trying to figure out what it was about this guy that enabled him to sucker women so thoroughly. Angie didn't look or sound stupid, but apparently she'd not only taken him into her home, but her heart. Maybe Quent had super-duper pheromones or something.

"Not exactly," Dawn said. "I live about two miles from here."

"Why didn't you tell me you had friends in the Springs, honey?"

"I'm not his friend, Angie. I'm his wife."

Quent closed his eyes. His groan sounded more angry than pained.

Ross deeply regretted the man's injured state. Now would be an excellent time to shout, "And I'm the best man he played for a chump!" then wade in with both fists flying. But no amount of anger could make him kick a guy as down as Quent. Instead, he clamped a hand on his cellular phone, giving Dawn a minute to regain her bearings before he called the cops.

Angie's broad, country-girl face wrinkled and her nose twitched like a rabbit's. Her smile turned into a puzzled grimace. "Wife?"

Dawn sighed. "We haven't been married long. It must have slipped his mind. Quentin?"

He groaned loudly and eased with excruciating slowness into a prone position. Even Ross winced along with the man's pain. Angie helped Quent's legs onto the bed. He wore slacks, but no shoes. Ross wanted to feel triumph at finally catching the creep, but felt pity instead. It irritated him—Quent deserved every bruise and scrape. Unhooking the phone from his belt, he held it up until Dawn looked his way. He waited for her go-ahead to call the police.

"Wife?" Angie repeated, watching Dawn apprehensively.

Eyes closed, teeth gritted, Quent whispered, "Leave us alone a minute, honey. Okay? Go grab a soda or something."

"Ex-wife, right?" Angie wrung Quent's shirt in her tanned hands. "You didn't say you were married. What's this all about? What's going on?"

Ross heard his opening. "Let me guess, Angie. Love at first sight, right? Has he asked you to marry him yet? Or is he just stringing you along for room and board, and maybe a loan?"

The girl gasped.

Dawn rested a hand on Ross's arm. She shook her head.

Quent's injuries precluded the pounding he deserved, but Ross had no intention of letting him off the hook. "He's a con man and a thief. He preys on women. Did you give him any money, Angie? Did you buy him plane tickets or give him a car?"

"Ross, please." Dawn beseeched him.

He'd been waiting too long for this to be silent now. He grasped the foot rail on the bed and loomed over the battered man. "We met Galena. Did she do this to you? Too bad she didn't invite me to the party, I'd have held you down while she broke all your ribs. Your legs, too, and maybe your arms."

"Ross!"

Angie threw down the shirt. Fists clenched, she advanced stiff-legged on Ross. She probably hiked, biked, skied and mountain-climbed, and looked more than willing to use all that hard-earned muscle to shut him up.

"He's wanted in two states that we know of," he told her. "Fraud, embezzlement, bigamy, larceny. The FBI is looking for him, too. He's a crook, Angie."

Angie halted in her tracks. She shifted her uncertain gaze between Ross and the man on the bed. "Timmy's a real-estate broker from Boston."

"Tim Wiley is an alias," Ross said. "He told us his name is Quentin Bayliss. His real name is Carter."

Quent groaned again and clutched his ribs. "Dawn, darling, don't listen to his lies. He's got it all wrong. I meant to tell you everything, but my life is in danger and I couldn't drag you into it. The only way I could protect you was by hiding out. I love you, you're the most wonderful woman in the whole wide world. The pain in my body is nothing compared to the pain in my heart knowing you were so close, but so unobtainable."

"Disgusting son of..." Ross thrust out an arm. "What did I tell you, Angie? He's a liar and a thief. And now he's going to prison." He opened the telephone.

Dawn stopped him. "Wait."

"Wait, nothing!" He shrugged away from her hand. Something was wrong with Dawn. She was too calm all of a sudden. The way she gazed at Quent made his stomach bunch into an ice-cold knot while cat claws crawled up his spine.

"Timmy?" Angie whispered.

Quent locked gazes with Dawn. He was making at an effort to smile, but it cost him. Sweat beaded on his forehead. He panted rapidly.

"Tim!"

Without so much as a glance, he murmured, "Beat it, Angie. I'll give you a call."

The young woman burst into tears and fled the room. Filled with a mixture of pity and relief to have saved her from making a real mistake, Ross watched her go. "Do I call the police, or do you want to do the honors, sweetheart?"

Dawn went to the chair beside the bed and sat. Poker-straight, her pocketbook perched on her lap, she continued her quiet perusal of Quent's battered face. Ross questioned her with his eyes. Where was her indignation? Anger? Why wasn't she pumping Quent for answers? Her face revealed nothing at all.

He pressed nine on the phone. It beeped. "I'm calling."

"I'd like a few minutes alone...with my husband." Her cheeks and forehead tightened and her eyelids drooped. The mournful expression lasted only a second. She drew a deep breath and placed a hand atop Quent's. "Please don't call the police, Ross. I appreciate all you've done for me, but I'd prefer to handle it from here."

Quent lifted his eyebrows. Not even swollen flesh and blackened bruises lessened the gleam of satisfaction in his eyes. He entwined his fingers with hers. "Oh, darling, you don't know how much I've missed you, but I couldn't contact you. It was too dangerous and I've been so afraid. Not for me, but for you.''

"For me?'' she asked sweetly.

Ross's mouth fell open. If a fifty-pound bag of concrete had dropped into his gut, he couldn't feel more stunned. "Don't listen to him. He's lying.''

"Please, Ross, this is my husband. I have to hear his side of the story.'' She lowered her face. "We don't know for a fact he's the man the police are looking for.''

His heart pounded painfully and he nearly dropped the telephone. He held onto the foot rail so tightly his hand ached. "Don't do this.''

Her throat worked convulsively. "I made my position perfectly clear. This is my husband and I owe him my loyalty...and every benefit of the doubt. Thank you so much for all you've done, but I'd like you to leave now. I'd like to talk to my husband.''

"No.'' He rattled the bed and Quent yelped. Ross rattled the bed again. "Dammit, Dawn, I love you!''

She leaned forward as if to rise, then went rigid, remaining firmly seated. She stared blankly at her husband. "I take my marriage vows seriously. For better or worse, until death do us part. This is my responsibility and not your problem anymore. Please leave.''

Ross turned his incredulous gaze on Quent. He couldn't believe this was happening. He loved her. He was madly, hopelessly, gloriously in love with Dawn and if she asked him to lie down at her feet and die, he'd do so with a smile on his face.

But this?

"I'm a Lovell, Ross,'' she said quietly, and finally looked at him. She stared directly into his eyes. "I know my duty. I know what I must do. Please understand.''

"He's a liar.'' The best he could manage was a husky

croak. As if from far away he heard hospital noises: the squeak of rubber soles on the linoleum floor, quiet voices, carts rattling. But the sound that grabbed him was that of his own heart breaking. "Don't do this, sweetheart."

"Don't make this any more difficult than it must be."

A glance at Quent, lying there so helpless and hurt, making spaniel eyes at Dawn, made Ross suspect this was some kind of girl thing. As tough as his sisters were, nothing could turn them to mush faster than a wounded animal. Seeing Quent wounded obviously made Dawn forget how the man had wounded *her*.

Aching and dazed, unable to see anything except her beautiful eyes telling him goodbye, he backed away from the bed.

Good thing he was in the hospital—his chest was about to explode. He walked slowly out of the room. With every footfall he prayed she'd call his name and tell him she was only kidding...she didn't mean it...she loved him. He reached the door and paused. A passing nurse gave him a compassionate look, faltering in her step as if expecting him to ask for assistance. He realized he must be wearing his feelings on his face, and if that was so, he must look like a dying man. He caught the door edge, gave it a jerk and pulled it shut.

Still, she didn't stop him.

"BRAD," HE SAID QUIETLY. Talking hurt, but talking was the only thing capable of getting him out of here. Ross Duke, whom he'd sorely underestimated, was going to call the cops. He felt as certain of that as he was certain that he hurt as he'd never hurt before.

"Brad," Dawn repeated slowly. "As in Bradley Ellis Carter?"

How, how, *how* had she learned so much? A sick sensation nagged him—he'd underestimated her, too. Moving only his eyes, he studied her. She looked different. The dark red dress with the short skirt was certainly different, and so was the way she wore her hair. But that wasn't it, not really. Her eyes, he finally decided. Something about her eyes had changed. She no longer looked like an awkward fourteen-year-old on her first day in a new school.

"I'm sorry I couldn't tell you my real name."

She snuffled and shuddered. Muttering an apology, she reached inside her pocketbook, fumbled around and brought out a handkerchief. Handwoven Irish linen, he noted. She dabbed at her eyes.

"You couldn't tell me? Why not?"

He lowered his voice. "Witness Protection Program."

She lifted her eyebrows.

Her credulity sent his mind racing. "It's true about me being a real-estate developer from Boston. But I got mixed up with the wrong financial backers. I discovered they were using my corporation to launder drug money." He paused for dramatic effect and lowered his voice. "I testified against the mob."

"I see."

"They gave me a whole new identity, the works. But something went wrong. A bad cop snitched on me. I had to hide not only from the mob, but from the feds. They trumped up charges against me, put out phony warrants. I don't know who to trust anymore. I had to leave you because they found out about you and I was afraid they'd kill you or kidnap you to get back at me."

"Oh."

"I love you so much, darling. It's been hell not being able to contact you, but I'm sure the mob has you under surveillance. I couldn't take the chance."

She nodded. "And Galena? Is she a mobster?"

Her knowledge surprised him, scared him. Think, think, *think,* he ordered himself. He'd refused pain medication in order to keep his head clear, but pain fogged his brain. "What's the deal with you and Ross? Didn't take you long to replace me."

Anger flashed in her eyes. She didn't look mousy at all, or dowdy or plain. She was beautiful. And she was touchy about Ross Duke. He could use it against her.

Dabbing at her face again, she said, "I know about Utah and California. I know you stole from Galena. She's the one who did this to you, isn't she?"

"She's a hired hit woman. I barely escaped—"

"I can't help you if you keep lying to me."

Prickling with mingled suspicion and hope, he clamped his mouth shut. She was definitely different from the insecure, poor little rich girl who'd trotted down the aisle with him.

"You're my husband, Quen—Brad. You may have married me under false pretenses, but there was nothing false about the vows I took. I take my responsibilities very seriously. It's the way I was raised. It's the way I must be."

"That's why I love you so—"

"Hush." She pressed a finger to his lips. "You talk too much. Now I would like you to listen." She waited a moment before settling back on the chair. "You are in a lot of trouble. The police are looking for you. The FBI are looking for you. Galena is looking for you."

He closed his eyes, hating his helplessness, hating knowing he was trapped like a rat.

"For better or worse, I married you. I don't think it can get much worse than this. I can't help you, however, unless you tell me the truth. I must be able to trust you."

Now the inner radar clamored. *Trust?* He peeked at her, seeking any trace of anger or vengeance. Her blue eyes regarded him solemnly. "Get me out of here, Dawn. I'm scared and I need a place to rest."

"First we have to talk." She lowered her gaze. "No more lies between us."

"I told you the truth, darling. I'm in the Witness Pro—"

"That's a lie." She stood up and gazed down at him with weary resignation. "You have a choice. Either you tell me the truth, or I'm calling the police and you can talk to them."

Truth...truth was for chumps and suckers. His ribs twinged and his lungs cramped. He squeezed his eyes shut against the pain. Each agonized breath reminded him of his helplessness. Resentment swelled, at her, at his situation, at his inability to run. Little Dawn was going to pay for this one.

"Make up your mind," she said.

Her calm, reasonable voice was getting on his nerves. She made him feel like a stupid kid, forced to sit still for a lecture. She would pay for that, too.

"You emptied my bank accounts. You emptied my house. You broke into my father's safe and stole everything inside. You used the name of a Denver businessman when you married me. You're a con artist and a thief."

He opened his eyes and shakily wiped sweat off his brow. Raising his arm caused his torso to creak. Busted ribs were a killer. "Sit down."

She sat.

"Yeah, I cleaned out your house, but I had no choice. My life is in danger and that's God's honest truth."

A ripple of distaste passed over her features.

"Okay, okay, I'm not in the Witness Protection Program, but I did mess with the wrong people. It wasn't my fault, I'm just a businessman and I got sucked in before I realized who I was dealing with. I had to go into hiding, but no matter how many times I changed my name and address, they found me. There's a contract on my head. Say what you will about my methods, but see what you'd do if you had a bull's-eye on your back. When it comes down to a choice between your scruples and your skin, you'll take your skin. Trust me on that.''

"So you took my money?"

"I hated doing it, darling, you can't know how sorry I am. But I kind of worked a deal. I pay them off, they leave me alone. I was desperate. I didn't want to do it to you, but I figured you'd rather have me alive than dead. Besides, you got the trust fund. It's not like you're poor or anything.''

"Why didn't you tell me? I would have helped you."

"I figured the less you knew, the better." Picking up momentum from the sound of his own voice, he rolled with the story. "Then they double-crossed me. They lied to me! They got to me at Elk River. Galena is a contract killer. She waited until I gave them everything I had, then came after me. The only way I could save you was to run.''

"Hmm.''

"I had to make sure you didn't know anything or they'd come after you. And their methods aren't pretty. Not pretty at all. If they suspected you knew where I was, they'd have hurt you. I know it for a fact.''

"I see.''

Encouraged, emboldened, he managed a smile. "I screwed up. I know I made a big mess of things, but damn, I love you so much. You're the moon and stars to me. I shouldn't have married you, but I was so crazy in love I couldn't help myself.'' He reached for her hand. "I was weak, I did a dumb thing, but I couldn't help it. You're so beautiful and smart and brave. You're the most exciting, loving woman I've ever met in my life. I wasn't thinking straight.''

She kept her hands on her pocketbook, out of reach. "Why did you use Quentin Bayliss's name?''

"Because the people after me know about Tim Wiley. I couldn't risk the public record. I couldn't risk endangering you.''

"But you did use the name Tim Wiley to register the car and rent the storage units in Fountain.''

He did not consider himself a violent man. Violence was for apes and dopes, but a murderous rage built within his aching chest. Dawn was a small woman with a thin, fragile neck. He saw her helping him into her house, turning her back, leaving her throat vulnerable to his clutching hands. "I've been on the run a long time. Using a lot of names scatters the scent. It's got nothing to do with fraud.''

Once she was dead, he'd take her father's old Caddy and *hasta la vista*, Colorado. Who knows, violence might even be fun. "Darling, I'm hurting. I'm scared. I can't think. Get me out of here.''

"Where is my money?''

"I told you, darling, I bought off the killers. They double-crossed me and sent in a hit man anyway. It's gone. Every penny. Look at me. Do I look like a rich guy?'' He could smell her disbelief. Her calmness, however, confused him. No tears, no accusations, no anger, no nothing. Just sitting there with her hands on that clunky purse, her feet flat on the floor, her big eyes watching him with a steadiness that rattled his nerves. He'd had her pegged. Rich, lonesome, insecure, naive, gullible...she wasn't acting right. His rage bubbled closer to the surface.

"As your wife," she said, "I will do everything possible to help you. In return, you must give me cause to trust you."

Trust again... He saw her game now. Did she really think he'd roll over and tell her where he'd transferred the money? He smiled as best he could. Another pang in his chest caught him by surprise and he groaned. She gave a start and gasped. That pleased him. He groaned piteously, gratified when her cheeks paled.

"I'm hurting bad, baby. Real bad. But you have to get me out of here." He waved weakly in the direction of the shirt Angie had dropped. "I have a phobia about hospitals. I have a recurring nightmare about dying in a bed just like this. I can't think here. Let's go to your place and talk. Okay? We'll work all this out. Let's go to your place and I'll tell you everything. Everything you want." He smiled as pitifully as possible. Not much of a stretch, considering how he felt. "I love you, darling. I've never loved anyone as much as I love you. Ours will be a marriage made in heaven. Just get me out of here."

Covering her mouth with a hand, she barely breathed. She spoke between her fingers. "How did you get hurt?"

Knowing he'd hit the mother lode of sympathy, he shuffled through stories before settling on the truth. "Galena ran me off the road. Another couple yards and I'd have gone off the side of the mountain. I was never so scared in my life. There's my car stuck and she's coming back for another shot at me, so I took off into the woods. Pitch-dark, can't tell up from down, and she's shooting at me!"

"Oh, my."

"She meant to kill me." He paused for dramatic effect,

pleased by the whites showing around her irises. "Then I fell off a cliff."

"Oh my!"

"I don't know how far I fell, but I was all beat up. Then I hid under some rocks, scared to death she was gonna get me. The next morning I could barely move."

"That's when Angie found you."

He searched her eyes for clues. Was that funny catch in her throat jealousy? He hoped so. "She's a nice kid. I gave her that cock-and-bull story to keep her out of trouble."

"Because of the mobsters?"

"That's right. There's nothing going on between us. She gave me a place to crash and doctored me up as best she could."

"Why didn't you call me? I've been worried about you."

"I couldn't take the chance. Your phone could be tapped. Mobsters could be tailing you."

The corners of her mouth twitched and she covered her lower face with a hand. She wore her wedding ring.

"I'm telling you the truth, baby. You're the only woman I've ever loved. I'd never cheat on you. Especially not with a ding-a-ling like Angie. Get real! She's not grown-up enough to be a real woman. Real, like you. Help me get dressed. Let's go. I gotta get out of here." He struggled to sit upright. A dull, white-hot knife sawed at his rib cage.

Dawn stood and pressed a hand against his shoulder. "Stay still. You're in no shape to go anywhere. I'll speak to your doctor and see what he says."

He grabbed her hand. "Come on, Dawn! Just help me up and give me my shirt. Please."

She lowered her face until he could smell the sweetness of her toothpaste. "What did you do with my money?"

"Help me out of here and I'll tell you."

The door opened. Expecting a nurse or orderly, it took him a few seconds to recognize the woman who peered around the door. He groaned again, this time more from fear than pain.

Galena Carter, wife number six, tossed her blond hair away from her face and stalked into the room. She closed the door firmly behind her. Dawn staggered, struck the chair with the back of her knees and sat down with a thud. Galena pulled the .32 automatic from her purse and pointed it straight at his heart.

"I knew it," she said. "You've been helping this low-down, belly-crawling snake all along. Both of you are dead meat!"

Chapter Fifteen

Ross pushed through the glass doors and turned in the direction of the parking lot. He'd helped Dawn, gone above and beyond any ethical or legal obligations, laid his heart at her feet and what did he get in return? A kick in the teeth and see you later, chump!

Couldn't she see how much he loved her?

He spotted Angie. The girl leaned against a lamp pole as if it were the only thing keeping her from sprawling on the concrete. With her face buried in her hands, she sobbed.

Chalk up another broken heart for Carter-Venetucci-Bayliss-Wiley-etcetera.

Ross stared at the hospital doors, hoping beyond hope to see Dawn hurrying after him. A woman helped a man on crutches over the threshold. Ross squinted against bright morning sunshine, watching, waiting, hoping, but after the man and woman passed through the doorway, the doors closed.

"You deserve him," he muttered, but didn't mean it and hated himself for not being able to mean it. He shoved his hands in his pockets and rocked on his heels.

Temporary insanity. That's what it was. Stress and sleep deprivation had made Dawn crazy. She needed to see Quent for the crook he really was. Refusing to consider that Dawn might hate his guts forever, he whipped out his telephone and wallet. He found Detective Goldenberg's card and dialed the number. He glared up at the hospital. She'd thank him for this. She'd realize who really loved her. It took several minutes before he reached the detective.

"This is Ross Duke," he growled. "I've got him."

The detective's excitement traveled over the airwaves as he demanded to know the details. After promising Ross he'd be there immediately, he ordered Ross to contact hospital security.

Ross snorted in derision. "Trust me. He's in no shape to give anybody a problem." He closed the telephone with a satisfying snap.

He glanced at Angie and his heart went out to his fellow victim. "Hey, Angie. Are you okay?"

She jerked up her head. "He's married!" she wailed.

"Yeah, all over the place." Tentatively, he touched her shoulder. "Can I do anything for you?"

She shook her head so hard her hair whipped like a honey-colored flag in a windstorm. She hiccuped loudly and used her T-shirt sleeve to wipe her face. "He—he lied to me! I saved his stupid life and he lied!"

"That's what he does best."

"I fed him and gave him my bed." Sobs punctuated her words. "I—I—I bathed him!" She slammed a fist against the metal pole. "I'm not stupid, but he fooled me anyway. I want to kill him!"

Ross stiffened, staring hard at the sobbing young woman as she recited a litany of Quent's crimes. Dawn knew all about his crimes and how he lied and what he'd done to her. In spite of her vulnerabilities, she was not now and never had been a stupid woman. She made mistakes, but she learned from them—and she was a fast learner. He turned around slowly, lifting his gaze up the hospital walls, searching windows as if he could see Quent's room.

"I know my responsibility..."

"Hey, Angie. The cops will be here any minute. Tell them what that creep did to you."

The young woman recoiled. "And let everyone know what an idiot I am?" She scrambled away and ran across the parking lot.

Ross returned to the hospital. Like a skipping record, he kept hearing his own advice: To know the artist, look at the art. Forget what Dawn had said, look at her actions. Beginning with that wine-red dress. She'd worn it for him, to look pretty, to show him she cared about his opinion. Her kisses, the endearing, shy way she gazed into his eyes. Her laughter, her trust. When she'd entered Quent's hospital room, she'd been loaded for bear and out for blood. That eerie calm of hers indicated fury.

Fury directed at Quent.

At the elevators, he punched a button.

Look at the art... Why didn't she want him calling the police? Why throw him out of the room as if she had no more use for him than she had for yesterday's newspaper? Why all that malarky about responsibility to her husband and thank-you-very-much, Ross, but there is nothing between us and there never will be because I'm a married woman?

The elevator door *shussed* open and he stepped inside, sharing the car with an orderly accompanying an elderly man in a wheelchair. The old man was saying, "Don't let her fool you. Mama's worried sick. She just grouches like that so I don't worry about her."

The orderly nodded in understanding.

"I know all that old woman's tricks."

"I'm not taking it personal, sir."

Ross faced the door, pretending not to eavesdrop, but he heard. And he understood about appearances being deceptive. He recalled Dawn giving Deputy Longbow the devil—even though he'd scared her half to death with his not-so-subtle interrogation. Dawn holding her head high in the face of his family's suspicions about her moral character. She had class, and she was also skilled at hiding her emotions.

By the time the elevator stopped, he'd figured it out. Dawn wanted her money back and the only way to get it was to make Quent believe he could still play her for an idiot.

He stopped outside the door, regretting now that he'd called the police. As soon as Quent saw a uniform, he'd clam up.

A passing nurse gave him a curious smile and he smiled in return. He leaned against the wall and folded his arms, thinking. He could bust into the room, acting out of control and threaten Quent's life. Let Dawn beg him to not hurt her husband.

Or, he could announce he'd talked to the police, but nothing was going to happen unless Dawn lodged the complaint. Quent might jump at the opportunity to return Dawn's money rather than have her testify against him.

Pondering the best way to stage the confrontation, he stroked his jaw. This had to be better than any of his speeches, lectures or seminars. The stakes were too high to leave anything to chance.

"How did you find me, Galena?" Dawn asked, keeping her voice as friendly and nonthreatening as circumstances allowed. She wished she hadn't sent Ross away. Sweat formed high between her shoulder blades and trickled down her spine. She glanced at Quentin—Brad, whatever his name was—and was tempted to bop him on his bruised nose to show they weren't in cahoots.

"I have spent five years searching for this man. Compared to finding him, following you around town was a cakewalk," Galena said, advancing. The hand holding the gun trembled, but she kept it trained in the general vicinity of Quentin's chest. "Now I find you playing nurse."

"Help." Quentin's plaintive whisper touched Dawn's ears.

The plea failed to touch her heart. "Shut up," she muttered, more to the inner voice than to Quentin.

Dawn asked, "Are you married to this man, too?"

Galena gestured with the gun. "I wish I could say we belonged to an exclusive wives' club, but how exclusive can it be when there are more than thirty members?"

"Thirty?" Her mouth dropped agape. "You defrauded thirty women, Quentin? This is unbelievable."

"She's lying! You're the only one for me, darling. I love you. You're—"

"Shut up," Dawn and Galena said in unison.

At the foot of the bed, Galena shifted the aim of her pistol to Quentin's crotch. "I had an art gallery. It took me ten years to gain a reputation, to start drawing in the best artists and sculptors. He cleaned me out and the insurance wouldn't cover it. The police wouldn't do anything because we were married. I had to sell my house to pay back the artists and to cover his bad checks and credit-card bills. I lost everything, and no one would help me."

Cringing in sympathy, Dawn clucked her tongue. "Is that why you helped him steal from me?"

Galena pushed back her hair and lifted her tearful eyes to the ceiling until they cleared. "I didn't! He told me you understood he had debts to repay. He was supposed to have a cashier's check for me after the wedding." She dashed a hand at her nose.

Quentin's eyes rolled wildly in their sockets. Dawn guessed by the working of his mouth he was trying to tell her to use the call button to summon help. Unable to raise an iota of sympathy, she ignored that, too.

Turning her thoughts to practical matters, Dawn crossed her arms and frowned at nothing. She wished desperately for Ross's calm, clever presence. He'd know how to explain things to Galena. "I wish I could help you, but he's stolen everything from me as well." She smiled. "Would you please put the gun away? Shooting him won't get your money back."

Quentin groaned loudly and clutched his bandaged ribs. "Wait a minute," he gasped. "Whose side are you on? Dawn, darling, love of my life—"

"Be quiet." She directed a firm nod at Galena. "I'd hoped he would tell me where he put my money."

"You can't deal with him. Even if you have him arrested, he'll get out on bail and skip town."

"Not this time. Trust me. You see, I have—"

The door burst open and Ross strode into the room. "You aren't holding me back this time, Dawn! This time I'm—" He froze in midstride and midspeech. He stared at Galena's gun.

The woman jumped and let loose a high-pitched shriek. Losing her grip on the gun, she grabbed wildly for it. Scrambling, she slipped, nearly fell, then ended up with the gun pointing at Ross. He blinked once, twice, then flung his hands in the air.

Dawn froze, her heart in her throat. Galena's face had

lost every trace of color. Her eyes were twin moons. Cords stood on the backs of her hands, and as easy as breathing she could pull the trigger, shooting Ross. Dawn shifted her gaze to Ross and guessed he was imagining the same horrible scenario.

Logic and reason said to stay very, very still. Her heart told her otherwise. Forcing a smile, she said brightly, "Galena, please lower the gun. I'd hate for there to be an accident." The woman glanced at her. Consciously ordering her feet to move, Dawn walked to the end of the bed and put a companionable hand on the woman's shoulder. "I understand how he drove you to this. I'm sure Ross understands, too. We'll get our money back, but we'll do it legally."

Galena lowered the gun and hung her head. Covering her eyes with a hand, she burst into tears. Queasy at the thought of touching something so dangerous, Dawn reached for the gun. She grasped it gingerly by the butt and pulled it from Galena's limp fingers.

"Call security!" Quentin rasped. "She's a crazy woman!"

"Shut up," Dawn, Ross and Galena said in unison.

Ross took the gun from Dawn just as the door opened. Ross dropped the gun in his pocket. Three uniformed officers and Detective Goldenberg walked into the room.

Ross wrapped an arm around Dawn's shoulders and guided her away from the bed. "Here he is, detective. Gift-wrapped."

The detective had a sheet of shiny fax paper. He looked between it and the man on the bed. "Bradley Ellis Carter, you're under arrest." He nodded curtly at the officers.

"I'm not Carter! This is a mistake!"

Goldenberg squinted at Galena.

Dawn exchanged a look with Ross. Quentin had pushed Galena over the edge. Dawn understood. She felt compassion. She found compassion in Ross's eyes, too. Ever so slightly, he nodded.

"Detective," Dawn said as she put her hand on Galena's bowed shoulder, "this is Galena Carter. She's a victim, too. Without her help, we probably never would have found Quent—Brad, whatever his name is."

"I thought you said she assaulted you."

Meeting the woman's tearful eyes, Dawn made her voice casual. "Assault is probably too harsh a word. I'm willing to let bygones be bygones if it means this man goes to prison."

"You can't prove nothing!" Carter yelled. He flinched and winced as the officers helped him upright.

"I think I can." She reached inside her pocketbook and pulled out her memo recorder. She pressed the rewind button. "We were interrupted, but I think there's enough here to send him away for a long, long time."

She pressed the Play button. Her voice, sounding a bit tinny and muffled, but clear enough, said: *"Why did you use Quentin Bayliss's name?"*

Quentin's voice came through clearly: *"Because the people after me know about Tim Wiley. I couldn't risk the public record. I couldn't risk endangering you."*

"But you did use the name Tim Wiley to register the car and rent the storage units in Fountain."

"I've been on the run a long time. Using a lot of names scatters the scent. It's a trick I learned. It's got nothing to do with fraud...."

"Where is my money?"

"I told you, darling, I bought off the killers. They double-crossed me and sent in a hit man—"

Confident the police would be able to sort out the

truths from the lies, Dawn shut off the tape. "I recorded our entire conversation. He told a lot of lies, but there are some truths in here as well." She smiled up into Ross's beautiful eyes. "I know my responsibilities, Ross. Putting Quentin in prison is number one."

"THERE'S SOMETHING up your sleeve," Dawn said as Ross opened the passenger door of the Lexus and took her hand to help her out. She inhaled deeply of the fresh mountain air tinged with the warm scent of wood smoke. She gazed at Elk River Lodge, feeling a tug in her heart. She hadn't been here since summer, when the park rangers had found the Lincoln. Now, two weeks before Christmas, the lodge wore a mantle of crisp snow and the spruce trees looked blue. Smoke curled from the lodge's many chimneys. A couple carrying cross-country skis entered the lodge's main doors.

After the warmth of the car, the air seemed especially cold. She shivered inside her coat. "Come on, Ross, what are you up to? You've been teasing me ever since we left the Springs."

Ever since they'd caught Quentin, she and Ross had been dating steadily. Throughout the legal morass of getting her marriage annulled and recovering the property Quentin had stolen, Ross had been her lifesaver, her rock. Quentin had emphatically denied cleaning out her bank accounts; he'd tried to use restitution as leverage to keep from being extradited to California to face federal fraud indictments. It hadn't worked, and California had him anyway. Dawn figured it would be years before anyone could trace the convoluted paper trail and she recovered her money. Even if they did find all his foreign bank accounts, she'd have to stand in line. His crimes stretched back over twenty years.

In the end Dawn decided being poor didn't matter all that much. She liked the college students who rented rooms in her house. Connie had convinced the board members of the Children's Betterment Society to make the job of office manager a paying position. Ross hadn't been thrilled that Dawn wouldn't be working for him, but she preferred dating him to working for him, anyway.

This evening, she knew, wasn't a regular date. He'd told her to dress up, but hadn't told her where they were going. Since it wasn't her birthday or a holiday, she was wildly curious as to why he'd chosen Elk River.

They entered the lodge, and she balked inside the lobby. "Okay, we're here. You have to tell me what's going on."

He wagged a finger in front of her nose. "Curiosity killed the cat. Here, give me your coat."

Sighing with impatience, she gave up her coat. The lobby was empty except for a young woman Dawn didn't recognize working behind the reception desk. "Where is everybody?"

"Come on." His face alight with mischief, he tugged and urged her toward the private wing. He led her into the Duke family's dining room.

Illuminated by dozens of candles, the room looked like a fairy palace. The big table was laid with snowy linen, and silver bowls and vases held arrangements of red roses. Dinner service for two was laid at the far end of the table. Champagne chilled on ice. Telling herself she should be used to his sometimes silly, romantic impetuousness, she pressed a hand over her fluttering heart.

"It's beautiful," she breathed.

"It pales in comparison to you." He held a chair for her and she sat. "By the way, have I told you how gorgeous you look tonight?"

Smiling, she lowered her face. She'd splurged, dipping into her tight budget to buy an exquisite cocktail dress in black velvet with a low-cut bodice and fitted waist. Her only jewelry was the little, gold puff-heart on a chain Ross had given her as a birthday gift. "Yes, you have, but thank you." She thought he looked pretty darned gorgeous himself in his black tuxedo and starched white shirt.

He made a show of opening the champagne, releasing the cork with a faint, luxurious pop and filling two crystal flutes.

"It's not my birthday. Or a holiday. Or even the anniversary of when we met. Please tell me what you're up to, Ross."

He glanced at the swinging door leading to the kitchen. "Okay." He went to the door and pushed it open a few inches. He said something she couldn't make out before he returned to the table.

Hands in his pockets, he faced her. Candlelight sparkled in his gray eyes. "I love you, Dawn. I think I fell in love the first minute I met you. You're special and you're wonderful and I've never been so happy in my life."

Emotion rose in her throat. "I love you, too. Because of you, I have a life."

He pulled a small velvet-covered box from his pocket and lowered himself to one knee. "You know I'm not one for conventions, but this one is too good to pass up." He opened the box, revealing a diamond ring with a sparkle to rival his eyes. "Marry me."

She couldn't speak. Tears blurred her vision.

A soft ting-a-ling startled her. A ding, then a soft bong, then tinkles and chimes and musical trills filled the dining room. Ross's family filed into the room—the Colonel,

Elise, Janine, Megan and Kara. The chef joined them, and Stefan and Nancy the housekeeper, and other employees. Connie was here, and some of Dawn's friends she worked with at the Society. Each person held a bell. Crystal bells, silver bells and even a bell-shaped wind chime that Kara tapped with a small mallet.

Dawn covered her mouth with her hand. Tears of joy streamed down her cheeks.

"Are these enough bells for you, sweetheart? If you need to hear more, I can rustle them up somewhere."

Janine laughed. "Say yes, already, Dawn!" She gave a silver service-bell a jangling shake. "I promise, I'll give you guys a great deal on a cabin in the Honeymoon Hideaway."

"Hurry and answer him, my darling, I'm dying from the suspense," Connie called.

With the bells in her heart pealing to drown out the sound filling the dining room, Dawn extended her left hand and said, "I love you, Ross Duke, with all my heart. Yes, oh yes, I'll marry you."

Imagine that you've traveled far away, to a place of heady danger and luxurious romance nestled high in the Colorado Rocky Mountains. The bellhop has left your bags, and you're about to unpack in a room you'll share with a sexy man....

Welcome to the

Honeymoon Hideaway

This summer, reader favorite Sheryl Lynn brings you this exciting duet in June and July. Don't miss her upcoming romantic mysteries:

#424 THE CASE OF THE VANISHED GROOM
#425 THE CASE OF THE BAD LUCK FIANCÉ

Harlequin Intrigue invites you to make your vacation escape to the HONEYMOON HIDEAWAY!

HARLEQUIN®

I N T R I G U E®

HMH

Take 4 bestselling love stories FREE

Plus get a FREE surprise gift!

Free Gift Offer

With a Free Gift proof-of-purchase from any Harlequin® book, you can receive a beautiful cubic zirconia pendant.

This stunning marquise-shaped stone is a genuine cubic zirconia—accented by an 18" gold tone necklace. (Approximate retail value $19.95)

Send for yours today...
compliments of ✦HARLEQUIN®

To receive your free gift, a cubic zirconia pendant, send us one original proof-of-purchase, photocopies not accepted, from the back of any Harlequin Romance®, Harlequin Presents®, Harlequin Temptation®, Harlequin Superromance®, Harlequin Intrigue®, Harlequin American Romance®, or Harlequin Historicals® title available at your favorite retail outlet, together with the Free Gift Certificate, plus a check or money order for $1.65 U.S./$2.15 CAN. (do not send cash) to cover postage and handling, payable to Harlequin Free Gift Offer. We will send you the specified gift. Allow 6 to 8 weeks for delivery. Offer good until December 31, 1997, or while quantities last. Offer valid in the U.S. and Canada only.

Free Gift Certificate

Name: _____

Address: _____

City: _____ State/Province: _____ Zip/Postal Code: _____

Mail this certificate, one proof-of-purchase and a check or money order for postage and handling to: HARLEQUIN FREE GIFT OFFER 1997. In the U.S.: 3010 Walden Avenue, P.O. Box 9071, Buffalo NY 14269-9057. In Canada: P.O. Box 604, Fort Erie, Ontario L2Z 5X3.

FREE GIFT OFFER
084-KEZ

ONE PROOF-OF-PURCHASE

To collect your fabulous FREE GIFT, a cubic zirconia pendant, you must include this original proof-of-purchase for each gift with the properly completed Free Gift Certificate.

084-KEZR